TITLES BY MAXIE DARA

A GRIM REAPER'S GUIDE TO CATCHING A KILLER

A GRIM REAPER'S GUIDE TO CHEATING DEATH

A GRIM REAPER'S GUIDE TO LIVING TWICE

PRAISE FOR MAXIE DARA'S S.C.Y.T.H.E. MYSTERIES

"I'd follow this grim reaper anywhere. Wildly creative and impossible to put down, sure to induce both belly laughs and tears, *A Grim Reaper's Guide to Catching a Killer* is full of heart and soul(s)."

—Laura Hankin, author of *One-Star Romance*

"Witty, moving, and with a mystery that'll keep you turning pages late into the night, Dara's debut is a creative, laugh-out-loud novel about the business of death, and what it can teach us about family, love, and the best parts of being alive."

—Claudia Lux, author of *Sign Here*

"I was hooked right away by the inventive premise of Maxie Dara's *A Grim Reaper's Guide to Catching a Killer*, but it was the relationships that really did me in. I loved watching Kathy bond with Conner, a dead teenager, and work through her relationship with recent-almost-ex-husband Simon, all set against the backdrop of a surprisingly corporate job in human soul logistics. Funny and warm and full of little moments that kept me guessing, *A Grim Reaper's Guide to Catching a Killer* is a delightfully fresh mystery!"

—Alicia Thompson, *USA Today* bestselling author of *Love in the Time of Serial Killers*

"Sure to lighten the darkest mood. Come for the mystery, stay for the punched-up pairing. This new series is one to watch."

—*Kirkus Reviews*

“Fun and lighthearted despite the presence of death, the characters are relatable and funny, and the paranormal aspects are balanced with the ordinariness of Kathy’s messy life. The ending fleshes out this creative premise and sets the book up for the next in a heartwarming series.” —Booklist

“This debut paranormal mystery offers humor, love, and a strong cast of characters who form a found family.”
—*Library Journal* (starred review)

“Witty. . . . A long list of suspects, a dark sense of humor, and surprisingly weighty meditations on mortality carry the day. It’s a killer good time.” —*Publishers Weekly*

A GRIM REAPER'S GUIDE TO LIVING TWICE

Maxie Dara

BERKLEY MYSTERY
NEW YORK

BERKLEY MYSTERY
Published by Berkley
An imprint of Penguin Random House LLC
1745 Broadway, New York, NY 10019
penguinrandomhouse.com

Library of Congress Cataloging-in-Publication Data

Names: Dara, Maxie author
Title: A grim reaper's guide to living twice / Maxie Dara.
Description: First edition. | New York : Berkley Mystery, 2026. |
Series: S.C.Y.T.H.E. mystery
Identifiers: LCCN 2026015521 (print) | LCCN 2026015522 (ebook) |
ISBN 9798217187454 trade paperback | ISBN 9798217187461 ebook
Subjects: LCSH: Grim Reaper (Symbolic character) |
LCGFT: Paranormal fiction | Cozy mysteries | Novels
Classification: LCC PR9199.4.D368 G75 2026 (print) | LCC PR9199.4.D368 (ebook) |
DDC 813/.6—dc23/eng/20260608
LC record available at https://lccn.loc.gov/2026015521
LC ebook record available at https://lccn.loc.gov/2026015522

First Edition: November 2026

Printed in the United States of America
1st Printing

The authorized representative in the EU for product safety and compliance is Penguin Random House Ireland, Morrison Chambers, 32 Nassau Street, Dublin D02 YH68, Ireland, https://eu-contact.penguin.ie.

To your dog. Please tell them I say hi.

A GRIM REAPER'S GUIDE TO LIVING TWICE

Collections Agent Training Manual

Death: it's a living!

Welcome to S.C.Y.T.H.E.: a business by trade, a family at heart. In this manual, you will learn the basics of what it means to be a Collections Agent for the world's leading afterlife transport and security company. Please read it through with care and fill in the activity sheet on page 23 for your department manager.

Dispelling Common Myths

It is important that our employees understand as much as is relevant to their position so as not to harbor potentially harmful misconceptions about the afterlife industry. The following is a list of commonly held beliefs or rumors about the functions of death that hold no basis in reality:

Myth: Ghosts often or exclusively haunt cemeteries

Reality: Ghosts are prone to haunting where they lived or died, and very few people do either in a cemetery!

Myth: When interacting with essences, one must be careful to avoid contact with ectoplasm
Reality: Essences are entirely formless and unable to physically interact with the living, including through substances popularized by the historically inaccurate 1984 film *Ghostbusters* and its sequels.

Myth: There are areas on this earth that Death cannot see, known as Blind Spots
Reality: Death, like oxygen, gravity, and spiders, is ever present across all corners of the world.

Myth: The overtaking of a body by a disembodied soul, known as possession, can occur under specific circumstances
Reality: Only one soul can ever enter a body throughout the duration of its existence. As such, possession is not possible.

1

The thing about dead bodies is they always look slightly disappointed. Something about the way the lips fall after rigor mortis fades, probably. Whatever it was, it was the least of Jack McCoy's worries. Because the thing about Jack McCoy was that as comfortable as he was with other people's disappointment, he'd never been quite so comfortable with death. Which made his nine-to-five a daily disappointment of its own. Because the other thing about Jack McCoy was that he worked as a grim reaper, though he'd never say as much to his colleagues. Around the office, Jack's fellow soul harvesters preferred the term "Collections Agents." Jack didn't care what he was called or what his colleagues preferred, but he needed to fit in, so Jack was a Collections Agent too, in the Murder department of S.C.Y.T.H.E.—Secure Collection, Yielding, and Transportation of Human Essences—where he'd now worked for just shy of two months, though his host body had worked there for decidedly longer.

Because the other other thing about Jack McCoy was that he was dead.

Not quite so decisively dead as the corpse in front of him,

mind you. No, while Jack had lucked out and possessed the reaper S.C.Y.T.H.E. had sent to collect his soul, this guy was fully committed to the bit. Jack tapped a waxy, outstretched finger with the toe of an orthopedic Mary Jane pump.

"Could you not do that?"

Jack looked from the body on the ground to the soul hovering just to its left. They would have been fully indistinguishable from each other if not for the soul's slight transparency and the fact that his skull and brain matter weren't currently visible.

"Sorry."

"It's fine," said the soul. "It just tickles a bit is all." He examined the incorporeal finger corresponding with the fleshy version Jack had prodded.

Jack glanced down at his own hands, heavily weathered and spotted and sporting a manicure in a pearly peach. Well, they weren't his hands, exactly, but they'd begun to feel less foreign these days. The arthritis in the first two knuckles of the right hand, the weakened grip strength, the wedding ring he would pawn for a pretty penny if he thought he had any chance of getting away with it. He wasn't exactly driving a Ferrari here, but he was beginning to get used to the ride.

"What now?" the soul asked.

The real answer to that was something Jack had decided was none of his business when the question first occurred to him nearly two months ago. The guy in front of him would find out for himself soon enough, so Jack just offered a shrug.

"Come on, we're going for a drive."

They were the very same words Margaret Chen had said to Jack when he'd died, in the very same voice, and they seemed to offer as little comfort now as they had then.

Hovering over his own body back then, untethered and unable to fully comprehend the situation, Jack hadn't particularly wanted to go for a drive. What he'd wanted was more of the life he loved. It was all he'd ever wanted. And if he couldn't have that back, he'd take the next best thing. Taking, after all, was one of the things Jack did best. He just needed a plan.

Breaking into a house was easy; you just watched and waited for everyone inside to leave and then made yourself at home.

Margaret had given her client an impatient look, but Jack ignored it. His brain, or whatever did the thinking for him now, whirred the way it always had when the seed of a scheme took root. Something had begun to blossom, but it wasn't quite there yet. Jack needed more time; something the old woman in front of him seemed unwilling to provide. Which was fair, Jack decided. She probably didn't have an excessive amount left of it herself.

Margaret had checked the fine gold watch on her wrist then and looked out a nearby window of the empty club, into the great blue eternity of the sky beyond. And for a very brief moment, her spirit wasn't quite so heavy in its shell. Jack had seen it in her eyes, the gentle vacancy we all allow ourselves from time to time when we're especially tired or bored or dealing with an uncooperative disembodied soul. But there was something more. It was as though this woman had suddenly felt the weight of all her years landing on her all at once, the barrier keeping them at bay nudged away by Jack's stubbornness, or by a tucked-away sadness, or by the person attached to the wedding ring she absently stroked with her thumb. Maybe by it all. And for barely a blink, her eyes said she was done here. Jack had seen it, and it was as good as an empty house. And suddenly that seed of a scheme was a flower.

Without a single thought to the implications, he'd leapt forward and through the old woman, a tick attaching to its host. There was darkness for a moment, and Jack had nearly felt as though he'd died again. But that wasn't it. His eyes had been closed, he realized, and when he opened them, he knew they weren't his eyes at all. The world looked blurrier, and the ceiling was higher than it had been. And his boob itched. And he had a boob. Two, in fact. And just like that, Jack had possessed the body, and by extension the life, of Margaret Chen. He'd committed his final heist.

Or so he thought.

THE OFFICE WAS BUSTLING BY THE TIME JACK GOT BACK JUST AFTER the lunch hour. No one in this place ever dawdled or took a slightly-too-long nap in their car or had a slightly-too-boozy afternoon meal, so Jack couldn't either. He bobbed a cottony, silver-white head at everyone he recognized and everyone he didn't, just in case, before snaking across the bland gray office and sinking into the battered rolling chair in his cubicle that wasn't actually his cubicle.

His new face stared up at him from a photo in a silver frame on the desk, several years younger and pressed to the cheek of a man Jack had come to know as Wesley. Wesley was also dead, which Jack figured was the only thing they'd have in common. The man in the photo was dressed in a navy sweater over a button-up, like something you'd see on a lawyer at a country club on the way to a lobster dinner. Margaret had clearly done well for herself. Jack could feel her small spark of pride, emanating from somewhere indecipherable, at the thought. Her spirit was mostly dormant since Jack's takeover, but Wesley always brought her briefly back to life. In the photo, she stood primly beside her late husband, a cream cashmere sweater tied jauntily around her shoulders. He knew from experience how much time went into styling that stiffly curled hair—something Margaret had mastered but he decidedly hadn't. In life Jack would have looked at Margaret and Wesley as ideal marks, but even in Margaret's own skin, her wealth was beyond his grasp, her bank accounts secured with information she kept locked away in a part of her he couldn't access. For now that was fine, because whether she'd meant to or not, she'd given him access to something far more important to a dead man.

Jack gave the photo a salute and cracked open the ancient laptop in front of him to begin writing up a report on his morning collection. It was a pretty light day in Murder. Jack had only one more file on his desk, which meant the rest of the day would be paperwork. This was his favorite kind of day, which would have seemed laughable to him a few months ago. Paperwork (or anything with the word "work" attached, frankly) wasn't exactly in Jack's wheelhouse, but it beat seeing gunshot wounds and blunt force trauma up close, so he'd learned to adjust.

When he finished his report, he flipped open the lone file and scanned for an address, then braved a glance at the cause of death so he'd know what he was in for. What Jack *didn't* check was the client's name, because that never mattered to him. What Jack *should have* checked was the client's name, because that was about to matter quite a bit. Maybe, if he had checked, he could have prevented what was about to come. But, like paperwork, forethought wasn't in Jack's wheelhouse, so instead he closed the file and headed toward the beginning of his own downfall.

2

A stabbing in a back alley struck Jack as a little cliché. Not that he had much appreciation for the more creative murders, mind you, but, inadvertent pun aside, this whole setup felt a little hack.

He pulled up to the curb in Margaret's Mercedes and peered down the alley to the body sprawled across the pavement, a pair of sneakers peeking out from behind a dumpster. No blood was visible from this vantage point, for which Jack was grateful. It gave him an extra moment to steel his stomach. He unbuckled his seat belt and adjusted Margaret's hair without thinking; one of the leftover tics of his host, who apparently found it a faux pas to arrive at a crime scene with flyaways.

The air outside was brisk, the last of winter's chill still clinging to the breeze like icicles to an awning. Jack wrapped his tasteful burgundy peacoat tighter around his borrowed torso and moved toward the alley.

When he had decided to inhabit the body of Margaret Chen, he hadn't considered all it would entail. He hadn't really had time to think it through, but even if he did, he probably wouldn't have taken it. He rarely did. All he knew in that fateful moment was that he was dead and he didn't want to be. That Margaret was alive and seemed just apathetic enough about it for Jack to hitch a ride. And before he knew anything more, he was wrapping the life of an eighty-three-year-old grim reaper around himself as tightly as he wrapped her peacoat now. With that life came an unexpected amount of death, and Jack found himself reluctantly walking toward it again.

The body in the alley lay face down, sprawled in a way you had to be fairly dead to achieve. Blood had deepened the dead man's charcoal gray jacket to black in three different places on his back, the shredded fabric peeled back just enough to reveal torn skin. Jack averted his eyes and put them to more productive work locating the recently evacuated soul. It wasn't hard to find; they rarely were. Souls tended not to stray too far from their bodies immediately after death—the last tether they had to life.

He recognized the scar first: a raised crescent that traced a puffy cheekbone and curved just under the left eye. According to the scar's owner, it was the result of a broken bottle wielded during a drunken brawl. According to fact, it involved a stoned *Peter Pan* rewatch and a mental lapse regarding the concept of gravity.

Dale Keegan was thirty-three, a year younger than Jack. Not an ideal age to die. Jack might have taken a moment to reflect on that, or maybe on the disconcerting connection to his recent past currently hovering in front of him, but he didn't get the chance. Dale's glance shot up from where it had been lingering on his own discarded body, his eyes landing on Margaret in her tasteful coat before widening.

"Jackie?"

Jack froze. To the outside world, he was a five-foot-nothing octogenarian with a four-step skin-care routine. Jack didn't exist; couldn't exist. It was what allowed him to continue existing at all.

Before he could say anything, Dale's essence continued. "Holy shit, is that you? What the hell are you doing in there?"

"I—" For the afterlife of him, Jack couldn't think of what words belonged on the end of that sentence. He was too busy trying to figure out how Dale could recognize him behind his geriatric disguise.

"Damn weird day, man. Got stabbed a few hours ago and now one of my best friends is an old lady. What's up with that?"

Jack found himself looking over his shoulder, as if anyone else could hear Dale's words. "Hey, I need you to keep it down, okay?"

This elicited a knowing grin from Dale.

"Nice to see you're up to your old tricks," said the spirit.

Though possession was definitely a *new* trick for Jack, he couldn't argue his track record of often questionable life choices. They were the foundation of his whole relationship with Dale. They were work friends of a sort—work that would have ended in a decent jail stint if they ever got caught.

"You on the run, Jackie? Seems unnecessary if you're already dead, but you always did manage to get yourself in over your head more than most."

"Can you stop saying my name now?" said Jack. This neighborhood was always swarming with agents from his department, and the last thing he needed was a colleague overhearing this conversation. "What the hell happened to you, anyway?"

"One of the Winston brothers finally caught up with me." Dale shrugged. "Can you believe it took the dumbasses this long?" He glanced back down at his body, head cocked in consideration. "Oh well, it was fun while it lasted. But what's your deal now, Jackie? Hiding out in an old lady, what's that all about?" Jack probably could have—*should* have—explained the whole situation. About the opportunity to stay alive, about Margaret, about S.C.Y.T.H.E., which, back in the day, would have led him to come up with some half-cocked scheme to use Margaret's unassuming appearance for nefarious purposes. At which point Dale would have egged him on to do something profoundly stupid. And illegal. And fun. But now the only chance Jack had to avoid being a bodiless spirit like Dale was to fully embrace the role of Margaret, and that meant leaving all those habits behind.

"Let's go for a drive," Jack said instead. In his mind he was already halfway to dropping Dale off at the processing warehouse.

"Great idea, Jackie. To Billy's?"

"No, not to Billy's, dude. I have a job to do."

Dale's eyes lit up at that. "Can I get in on it?"

"Not that kind of job."

"Then what— Oh." Dale looked at his feet, the left of which a cockroach was currently scampering through. "You're a working man now, Jackie, I get it. You died and the old ways died with you."

"It's not like that," Jack said, too quickly. "I have to keep up appearances, that's all."

"Well, if that's all," Dale tried again, "then a quick stop at Billy's won't hurt, right? One last time? For a dead man?"

It was tempting. Jack couldn't deny it. Billy's All-Day Diner sat at the end of a lonely street, its sign holding up only moderately worse than its decrepit interior. It had failed so many health inspections that Billy had nearly been forced to close, each time prompting a standoff between the restaurant inspector and the neighborhood that ended with the inspector threatened, coerced, or—in one case involving incriminating feet pics—blackmailed out of town. They'd gone through roughly six inspectors by the time Jack graduated high school.

Jack had never left one of Billy's booths without dragging his friends into some twisted scheme or other. It was a den of greasy eggs and sin, from which nothing good ever emerged. A place in which Margaret would never have been caught dead and, frankly, one Jack shouldn't be either, even if it was one of the few tangible remnants of his old life; a life he craved more than Billy's famous hash browns. He looked at his dead pal, and his heart, which was also Margaret's heart, gave a reluctant pang.

"Billy's," he agreed, sealing his fate with a single word.

3

Nothing had changed since the last time Jack had sipped a black coffee in one of Billy's peeling red diner booths over three months ago. The stains on the walls were the same, the burnt coffee in his cup was the same, even the cup itself was probably the same one he'd drunk from last time. The only difference was in the looks he received walking up to his usual booth wearing the costume of a wealthy eighty-something, and even those were short-lived, thanks to the strict mind-your-business ethos of the neighborhood. Jack had counted on that attitude to come in clutch for what was about to appear to onlookers to be a conversation between Margaret and herself.

Jack took another sip of his coffee, waiting for Dale to get on with whatever final words he had, but the man across the booth simply stared, occasionally shaking his head in what appeared to be wonder.

"What?" Jack finally asked.

"I just can't believe it. You hacked death. I mean, if anyone was gonna, it would be Jack McCoy, but still."

Jack took another sip.

"Any chance you got another spare body lying around I could hop into?" It was a joke in tone, but Jack could hear the tint of a plea coloring the edges. "It's just, Savannah's gonna be a wreck, you know?"

"I got lucky," Jack said, almost apologetically. "The reaper assigned to my case gave me an in and I took it, but I'm pretty sure this isn't standard protocol."

"Is that what you are now? Some sort of grim reaper?"

"Basically," said Jack. "Though they get real testy when you say it like that."

"So you know everyone who's gonna die before it happens?"

Dale spoke with the kind of awe he'd previously reserved for Jack's most brilliant schemes, and for a moment Jack considered not correcting the assumption. It couldn't do any real harm; Dale wouldn't be sticking around for much longer anyway. But that would only lead to more questions, which would only lead to the need for more lies, and frankly, Jack didn't have the energy for that anymore. Being in your eighties really took it out of you.

"Not quite," he said. "I just get files for whoever's dying each day."

"Oh," Dale replied, awe fading quicker than sunshine in midwinter. "That's still cool, Jackie."

Jack took another swig of his coffee in reply. The bitter, mildly tangy sludge coated his throat in the comfortingly off-putting way it always had.

"So where do the files come from?"

Jack completed his laborious swallow. "Huh?"

"The dead people files. Where do they come from?"

Jack contemplated another sip of his coffee, but he wasn't entirely convinced his new body could handle whatever weapons-grade ingredients Billy put in there. In truth, Jack had never given much thought to the S.C.Y.T.H.E. chain of command, less out of a lack of curiosity and more because his afterlife depended on keeping his head down and not asking too many questions.

"They're just on my desk when I get there in the morning," he admitted finally.

"Sure, but who writes them?"

This wasn't right. The tone in Dale's voice. The glimmer in his eyes. Jack knew them too well. They used to be his. He shifted in the booth, lifting a shred of fabric off his seat with the motion.

"Hey, tell me something. The whole world looks at me and sees Margaret Chen, right? So how come you can see me in here?" he asked, trying to change the subject.

"I guess now that I'm dead it's easier to see the soul under the body. And I'd recognize you anywhere," said Dale.

Jack considered this for a moment. Had his other collections been able to see him too? Were they confused as to why there was a young man hanging out in the shell of an old woman? No one had ever said as much, but it certainly would explain a few odd looks he'd attributed to the confusion of being recently dead.

"Anyway," Dale said, dragging Jack out of his thoughts. "You were saying?"

"I was?"

"Yeah. About the files. About who writes them."

Something pricked at Margaret's neck. Jack didn't like where this conversation was going, but it felt like that impressively spherical boulder from Indiana Jones, picking up speed and difficult to dodge now that the booby trap had been triggered.

"Above my pay grade," Jack said into his mug. "So, how's Savannah? Still waxing eyebrows?"

"Yeah, yeah, she does pubes now too," Dale said, his tone distracted. "Look, Jackie, I have an idea."

The words struck Jack as wrong, not because they didn't belong here, in this booth, where they'd been uttered a million times before, but because it should have been Jack who said them.

"Oh," said Jack, a discordant combination of nostalgia and dread running through him.

"Look, after everything that happened back in the day, you always said we'd do one last big job. You promised it and everything. Said I might even get to try being in charge and stuff, remember?"

"I remember."

"And we did some little stuff together, sure, but nothing like the way it used to be. And I kept hoping . . . but then you died and, I mean, things were never gonna get very far without you. But now you're here again, and you did always used to say that any opportunity for taking is ours for the taking, right? We could finally do it, that last big job. You and me."

Jack pressed his lips together. He'd loved his life before. The small-time heists and robberies committed shoulder to shoulder with his dearest friends. But this was his afterlife, and the rules were different. Still, before he could help himself, he was saying, "What are you thinking?"

Dale's face brightened, his back held a little straighter. "Jackie, this is the kind of thing you would've come up with in your heyday, I swear it. Okay, think about it. Folks could know in advance when they or someone they love is gonna kick it, right? How much do you think info like that would go for? Loads! So what we do is we find out where they keep whatever Master List they're working from and we take it. Sell it off. Sav could get a cut of the money. So could the rest of the gang. Or you could blow it all in Vegas. Who cares? We'd have pulled off the most badass heist in history. We'd be legends."

There was a part of Jack—one so far removed from Margaret he could feel her essence shudder as he thought it—that felt a sense of pride in that moment. Dale was right, this was exactly the sort of scheme he'd have come up with not long ago, the sort that would have seen them rolling in the proceeds of a bad job well done. Dale had never been an ideas man, but he'd hung on Jack's every word for long enough that something had clearly rubbed off. Something that, under different circumstances, Jack would have happily nurtured. But in his current skin, he didn't have that kind of luxury. Jack shook his head. "I like it, but we can't. I need to keep my cover or else I'll end up dead. Well, dead-dead. I can't risk it."

"Dead-dead." Dale stared down at his semitransparent hands resting on the table. "Can't imagine what that would be like."

Jack didn't say anything. There wasn't anything to say. He'd caught a lucky break, the way he always had, and Dale hadn't, the way he never did. It hadn't ever really been fair, the way Jack could always make shit hit the fan without any of it landing on him. But he'd always reasoned that life wasn't fair, and now he decided death wasn't either. It wasn't his fault. He was just a leaf on the stream. But who was he to refuse a gift when offered to him?

"C'mon, Jackie, how many times have I taken the fall for you? How many nights have I spent on the couch or has Eli spent in jail because of something you pushed us into? You can't risk being dead-dead, but you have no problem shuffling me off without keeping your promise? And the other guys, what are they gonna do with us both gone? This could really help them."

"They'll figure it out," Jack lied.

Dale shook his head, his focus back on his hands.

"Jeez, Jackie. You become an old woman once and suddenly it's like I don't even know you anymore. The Jack McCoy I know would've jumped at this so fast. Hell, he'd have come up with it himself. But I guess he's gone, huh? What's the point of continuing on with life if it isn't even your life anymore?"

Jack was no stranger to those words. He'd thought them himself at least once a day since he'd become Margaret. When he looked in the mirror and saw plucked brows and designer cashmere sweaters reflected back at him; when he had to care about emails finding their recipients well or circling back to a topic he didn't give two shits about; when he drove through his old neighborhood and caught a glimpse of the life he left behind. He often found himself aching for his old friends, his old schemes, his old world. And then he would tell himself he didn't, and he'd carry on as Margaret, and the feeling would eventually pass. But to hear those words from outside his own mind made them hit with more weight, the kind of weight that would have knocked his frail new body over if it were standing upright.

In life, Jack had never taken the time to consider a decision before making it. In death, he'd had to learn to adjust to considering things from Margaret's perspective first, so no one realized she wasn't the one steering the ship. But old habits died hard, and as much as Jack wasn't willing to do the same, the words left his mouth with as little forethought as an exhale.

"We'll have to be careful about this. And we'll need some help."

4

Her

August 2002

The heat of the sun poked its way through the cracks of Fort You Again like a toddler's sticky fingers, leaving foreheads slick with sweat. Frankly, the fact that the flimsy sticks and tarp scraps that made up the fort had held up this long was verging on miracle territory. It had been a late summer day like this when the six of them ran off into the deepest depths of the remotest woods they knew—the quarter-acre patch of spindly trees at the end of Jack's street—and built their headquarters from fallen branches and whatever supplies they could sneak out of their parents' garages without getting caught. At the time, Fort You Again had been an impenetrable fortress that would surely stand the test of time. These days it was patiently waiting for a Big Bad Wolf to come put it out of its misery. They'd have to find a new place to meet soon. Jack couldn't ignore that, no matter how much he wanted to. But there was something to be said for tradition, even when that tradition came in the form of sweat in uncomfortable places. He looked out over the gathered faces from his perch on a tattered beanbag chair.

"Well?" Eli prompted impatiently, fingers tapping on the thigh of his baggy jeans.

"I'm waiting for everyone," Jack said, gaze scanning the forest beyond the fort through the cracks in the wall of branches.

"She's not coming, dude."

"I'm waiting," Jack said again, the authority in his freshly changing voice wavering slightly.

Eli rolled his eyes and mouthed something at Carter from behind his hand. Jack decided not to care. Eli had been moodier than usual lately, and that was a pretty high bar to clear. But that was the price you paid for having an Eli in your group, and as far as Jack was concerned, it was worth the cost. For all his scowls and sharp retorts, when push came to shove, Eli would be the one doing both the pushing and the shoving on his friends' behalf.

Jack had selected the You Agains with great care, each of them an essential ingredient in the schemes he was forever cooking up, and Eli was no exception. But right now, one of those ingredients was missing. An important one. The one that brought the most flavor, at least as far as Jack was concerned. And he wasn't about to attempt this recipe without her.

He chanced a look at his Spider-Man watch. Maybe she really wasn't coming.

How much longer could he stall? Carter had stopped doodling on his jeans by now, the grotesque ink faces that peered out from mucky denim staring at Jack with the same impatience as their creator. It wasn't angst that pulled Carter's arms across his chest the way it was with Eli. Carter was the no-nonsense type, which meant his annoyed posture was the result of disapproval. That was always worse.

At least there was Dale. Despite the need for a man-to-man conversation about his recent decision to start frosting his tips, Jack could always count on Dale to be perfectly complacent and compliant. It was why Jack had selected him as his right-hand man. You needed that kind of thing as a leader; someone who wouldn't cross their arms in frustration or disapproval but would smile up at you with all the earnest reverence of a little kid playing with a slightly older kid. At least he had one You Again on his side.

Jules, meanwhile, wouldn't meet his eye from where she sat across the fort, tiny and as aggressively fearless as a Yorkshire terrier. She knew something. The youngest of the group and the most apathetic toward the conventions of the world, Jules always knew something, though it was usually a weird something, and often pertained to worms. Still, if their missing member had told anyone she was bailing, it would be Jules.

Jules lifted her chin defiantly as Jack shifted in his beanbag throne, trying and failing to haul himself to his feet from the unrelenting clutches of his squishy seat so he could begin the necessary interrogations. Whatever Jules knew, he needed to know too. Especially if it was going to validate the worry currently sitting like a rock at the base of his stomach. Could this really be the end of the You Agains as he knew them? All because his favorite member had been inconsiderate enough to go through puberty and start caring about what other people thought was cool?

A twig snapped just outside the fort; combat boots stomping over earth, the swoosh of a sundress against overgrown shrubs. Jack's back straightened at the sound, his heart giving a quick jolt against his rib cage as he sank back onto his beanbag. He caught Eli's eye and flashed an I-told-you-so grin. Then, as subtly as possible, he sniffed his pits to make sure they hadn't grown too oniony in the summer heat and swept back the strands of hair sticking to his forehead. A smug smile ran across Jack's lips as the fort door flap swung back. He had known he was right to wait. Never doubted it for a second. When it came to his schemes, he'd never even think to start cooking until every ingredient was in place. That, he decided, was a promise. It was all the You Agains against the world, just the way it was meant to be.

"YOU REALLY DON'T THINK WE SHOULD JUST DO THIS OURSELVES?"

"I'm not doing this without everyone, man." Jack folded his arms over his recently acquired bosom and turned away from the passenger seat of Margaret's car, where Dale's essence sat.

"I hear you, Jackie, but how do you expect to convince any of them that you're who you are? Or that I'm here with you? Eli don't even believe the earth is round, bro. He's not gonna believe you're living in a little old lady."

"Which is why we're not starting with Eli," Jack said on a huff.

He narrowed his eyes at the house across the road: a squat little single-story redbrick with a sloped roof and a yard polka-dotted with dandelions. Carter would be the easiest get, and once they had him, the others would surely fall into line. They always had. And though a few inconsequential things had changed over the years—beer bellies and receding hairlines and Jack borrowing someone else's body—what truly mattered never would. His army would be ready to go into battle at his side, just as they always had.

He unbuckled his seat belt. "You coming?"

Dale obediently passed through the passenger-side door, his skepticism quickly withering in the face of Jack's authority. It was a dynamic that had always served the group well. After all, Jack was good at what he did, and Dale was good at telling that to everyone.

Just now, Dale expertly followed Jack up the stone slabs to Carter's front door. Jack readjusted the blazer of Margaret's hot pink Gucci pantsuit and gave the door a rap. He was enough of a presence in this body for Dale to have recognized him; surely some of that famous Jack pizzazz would be visible to the living too, at least when they knew him as well as Carter did.

A moment later, Carter was in the doorway, beige Henley stained with ancient spray paint splatter, the archaeological remains of shenanigans past. His obsidian eyes searched the small woman on his front step, apparently coming up empty.

"Can I help you?"

Okay, so Jack was going to have to pizzazz a little harder than he'd expected. But that was all right. Aside from dying, he'd rarely faced a challenge he couldn't meet.

"Dude, it's me," he said in a voice that wasn't his at all. "It's Jack. Jack McCoy. I've got a mark for us."

Carter's blank expression melted into a furrowed brow before his entire head gave a small shake on a disappointing sigh. "Jesus Christ," he barely muttered. "How much?"

Jack's face did an instant replay of Carter's expression journey as he tried to suss out the meaning behind his words.

"How much did he pay you for this stunt?" Carter continued, apparently attempting to fill in the blanks for Jack and failing miserably.

"Huh?"

"Jack," said Carter.

"Yes?" said Jack.

"No, I mean how much did Jack pay you to show up here and be weird?"

Dale cleared his throat. "I mean, that is something you'd do, man."

Jack couldn't really argue with that. Actually, now that Carter mentioned it, he suddenly wished he'd set up this kind of prank before kicking the bucket. He'd never had any intention of resting in peace, much less letting anyone else do the same after his death. Though that reputation didn't help him much right now.

"He didn't," Jack said. "I didn't. It's me, I swear. Look, I can explain."

Carter put a hand on the door. "Sorry, ma'am, not interested. He did enough damage when he was alive; I'm not dealing with his bullshit now." The door clicked shut in Margaret's face, leaving Jack blinking at khaki paint.

He wheeled on Dale. "The hell was that?"

"No idea, Jackie. He's one of those temperamental artist types, you know?"

"Since when?"

Dale shifted his nonexistent weight from foot to foot. There was more in him to say and it made him antsy, like a kid who had to pee. And like a kid who had to pee, he'd rather hold it in until he burst. That was fine. Jack would let him. He could wait. Besides, that wasn't his main focus right now. Carter was making this whole thing more complicated than it needed to be. Jack wasn't particularly accustomed to doors closing in his face; not in this world, anyway. Out there in the broader world, sure. Legitimate jobs were hard to come by and love was never to be. But here, among his people, in his neighborhood, everyone knew better than to say no to Jack McCoy. He was a man who got things done and who would always make a favor worth its while. But right now he was also Margaret Chen, and that presented certain difficulties.

"What now?" Dale asked, his pee dance reaching its final eight count.

"We try Eli," said Jack. This drew an incredulous silence from Dale. Jack had figured it would. If they couldn't get Carter, Eli was pretty much a write-off. But as far as Jack was concerned, they simply hadn't got Carter *yet*, and instead of waiting around, he'd rather waste their time attempting the impossible. It was more fun that way.

"I really think we could do this just you and me, Jackie."

"And I really think we do this the way we always have," said Jack. "With everyone."

"But you know we won't get *everyone*, right, Jackie? You know that. Not now."

Somewhere in a distance carved by time, in a past as dead as he was, Jack could hear the sound of combat boots stomping over earth, the swoosh of a sundress against overgrown shrubs.

"Let's get cooking," he said, a quirk in his lips. And with that, he traipsed back to the car.

5

Frankly, Jack had figured he'd never see Eli again. Not so much because he was dead but because Eli seemed pretty hell-bent on making sure he didn't.

As far as Jack knew, Eli was out of prison. That was handy. Jack figured it wasn't easy to get much done in prison that didn't involve building unnecessarily large biceps or becoming born-again, and neither would be much help with his latest scheme. Not that he knew much about the penal system beyond what he'd learned from *Orange Is the New Black*. Somehow, despite his penchant for petty crimes, he'd never suffered through more than a night in the slammer. The same couldn't be said for Eli. Like the ladies of Litchfield Penitentiary, Eli was something of an expert on life behind bars.

Meanwhile, Eli's life on the outside was based in an apartment building called Azure Heights, which was neither blue nor particularly tall, but did have one working washing machine and a rat colony that was still going strong after decades. Dale had to navigate to the complex. It had been nearly two years since Jack had last seen Eli and even longer since he'd been invited over for a beer. Not that they'd ever had a falling-out or anything. They'd simply outgrown each other over the years. It was something even a bad psychic could have seen coming. Still, Eli was an important ingredient in the You Again gang, and Jack figured it was worth a shot to see if that was still enough to get him on board.

He knocked at apartment 3A. Eli appeared a moment later in gray sweats and a frown.

"Yeah?"

Jack tried to force his new features into a more recognizable configuration, rounding his smile downward at the corners the way his old smile had; furrowing his brows so they sat lower on his borrowed forehead.

"This is going to sound crazy," said Jack, "but I need you to keep an open mind here. It's me. Jack. Jack McCoy."

"Huh?"

Dale shifted at Jack's side. "Here we go."

Jack forced his back a little straighter, trying to attain even a fraction of the height he once had. "Okay, so I was dead, right? You know that part. But I figured a way out of it. There was this old lady just standing there, not really using her body for anything, and I needed one, you know? Anyway, one thing led to another and now here I am."

Eli looked down at the old lady who was Jack. He gave a prolonged blink, his frown deepening.

"I swear it," Jack continued quickly, his arguments already primed on his tongue in the wake of his encounter with Carter. "Your middle name is Franklin," he listed off on his index finger. "We stole Principal MacNeil's car together junior year and did doughnuts in the high school parking lot until you threw up Froot Loops. You're afraid of butterflies and told me you'd kill me if I told anyone. It's me. It's Jack. I swear."

Jack steeled himself for rebuttal, ready for the inevitable disbelief and chastisement that was keying up to follow, but when Eli finally opened his mouth, all he said was, "Fuck."

Jack shot a glance at Dale, but before Dale could reply, Eli continued. "Get inside."

"Wait, what?" was all Jack could manage.

Eli turned from the door and disappeared into the apartment. Jack exchanged one last look with Dale, who shrugged his own bewilderment, before following Eli inside.

Apartment 3A hadn't changed much since the last time Jack had visited. The collection of fast food containers on the coffee table represented different chains, and the couch had an extra hole or two, but otherwise it was the same apartment it always had been. That was the upside of ping-ponging in and out of prison, Jack mused. Home upkeep was probably pretty minimal.

"Love what you've done with the place," Jack said all the same in an attempt to fill the silence. Eli bolted the door and gestured to the corduroy couch; a side-of-the-road find that had taken Jack, Eli, and Dale thirty minutes of sweating and swearing to carry back here in the middle of a heat wave. Jack sat. Dale slumped substanceless onto a cushion beside him.

In front of the couch, Eli paced, a fist held at his mouth. If Jack didn't know better, he would say Eli was gearing up to punch somebody. But Jack did know better, which was why he'd say instead that Eli was using every ounce of willpower within him *not* to punch anybody.

"Fuck," he said again instead.

"Crazy, right?" said Jack.

"No, not crazy," Eli snapped back.

"I mean, a little crazy," Jack countered.

Eli shook his head. "You didn't want to be dead, so you're not."

Jack crossed one dainty ankle over the other. "Right."

"Right," said Eli. "Because Jack McCoy always gets what he wants."

"Right," Jack said again, trying to catch up. "You said that like it's a bad thing."

"Why are you here?"

"I have a plan."

Dale gently cleared his throat.

"Sorry," Jack amended, "we have a plan. Dale's here too. He's also dead as of this morning."

Eli glanced from the elderly woman on one cushion to the empty spot on the other.

"Fucking hell."

"Yeah," Jack agreed.

"Dale's dead?"

"Yeah," Jack repeated.

"How?"

"Roy Winston," Dale offered. Jack repeated it and Eli let out a sigh.

"Okay," said Eli. "Get out of my house."

"I'm not lying to you, dude," said Jack.

"I know," said Eli. "It all adds up exactly right. Now get out of my house."

"Eli—"

"I'm done with your schemes, Jack. I've been done with them. You being dead doesn't change that." Eli walked to the door and ripped it open.

Jack rose to meet Eli's eye level, temporarily forgetting his new height. "But—"

"Does Savannah know about Dale?"

"What?"

"Does Sav know Dale's dead?" Eli asked again, propping the door open with his shoulder.

"I dunno," said Jack.

Eli's fist was at his mouth again. "No, of course you don't. You're just focused on what matters, like always, huh, McCoy? Go. I have some calls to make."

Jack's mouth hung open for a moment, catching dust particles. How had things gone upside down so quickly? Eli actually believed Jack and Dale were there in 3A, but for some reason he refused to help. Jack felt more confused than Eli seemed to be by the whole situation, which made very little sense under the circumstances.

"Hey, Jackie," Dale piped up from beside him, pulling Jack from his befuddlement. "Can you get Eli to tell Sav I'm okay? I don't want her worrying about me, you know? Thinkin' I'm burning in God's basement or nothin'."

Jack looked back up at Eli. "Message from Dale," he said through all the things he wanted to say. "Tell Sav he's all right."

"Don't involve me in this," Eli said. "Any of it."

Jack could feel Dale deflate beside him. He couldn't bring himself to look. Instead he gave a tight nod and walked out the open door.

* * *

BACK IN THE CAR, JACK FELT LESS CONNECTED TO MARGARET'S BODY than he had since he'd first tried it on. He was hovering somewhere near the surface, yanked loose from his tethers by the strange series of events that had taken over his afternoon. He'd felt this way before, back when he was still alive: as though he wasn't fully in his own skin. It always seemed to happen when life took a turn for the unexpected, but back then he was anchored enough to himself that he never actually thought he would be catapulted from his body the way he feared he could be now.

He was so close to getting his final hurrah. So close to one last caper. So close to really being alive again. And yet, they were no closer to actually getting the ball rolling than they had been before. But that wasn't what had Jack clinging to his host like a balloon on the verge of release from a child's careless hand. It was in the way Eli spoke, in how he held himself and how he looked at Jack as though he was looking not only through Margaret but directly through the soul inside as well. Something was wrong.

"I still think we could do it on our own," Dale said from the passenger seat.

Jack decided he hadn't heard that. He looked at the dashboard clock. It was nearly four. He needed to get back to the office and write up a report on Dale's collection before anyone got suspicious. The bright side of working in the Murder department was that you typically had only a handful of cases a day; some days not even that. The downside was that your paperwork was scrutinized more closely than in Accidents or Natural Causes, departments where agents had less thumb-twiddling time.

"I don't think this is happening," he said at last, finally putting the car into drive.

"What's not happening, Jackie?" Dale asked, heavy brown eyes still bright with the kind of earnest hope that made Jack squeamish.

Jack had to make a choice: protect his new life as Margaret, or let himself be Jack again for one more fleeting moment. But part of being Jack was having the You Agains at his side, and if that was off the table, the decision was an easy one.

"I need to get you moved on, bud," he said. "I have to get back to work."

"You're giving up?"

"Yeah," Jack conceded. It was a first, but the past few months had been full of those. At least this time it wasn't a bladder leak.

"That sucks, Jackie. That really sucks."

Jack couldn't argue with that. Still, he felt a little pang at Dale's words. Jack never liked to let his friends down. It was kind of his whole deal. He wasn't a particularly paternal man, unless you counted the class turtle he helped raise in fourth grade, but he took pride in taking care of his own. He let a sigh creep from his bottom lip, the air that escaped with it attempting fruitlessly to flutter through Margaret's stiffly sprayed hair.

"All right, tell you what. I'll drop you at my new digs on the way back to work. You can watch some TV or something and we can have a good catch-up when I get back after work. Have a heart-to-heart and shit. Then we'll get you going, cool?"

Dale shrugged. "I guess," he said. "I mean, yeah. Sure. Thanks."

It wasn't the level of enthusiasm Jack had been hoping for, but under the circumstances, he'd take what he could get. He'd just have to bullshit his paperwork on Dale's case a little. It was something he'd've had to do if they'd gone through with the initial plan anyway. And if there was one thing Jack could do in any body, it was bullshit.

Half an hour later and he pulled into the driveway of Margaret's mini McMansion, complete with a two-car garage and old-money beige stone walls with matching shutters.

"Damn," Dale said on a whistle. "I always said you'd strike it rich someday, didn't I, Jackie? Didn't know you'd be dead first, but still."

"It was a lucky possession," Jack said, boasting modestly. "Come on, I'll show you around."

Inside, the home glistened with the kind of polished marble and upper-middle-class white walls that stood as the antithesis to apartment 3A. Margaret had excellent taste in both house and house cleaner. Thanks to a small but formidable woman Jack knew only as Mrs. Shaw, who came by every Wednesday, the home was unfamiliar with concepts like dirt, dust, mildew, or a clean clothes pile that shifted from floor to bed to floor until their owner either finally folded them or they ended up back in the dirty pile, ready for the cycle to repeat itself.

Dale whistled again as they moved from the high-ceilinged foyer into the living room.

"Have a seat," Jack said, flipping on the ninety-inch TV and finding a college football game. "All right, hang tight. I'll be back in an hour or so."

Dale plopped onto a white leather couch cushion without argument, his focus immediately transfixed by the giant screen full of giant men in giant shoulder pads. Jack looked on for a moment with the same sort of paternal pride with which he'd once looked at his class turtle. Dale wasn't too different from that turtle, really. Dangle the right treat in front of them, be it lettuce or televised sports, and they'd do what you needed them to—whether that was crawling back into their tank when playtime was over or, Jack mused, crawling into a different kind of tank so he could get back to work knowing Dale was where Jack needed him to be for the moment. He'd always appreciated this about both Dale and Mr. Shellington, and he couldn't help but feel as though he'd trained them both well.

Satisfied with his distracted little turtle man, he left the house and headed back to work.

BY THE TIME JACK GOT BACK TO THE S.C.Y.T.H.E. OFFICES, A GOOD half of the Murder department was at their desks, wrapping up their respective days. Jack gave a polite bob of the head to two agents he vaguely recognized as he made his way to Margaret's cubicle. His office neighbor was a middle-aged man with razor-sharp features and the kind of hearing that meant a mouse couldn't fart in peace on the opposite side of the building without it being noted and, more than likely, commented on. Jack mentally referred to this man as The Eagle, though there was a good possibility that wasn't actually his name. Jack figured this was something Margaret should know, so he never asked, and besides, The Eagle suited him better than Ron or Tom or Bartholomew or whatever he was actually called.

Just now, The Eagle was clacking away on his keyboard as though he actually knew what he was doing in his job, which Jack considered both impressive and a bit smug. His tippy-taps stopped as Jack's heels clicked by, and The Eagle's sharp eyes landed on him. Jack gave a tight smile. The Eagle made a sound of acknowledgment and then returned to his keyboard, clearly swept away in his report-writing in a way Jack could never imagine and hoped he'd never have to.

Jack slid into Margaret's desk chair and cracked open the laptop that sat waiting for him on the desk. He opened a new document and typed Dale's name and case number into their designated columns at the top. Fiddled with the font for a moment. Then the font size. Then the color. These all had to follow the S.C.Y.T.H.E. standard, of course: Times New Roman, 12 point, black. The higher-ups had clearly taken inspiration from every high school essay rubric in North America. But the fiddling gave Jack time to think about exactly what he'd say about Dale's case. Processing would know Dale's essence hadn't arrived yet, so Jack would be screwed if he said otherwise and his manager took the time to do any cross-referencing. He remembered something he'd stumbled across during his crash research into the organization down in the S.C.Y.T.H.E. archives: a case involving a soul who wasn't with his body, only to be found later at a nearby park, so there was precedence for a missing essence, even if it was rare. But a story like that would raise too many questions.

He switched the font to Wingdings and was tapping his fingers on the desk, still pondering, when a phone rang. Jack stopped tapping and reached for his office phone.

"Secure Collection, Yielding, and Transportation of Human Essences, this is Margaret Chen speaking," Jack said down the line. In reply, a dial tone beeped in his ear. Jack's brows knitted. The phone rang again. Jack looked at the receiver in confusion for a moment, then replaced it and fished Margaret's cell phone from her purse. Its screen was blank save for the photo of Margaret and her husband, Wesley, on a postcard-perfect beach. The ringing continued.

Jack froze.

On the day he died, he left all his belongings with his body to keep things from getting more complicated than they'd needed to be: Sunglasses. Keys. A half pack of spearmint chewing gum. His wallet, containing his driver's license, seemed like an especially important thing to leave for whoever found the vacated corpse sprawled there on the sticky club floor. But his phone held every connection he had left to the living world, and in a moment of weakness, he took it. Of course, no one bothered texting dead men. Once the news got out and the Facebook notifications from people tagging Jack in farewell posts dried up, the phone went silent. But every once in a while, Jack found himself scrolling through his contacts, lingering on one in particular, thumb hovering just above the number with no reason to press it. It was the only time he bothered getting the phone out from the pocket of Margaret's laptop case these days. Except that right now it was ringing.

The Eagle's face slowly rose above the cubicle wall like a nosy meerkat, furry brows and receding hairline giving his position away. Jack swiveled his chair and dug out the ringing phone, curling over the device as he hit answer, as though his hunched position would muffle his voice.

"Uh, hello?" he half whispered down the line. When he dared shoot a glance over his shoulder, The Eagle's hands had joined his head above the wall, aiding in raising him up on his toes for a better vantage point.

"Jack."

Jack's borrowed heart hit the narrow rib cage surrounding it with such force that he jolted backward in spite of himself, his chair tipping precariously with the motion, one front wheel airborne. Jack shifted forward, sending himself hard back to earth in every way.

The voice that seeped with an unsteadying steadiness down the line was one Jack hadn't heard in more years than he'd let himself count. He found himself wondering if The Eagle could hear how his heart raced, how his breathing suddenly came fast and shallow. He had to say something. Something that wouldn't raise suspicion in either his colleague or the person on the other end.

"Yo," was what he came up with.

A brow ticked subtly upward above the cubicle wall. Jack tried to ignore it.

"I mean, yes?" he said carefully.

He heard muffled voices from the other end, indicating there were other people there. Then, "We need to talk."

"Okay," said Jack, too eagerly. "Yeah. Right. Where?"

"Eli's."

"Okay."

Before he could say anything else, a click sounded, and another dial tone blared in Jack's ear. He pulled the phone away and looked behind himself just in time to watch The Eagle quickly clamber back down into his own cubicle. Jack knew he didn't sound like Margaret right now. And right now, he couldn't bring himself to care. He opened the Recent Calls tab on his phone and found the caller ID at the top, half convinced he'd hallucinated the whole exchange. The name glowed softly back at him on the screen. Then, Dale's report still in Wingdings, he packed up and left the office.

6

Leaves

October 1999

Jack did not have a stomachache. What he did have was a gift for dramatics and a half-empty cup of banana pudding under his bed that looked remarkably like vomit when spewed across a planet-themed bedspread accompanied by gagging sounds.

It was just after ten a.m. and Jack was spooning the last remnants of a fresh pudding cup onto his tongue as he lounged on top of the fresh bedding his mom had laid out for him. She'd left for work soon after, which would usually be Jack's cue to lay siege to his castle, but today he was on a different mission. Breakfast complete, he flopped onto his perfectly healthy stomach and grabbed the phone receiver from its Garfield-shaped cradle on his bedside table. The phone had cost him twenty-five cents at a garage sale, which he'd dug out of the school vending machine when no one was looking. It was from that phone he'd made all his most pressing business calls.

Eli picked up on the second ring. Jack knew Eli was out of school for a dental checkup that morning. It was the main reason Jack had played hooky himself. That was one of the first life lessons Jack had ever learned: if you want to win the game, you have to think several steps ahead of the other players. He pressed the hard-earned Garfield phone to his ear. He was already winning.

"Eli," he crooned down the line, twirling the phone cord around his index finger.

"How'd you get out of school?" Eli asked, a hint of reluctant awe clinging to the edges of his words.

"Banana pudding."

"Okay," said Eli. "What do you want?"

"Ol' Mrs. Sullivan still offering ten bucks for someone to rake her leaves?"

"Nah, some high schoolers down the street already got there."

"Shit," said Jack, for only the fourth time in his nine years of life. The word still felt a bit strange on his tongue. "Well, leaves are always falling."

"Yeah."

"So it wouldn't hurt to go by there and ask."

"I guess."

"With some leaves."

"Oh."

"I'll bring a garbage bag and meet you in the woods by Fort You Again in half an hour, yeah? You bring your family's rake. We've got this. You and me. Five big ones apiece."

"I can't," said Eli. "My sister had a checkup today too and now I'm stuck with her watching me. I'm not allowed to go anywhere without her."

Jack gave a sympathetic tut. He didn't have any siblings, sure, but the concept of sisters always seemed unfortunate to him. He tapped Garfield's plastic nose thoughtfully. "She a narc?"

"Huh?"

"Would she squeal on us?"

"Nah, she's cool," said Eli. "But she'd never go along with it. Hanging with anyone under fourteen is way too lame for her these days."

"Tell her it'll be worth her while. She can have half of your cut."

"Hey! No, she can't."

"Look, do you want to make some money or not? Two bucks fifty richer is two bucks fifty richer, dude."

"Ugh, fine. I'll ask, but I can't promise anything."

"See you in half an hour, Eli."

"Hopefully."

"I'll see you in half an hour."

JACK WAS SHOVELING HANDFULS OF FALLEN LEAVES INTO THE OPEN mouth of a garbage bag when he heard the footsteps approach. It was later than he'd instructed, which meant Eli must have had to put some real work into convincing his sister to come along. That would earn Eli an extra quarter from Jack's own take. Fair was fair, after all.

Jack straightened and tossed a look over his shoulder. Eli emerged from the bronzed foliage, carrying his family's rake like a walking stick. He looked like Gandalf if Gandalf was a fifth grader in a neon yellow soccer jersey, which Jack figured he may have been at some point. Dragging her feet beside him was a real live teenaged girl. Her knees knocked a bit from where they poked out the bottom of a plaid skirt, there was a fading streak of pink in her sand-colored hair, and even from a distance, Jack could see an actual pimple on her chin. Jack studied her a moment, the way one might study a rare pygmy hippo on safari. A strange and mysterious creature, the teenaged girl. She looked sullen, never raising her gaze from the leaf-strewn ground, and yet she somehow commanded enough authority to keep pulling Eli's attention in her direction.

"Well, this is it," Eli said to his sister, tipping his head at Fort You Again, which sat proud and solid behind Jack. "And that's Jack."

"Huh." The girl lifted hazel eyes and ran them up and down first the fort and then Jack. She folded her arms. "Huh," she said again. Somehow she didn't seem particularly wowed by either.

"'Sup?" Jack tried. He flicked a rogue leaf from his hair. Her eyes were still on him, heavy with scrutiny. It was a weight Jack was used to carrying. You don't get suspended twice before double digits without the occasional weighty stare. But somehow hers dragged his usually proud chin a few inches lower.

"Greer," said the girl.

"I don't speak French," Jack said.

"That's her name, dork," said Eli.

"Oh," said Jack. "It's weird. I like it."

"'Kay," said Greer. "So, like, what are we doing here? Eli said we're raking Mrs. Sullivan's yard."

Jack's chin lifted again, his chest puffing slightly as he

prepared to dazzle this strange pygmy hippo with his brilliance. "Ah, but first we need something to rake."

Greer just stared at him. Those hazel eyes weighed a ton.

"So . . ." Jack took a deep breath. He hated having to fill in the blanks on his schemes. It was so much more satisfying when he could just say a quick cool phrase and get on with it. ". . . So we're gonna get some leaves and dump them on her lawn." He puffed a little more and waited for the usual admiration, but all that came was more staring. Jack's chest deflated. He opened the garbage bag again. "I'll just do it."

"This is a douche move, dude," Greer said at last. "She's an old lady. You can't rip off an old lady."

"Why not?"

"Because . . . I don't know, it's just wrong. Tell him, Eli."

Jack looked from Greer to Eli, who seemed caught off guard to suddenly be remembered by his sister.

"Maybe it isn't wrong to rip off *all* old ladies," Eli said carefully. "She did try to get rid of the Richardsons' dog that time, remember?"

Greer was quiet for a moment. "I do like that dog."

"She was so mean to it," Eli continued. "Didn't she even throw a croissant at it when it peed on her tulips?"

"An innocent dog." Jack shook his head somberly. "It could've been killed."

"Lulu ate the croissant," Greer said.

"It could've choked," Jack countered.

Greer shook her head.

"Besides, old lady or not, who hates dogs? No one worth keeping their ten bucks, that's who."

The girl cocked her head, not unlike a dog about to have a

baked good thrown in its general direction, and finally slouched her shoulders forward in defeat. "Fine. I guess it's the sentiment behind the croissant or whatever. Screw Mrs. Sullivan, then. How many more leaves do we need?"

A PIECE OF PAPER CLUNG WEAKLY TO MRS. SULLIVAN'S PERFECT white picket fence, still damp from the light rain of the previous day. On it were the words:

*$10 cash to rake this garden**
**must be raked during the reasonable*
hours of 6am–6pm, no exceptions

Jack opened the gate and ushered the others inside, dragging the bag of leaves behind him. Together the trio blanketed the perfectly manicured yard in a sheet of brown and yellow. Jack pocketed the empty bag and jabbed a finger on the doorbell. A buzz echoed through the compact stone house, summoning the dog-hater within. A moment later Mrs. Sullivan stood in the doorway, face carved downward to frame a frown that seemed as much a permanent part of her physiology as her silvery curler-set hair.

"Yes?"

"We're here to rake your yard," said Jack, indicating the rake in Eli's hands with a tip of the chin.

Mrs. Sullivan shook her head. "That won't be necessary, some nice boys from a few houses down already did the job."

"They clearly didn't do a very good job," Jack said.

Mrs. Sullivan's pale brow furrowed. She looked over the

cluster of children on her front stoop to the yard beyond and blanched.

"B-but it was only just raked last evening," she sputtered. "I don't understand."

Her focus shifted back to Jack, catching on something.

"There are leaves in your hair," she said slowly, pointing with a finger that bent like a fishing hook at Jack's forehead. "Young man, have you defiled my garden?"

"No," Jack said, mostly because he didn't know what "defiled" meant, but also because he wasn't going down without a fight. "There must have been a gust of wind."

"'Gust of wind' my eye," said Mrs. Sullivan. "You've got a garbage bag hanging out of your back pocket. What's a child need a garbage bag for?"

Jack winced. "Collecting . . . garbage," he tried.

For the first time since answering the door, Mrs. Sullivan looked to the other two children standing there.

"I know you," she said to Eli and Greer. "You're the Abrams kids. Do your parents know what you're up to? No? I'm informing them this instant."

Mrs. Sullivan gave a self-satisfied smile and took a step back into the house when something stopped her in her tracks. A whimper, small and pathetic. Jack turned to his left to see Greer's lower lip trembling. A fat tear freed itself from her right eye and traced a round cheek before leaping boldly off her chin.

"Please," Greer barely choked out. "We're sorry. We weren't trying to defile anything, promise. It's just that our friend here, Jack, he needs the ten dollars to get home. He was visiting his grandmother, who's very sick, and he used up all his bus money buying her flowers." She was sobbing now, snot streaming in time with her tears.

Mrs. Sullivan's frown creaked open and shut for a moment with nothing decipherable coming out. Finally she gave Greer's shoulder a brusque pat. "There now." She pulled a tissue from her sleeve and offered it to the crying girl. "That isn't dignified. Wipe up, child." Then, barely perceptibly softening, "Very well. I suppose the yard does need another raking. And if this is all as you say . . ."

"I swear on my grandmother's life," Jack said somberly. "However much of it she has left."

"Fine. Ring for me when you've completed your duties, then."

Jack nodded and Mrs. Sullivan disappeared. As soon as the door closed, Greer wiped her face with the tissue and turned to the boys as if nothing had happened. If Jack had to pinpoint it, he would say that was the moment he fell in love. Of course he wouldn't say it out loud, not to Greer or to anyone else. But it didn't matter, because from that moment on, his love for Greer became one of the things that made Jack, Jack. For the rest of his life. And then some.

7

And there she was. It was Greer who opened the door of apartment 3A. Greer who stood in the doorway. Greer who'd returned from the ether like a ghost. Which, Jack realized, was ironic considering his present circumstances, but still. Greer had vanished from his life over a decade and a half ago, and now, just like that, there she was.

"Wow," she said before he had the chance. But her "wow" wasn't filled with the awe his would have been. Hers was a stale pastry stuffed with disbelief and a trace of revulsion. "Okay." She stepped aside, effectively ushering Jack in, but he couldn't move, not yet. Somehow he was more confused to see Greer here than she was to see him in someone else's body.

She'd changed, of course. Her face was sketched with new lines and creases, like a treasure map that could lead you to the secrets of her recent past if only you knew how to read it. Her sand-colored hair held streaks of gray where faded pink had once been. The lankiness of youth was gone, replaced by soft flesh that had grown and shrunk and grown again over the years. Something panged deep inside Jack. He'd missed so much. He found the hazel eyes that looked out at him with the same scrutiny they'd held the day they met.

"Hi, Greer."

She tipped her head. It wasn't a nod, really, but it was an acknowledgment, and for now that would have to be good enough.

Jack uprooted Margaret's sensible heels and went inside.

As the door clicked shut behind him, Jack found himself looking between Eli and Carter, who both sat fidgeting on the corduroy couch. Greer swept past him and perched herself on the arm of the sofa. They all stared at Jack, wearing varying degrees of discontent.

Okay. This wasn't quite what Jack had expected when Greer had called, but then again, he couldn't really bring himself to expect anything in particular from that call. Did this mean they'd all come around to the plan? Their faces said no, but what else would bring them all together again like this?

"What's up?" He swung a plastic chair from what passed as a kitchen table into the center of the room and sat down, instantly regretting the seating choice. An octogenarian body required cushioning, Margaret's hips and lower back instantly reminded him. But it was too late, he'd committed to the chair. The silence in the room was too heavy and awkward to start making adjustments. He tried daintily crossing a leg.

"We need to talk to you." It was Greer who spoke first. It always had been.

"Sure," said Jack. "Is this about the plan?"

"It's about all of this." Carter waved a hand up and down Jack's body.

"This is fucked up," Eli added. "You get that, right?"

"Eli told us," said Greer. "Eli told us everything."

This was as good an excuse as any to get out of that medieval torture chair. Jack struggled to his feet with indignation and relief. “Wait, what is this? Some kind of . . . intervention?”

“You can’t go stealing a body, man,” Carter said. “Shit. It’s low even for you.”

“I didn’t mean to steal anything, it just kind of happened,” Jack protested.

“Just happened,” Eli repeated. “Right. Like taking the principal’s car for a joyride just happened. Like leaving me to take the rap for the bank thing just happened. Like Jules just happened.”

Greer immediately got to her feet at that. The air in the room hung uncomfortably for a moment before vacating it altogether. No one seemed to remember how to breathe.

“You went through life dragging everyone into your bullshit,” said Carter. “Now you’re trying to do it in death and it just . . . it has to stop.”

Jack forced an inhale. What the hell was he talking about? “I didn’t . . . I didn’t drag anyone into anything. We all wanted to be there, to do the things we did.”

“You think I wanted a rap sheet by sixteen?” Eli said. “Fuck that. Someone had to take the blame for all your schemes, and somehow nothing ever sticks to Jack McCoy.”

“I—” Jack tried, but in truth he had nothing to finish that sentence with, so it was almost a relief when Greer interrupted.

“You need to move on, Jack.”

But then it wasn’t a relief at all, not when he heard her words. Move on? She had to be joking. Jack might not be alive, technically speaking, but he was still living, and he didn’t want to give that up. Not yet. Not until he had one more chance to prove himself as the man he knew he was: the leader, the hero, the one everyone else looked up to. The man the world knew as Jack McCoy. Even if he was also currently Margaret Chen.

"I cannot believe I'm getting an afterlife intervention right now," he said. "Seriously? You're telling me that if you had the chance to not be dead, you wouldn't take it?"

At the group's collective silence, he changed tactics. "Listen, you're all struggling right now, right? And maybe I carry some responsibility for that. So I'm here to make it right."

Greer rubbed at her temples. "What are you talking about?"

"Dale and I, we've got a great idea for one last job. And it's not just the last job because we're dead, it's the last one because you'll never need another one after this. After this, you'll all be set for life. And then you'll never have to see me again. One last big job, like I always promised."

"You're fucking kidding me," said Carter.

"He doesn't get it, dude," said Eli. "I told you this was pointless." Then, unmistakably and unavoidably to Jack, "We've all lost enough thanks to your jobs. We're done. If you won't fucking rest in peace like a proper dead guy, then you can leave us out of whatever the hell you're planning."

For just a fragment of a moment, Jack felt as if he was back in his old body, a freshman getting kicked from all angles by the senior boys whose lockers he'd stolen weed out of. It had felt worth it then. He and the gang had all gotten high in Fort You Again, and the pain in his ribs and stomach was soothed by the memory of laughing so hard at Eli's impression of their math teacher that he almost threw up. But now, the metaphorical stomps on his solar plexus had no payoff. Now it was the people who'd always made the pain worthwhile doing the kicking. And for the life of him, Jack couldn't understand it. Eli's prison stints only occasionally resulted from one of Jack's schemes. Carter was doing some real job out in the world that he'd never complained about. And Greer, well, last Jack heard, she was still married to the guy she'd run off with after everything happened with Jules, and was a mom of two or maybe three. None were especially rich or successful, but that couldn't be blamed on Jack. He was just trying to make their lives better, just like he always had. But for some reason, none of them seemed to want his help. He winced at every bruise blooming under the strikes of their collective rejection. This was new.

Jack held up his hands. "Okay," he relented. "Okay." It wasn't, of course. As much as he appreciated a new life, what he actually wanted was a final taste of the old one. But it wasn't worth doing one last job without the people he did it all for, and they'd made it perfectly clear that wasn't going to happen. So being Margaret Chen would simply have to be good enough. "I'll leave you alone, then."

Greer's hazel eyes landed heavy on him. "That's it, huh? You're really just going to go back to living a stolen life? To keep taking from people. That's the plan?"

"You never used to mind."

"We're not dumb kids anymore," said Greer.

"Maybe that's the problem," said Jack.

"You need to move on," Greer said again, but Jack decided not to hear her.

DALE WAS STILL ON THE WHITE LEATHER SOFA WHEN JACK GOT home, still glued to the same game Jack had left on before going back to work. Jack let a small smile touch his lips. Now this was a true friend. This was someone who knew how to let Jack look after things instead of telling him he shouldn't go around possessing people.

Jack flicked the TV off, summoning Dale's attention.

"Oh, hey, Jackie," Dale greeted. "You just get in?"

"Yeah." Jack tried to run a hand through Margaret's hair, but it promptly got stuck in product. "We should get going."

"Oh," Dale said again. "Okay."

"Sorry."

Dale shrugged. "Hey, I got more time to hang around than most dead guys, I guess."

"Yeah," Jack said again.

"You okay, Jackie?"

Jack sniffed. Of course he was okay. He was always okay. That was his role in life. The guy who was okay, and who would make sure those he cared about were too. Even if he couldn't make things okay for Dale. Even if he was no longer allowed to do as much for the others. Being okay was all Jack had left.

"I'm okay," said Jack.

"Okay," said Dale. "I guess this is it, then."

"I'll take the scenic route to processing," Jack said. Both dead men tried a smile, but neither could quite manage it.

JACK FOUND HIMSELF WATCHING DALE FROM HIS RECENTLY BLURRY peripheral vision. Had he done right by Dale? He must have, or else Dale would never have been so loyal all these years. Sure, Jack was currently driving him to the last place he'd ever experience on this earth, which was a bit of a dick move if you really thought about it, but Dale got to watch that game, which was probably nice. And he was right, most dead guys didn't get to hang around this long. That was thanks to Jack. Jack even had to play fast and loose with company policy to make it happen. Granted, fast and loose was his favorite way to play most things, but still. It was objectively pretty generous.

Dale, for his part, just stared out the passenger window. Probably taking in the sight of trees and town houses and tantrum-throwing toddlers for the last time. If Jack really wanted, he could probably keep Dale overnight and get him to processing first thing in the morning. Give him one final night of drunken debauchery. But then, Dale couldn't actually drink or debauch in his current condition. And frankly, with the state of his new hardware, neither could Jack. No, he'd done all he could. This was what came next. What always came next. Still, he couldn't help but want to hold on. Not so much for Dale's sake, if he was honest with himself, but because this was the only real friend he had left. The last You Again on his side. The last connection to his old life.

Jack opened his mouth to say something, but all that came out was a wistful sigh, which wasn't like him. It was, if he had to guess, like Margaret Chen, and that realization made his butt cheeks clench. He was slipping loose of his tethers again. He could feel it.

A shrill ring erupted from the back seat. Jack nearly jumped out of his borrowed skin.

"You gonna get that, Jackie?" Dale asked after a second ring.

"Uh, yeah." Jack forced himself back into the front seat of Margaret's Mercedes and reached an arm behind himself, blindly fishing through the designer purse on the back seat floor for his old cell phone. Lipstick. Roll-on lily-of-the-valley perfume.

Switchblade. Phone. He wrapped his fingers around it and dragged it to his ear.

"Hello?"

For the second time that day, Greer's voice poured unexpectedly through the speaker.

"Where are you?" she breathed. Her tone was bordering on irritated, her volume hushed, but she'd called. For some reason she'd called. Whatever Jack said next could make or break whether that call continued.

"In a car." Probably break. He tried again. "I'm in the car with Dale. We're just . . . It's a long story."

"How far are you from Billy's?"

"The diner? That Billy's?"

"That Billy's," said Greer.

That Billy's was on the other side of town. "Not far," said Jack.

"I'm in the usual booth."

Before Jack heard the click from the other end of the phone, he was already turning the car around.

8

Greer held a mug that had likely never seen the inside of a dishwasher. A diamond winked out of a gold band on her left ring finger, a glimmer of something pristine and luxurious that didn't belong amid the easy grime of the diner. That didn't belong on her hand.

Jack slid into the booth across from her. Dale followed suit. Greer still hadn't looked up from whatever steamed in her mug. She took a sip. Dale shifted uncomfortably beside Jack, but Jack just looked on. He waited. Finally, she lifted her eyes.

"You drive a Mercedes," she said, and the words were so far from anything Jack could have anticipated that all he could do was repeat them like a particularly dense parrot.

"I drive a Mercedes."

"This . . ." She gestured at Jack's new body. "Her. She has money."

"Yeah."

Greer's gaze slipped back into her mug. "I wouldn't ask if I didn't have to."

"Ask?"

"For a loan. Just a loan. I'd pay you back as soon as I could."

"Oh," said Jack.

"I didn't know who else to ask. Sorry, I shouldn't— This was a mistake." She moved to rise, but Jack extended a hand across the booth toward her.

"Wait. Please." He held his breath until she turned back to face him. "How much?"

"Forty."

The worn booth cushion felt as though it had dropped out from beneath Jack at that. Dale sputtered a gasp beside him.

"Grand?!" the dead men spat in unison.

"This was a mistake," Greer said again, her movements quicker and more determined this time. "It's too much to ask after so long."

"It's not that," Jack said before Greer could fully finish her sentence. "I'd do it in a heartbeat, Greer. You know I would. But I can't." Greer said nothing to this, which told Jack everything he needed to know. She didn't believe him. She thought, honestly seemed to believe, that despite all they'd been through together and all she meant to him, that Jack wouldn't move heaven and earth, and hell too, for good measure, if Greer asked him to.

"Look, Margaret is loaded, sure," he said to Greer's profile. "But beyond her weekly paycheck, I can't actually access her money. I still don't really understand how this all works, but it's like Margaret gets to choose what parts of her thoughts and memories I have access to, and her bank details are tucked away somewhere she won't let me reach. I've tried. Believe me. Hell, as soon as I realized my host body was wearing real diamonds, I had a whole future on a beach in the South of France planned out. But her bank requires very specific details to get anywhere near her money, and every time I think I'm getting close to finding them in here, she moves them somewhere else. Somehow the stats of her favorite golfers are just lying around up here, but everything that actually matters is under lock and key."

Jack gulped in his first breath since he began his rant. In truth, it was as much a relief to get that off his chest as it was to see Greer warily ease herself back into her seat. This whole possession thing was still so new and confusing, and he'd had no one to talk to about it until now. It reminded him a bit of going through puberty, but at least sex ed had prepared him for those body changes.

"Okay," Greer said after a long moment.

"Yeah." Jack searched her face. "Wait, okay what?"

"I'll do it."

"Do . . . ?"

"It. Whatever it is. The job you tried to rope us into. You said there's big money involved, right? So whatever idiotic thing came out of the fucked-up mind of Jack McCoy this time, I'll do it."

"My fucked-up mind too," Dale corrected.

"Dale's here," Jack said absently. Greer's brow furrowed, her gaze shifting to the empty space beside Jack he'd tipped his head toward. Jack continued. "You will?"

"Yeah."

Jack ran his hands up and down his trousers. This was incredible. This was wrong. "What do you need the money for?"

"Jesus Christ, Jack. I just said I'm in. Isn't that enough?"

It was. It was everything. "Greer. What is it?"

Greer's face drooped back toward her mug. She shook her head, but not with her usual defiance. With something that looked almost like defeat.

A hand crept unbidden from Jack's lap back onto the table, inching toward hers again. But then he caught sight of the veins and the sun spots, the creases and arthritic bends. He wanted to comfort her, but not like this. Not with a stranger's hands. He retreated.

"It's my youngest," Greer continued, oblivious to the hand that wasn't Jack's. "She's been sick for a while now. We were managing as well as possible, keeping her stable, keeping our heads above water. But Curtis lost his job last month. I can't keep the four of us afloat on a hairdresser's salary, much less afford all of Mia's treatments. If this job is really a guaranteed payout, then I need it. My family needs it."

Her family. Greer's family. Greer's family with her husband. A man named Curtis. Who even went around with a name like Curtis? It was the celery of names: tasteless and weirdly stringy.

"I'm sorry," Jack said. "About Mia." And about Curtis, but this was probably not the moment to add that. What mattered right now was that Greer needed Jack just as much as Jack needed Greer. His army wasn't completely disassembled. Balance was ever so slightly restored to the universe. And to top it off, he could actually help. He could do something for Greer. It had been years since he'd been in such a position.

Greer nodded into her mug. "Thanks." She looked up again. "So, what is it?"

"What's what?"

"The job."

Jack looked over at Dale, who puffed up slightly beside him. Jack did his best to break down the nature of his job at S.C.Y.T.H.E. in as few words as possible.

"So the idea is, there has to be some kind of Master List

somewhere with all the details about people's deaths," Jack said. "Those details would be worth a ton."

"So the plan is to steal the Master List?"

"That's the plan," Dale confirmed.

"That's the plan," Jack reiterated.

"Right." Greer's hazel eyes bored into him again. "Do you actually know this list exists? Or where it is?"

"Above my pay grade." Jack waved a manicured hand. "But I'm sure I can find out."

"Jack, I'm not looking for 'I'm sure' here unless you actually are."

Jack shifted in his seat, trying to alleviate some of the weight from her gaze. "When I first jumped into this"—he gestured at his Margaret costume—"I didn't know anything about S.C.Y.T.H.E. or all the weird shit they do. But there's an archive in the basement filled with all kinds of info about the company. I spent hours in there reading up on the gig so I could play the part."

"You spent hours?" Greer cocked her head.

"Reading?" Dale added.

"I always do what I've gotta do for a job, you know that."

Both Greer and Dale nodded slowly at that.

"Point is," Jack continued, "if that list exists, there'll be information about it in the archives. I just need to do some digging."

LIKE THE REST OF THE S.C.Y.T.H.E. OFFICE, THE ARCHIVES WERE AN ode to fluorescent lighting, linoleum floors, and a particularly diluted shade of beige that would almost be eggshell if only it was brave enough. It required a key card for entry, which Margaret had left tucked safely in the front zipper of her laptop bag, and was overseen by a man somewhere between the age of 70 and 185, if Jack had to hazard a guess. The man, whose name Jack had never bothered learning, sat slumped in a rolling chair behind a little administrative desk, forever reading the same dog-eared old copy of a book called *Practical Pigeon-Keeping*, the author's appropriately feathered 1980s hairdo filling approximately one-sixth of the back cover. Today it was open to a page scattered with images of different feathers, each annotated by both the text and handwritten scribbles.

Jack cleared his throat. The man looked up from his reading material, apparently alarmed to be sharing the endless rows of shelves with another person. A pair of thick-lens glasses magnified his eyes to several times their natural size, giving him the look of a startled lemur.

"Oh, Ms. Chen," he greeted, lowering the glasses and becoming somewhat more human.

"Hi . . . you," Jack replied.

"Back again for some more research, are we?"

"We are," said Jack. "I'm looking for information on where we get our cases from. Maybe a list or something. I don't know, just spitballing here. Any idea what section I'd find that in?"

"Oh sure," said the man, adjusting his bow tie in a manner that Jack would almost call flustered. "Anything like that would be in Section 301 D."

Jack turned toward the row in question. "Great—"

"Of course, that section is only accessible to department managers and above."

"Ah," said Jack.

"It is lovely to see you again, Ms. Chen." The man gave a broad smile and slipped the glasses back onto his nose, ready to return to his book.

Shit. Jack was losing him. It hadn't been this hard before. The day after Jack took over Margaret, after struggling to understand how S.C.Y.T.H.E. and its agents worked, he'd slipped down here and told the startled lemur he needed to do some reading for a case. Asked for anything in the archives about this strange new world he'd stumbled upon and was pointed without issue toward a section full of training manuals and noteworthy case records. He'd returned every lunch break for a week and absorbed each drop of information he needed to pull off his disguise. Jack had never read for pleasure, and his school report cards didn't particularly favor the beginning of the alphabet, but when it benefitted him, Jack could be as studious as they came. All he needed was a point in the general direction of where to start. And the lemur wasn't pointing.

"So, pigeons," Jack tried, peering at the book.

"Magnificent birds," the man replied.

"Uh-huh," said Jack. "Great feathers. Very . . . gray."

"Not all of them," the man said, holding up a finger as if he'd just made a brilliant point in a presidential debate. "The pigeons we see on the street are only one species out of over three hundred. Though common street pigeons do have their charm, of course."

"Of course," said Jack. "I've always said it."

"Have you?" He waggled his glasses at that. "Why, Ms. Chen, are you a fellow chum of the Columbidae?"

"The . . ." Jack tried to remember if that was one of the STIs he'd learned about back in Sex Ed. The man continued to grin at him in a way that suggested probably not, so he said, "Yes. Of course. Who isn't?"

"I had no idea," said the man, leaning closer. "You know, I've dabbled in a bit of pigeon fancying here and there."

Once again, Jack found himself trying to decide if this was a sex thing. Well, he was just going to have to go with it. "You don't say." He rolled his shoulders back as far as he could, hoping to lift his bosom above his belly button. "I too have occasionally fancied pigeons."

This prompted a wet guffaw from the man. Okay, so he'd said something funny. That could be good. A flirty joke. Everyone enjoyed a flirty joke, even if it was unintentional. Jack ran fingers through his stiff hairdo and gave what he hoped was a seductive giggle.

"You know," Jack said, "I bet a handsome man like you is a bit of a rebel. I mean, pigeons? What else? Motorcycles? Drugs?"

"Oh, I've been on my best behavior since I left the military. Spent too many years having to make tricky decisions for the greater good. It's the restful life for me these days. Although"—the man leaned in farther, closing the gap between them and whispering conspiratorially—"last Sunday I went out for an early bird special, but it was only four-fifty. Saved fifteen percent off the suckers even though they don't technically start serving until five."

"Hot," Jack whispered back. "Listen, I'd never ask, but since you walk such a dangerous line anyway, do you think you could get me into Section 301 D?"

The man straightened and sucked his teeth for a moment. "Oh, Ms. Chen, I don't think I can. We have to abide by very strict rules here in the archives, you understand. It's an important job. There's a reason they don't put just anyone down here."

Jack ran a finger down one of the feathers in the book. "Not even for little old me?" For the first time in his existence, both of those adjectives were strikingly accurate.

The man fidgeted with his bow tie again. "You drive a hard bargain. I can't go letting you loose in there, of course, but I suppose it wouldn't hurt to show you around."

It was a start, Jack decided. He might not be able to do any actual research this way, but there was always a benefit to casing a joint. It would make coming back after hours a heck of a lot more efficient.

Jack batted his mascara-coated lashes and followed the man back through rows of shelves he'd perused only a few short weeks ago. The fluorescent lights above hummed like bugs trapped in a jar, restless and bleak. For a company devoted to the afterlife, the building that housed it was remarkably lacking in soul.

Aisle upon aisle of metal shelving units blurred together as they walked, centuries of dates written in changing hands scribbled across labels in front of weathered files. Between each row, a security camera blinked down. Jack tracked them as he walked, clocking blind spots in the nooks and crannies tucked among the endless shelves. Finally they reached a door at the very, very back of the bashfully eggshell labyrinth. A small bronze sign held onto the door by two reluctant nails, engraved with the words "Section 301 D—Authorized Personnel Only."

The man whipped a key card from the pocket of a pair of brown trousers that sat alarmingly close to his armpits. He tapped it to his forehead. "Good thing I'm authorized."

Jack attempted to swoon at this, though in truth he'd never quite figured out exactly what a swoon was. His best guess involved heavy breathing and a small wobble, though that may have come across more as a burp. The man didn't seem to mind. With a triumphant flourish, he swiped his key card and swung the door open. Although a patchwork of more fluorescent lights flickered to life, their ticking suggested they weren't thrilled at being revived. That wasn't something Jack could relate to, though he supposed he might have felt differently as a corporate lighting fixture.

Inside the small room were more metal shelves, which came as a bit of a disappointment to Jack, who had expected its top secret status to be accompanied by a little more oomph. He went to step inside, but the man gently tugged him back by the wrist.

"That's as far as I can let you go, I'm afraid," he said. "Still. Beautiful, isn't she?"

Jack summoned a few half-hearted oohs and aahs, his focus fixed on the shelves and their contents. He scanned past the reams of old files until he locked onto a corner at the back of the room piled with books and cardboard boxes. There were no labels to be found in that corner, and every surface appeared to be covered in dust, which all seemed promising. That would be where Jack would start when he returned. Which he would have to do, because the startled lemur beside him made for an unrelenting guard.

9

It was after eight p.m. and Jack was restless. He was always restless before a job. It was like his body knew how much adrenaline was about to hit and decided to get a head start on the process. Even in a different body, he found himself unable to sit still as the hours ticked by. Dale was back on the leather sofa, cracking up in sync with the laugh track of whatever sitcom they were watching. Jack had barely been paying attention when he turned the TV on. Within ten minutes of arriving home after work, he was already pacing. Half an hour and he'd made visible tracks in the white carpet. By now, most of the dust and crumbs brave enough to try making a life for themselves on the lower floor of Margaret's otherwise spotless house had been swept onto Jack's knee-high compression socks.

The man from S.C.Y.T.H.E.'s archives was called Gerard. This Jack had learned from the key card he'd nabbed during a flirtatious stumble that ended in tangled limbs and subtle but awkward pocket searching. Jack had to dodge a great many things during that faux stumble, but one thing he couldn't avoid was the promise of a date the following weekend. Which was fine, probably. Gerard didn't strike him as the sort to get too handsy on the first date, and Jack was too much of a lady to give in to anything if he tried. Plus it meant he now had the little plastic rectangle that would grant him access to a room full of answers. He ran the key card between his fingers as he paced, the smooth white surface a promise in his hands.

He checked his watch again. Time always seemed to move slowest when you had the least use for it. Jack smiled to himself. That was a thought he'd first had on the night he and the You Agains broke into the city library on a mission to find the dirty books they weren't allowed to read in the daylight. He was eleven and a half and nobody would tell him what an areola was. It felt like ages between the time school ended and when his parents finally went to bed. Dale, Eli, and Carter were sleeping over. They would meet Greer and Jules at the library, if only Jack could survive the wait. He'd learned a lot that night. Not what an areola was, unfortunately, but about the importance of timing when breaking and entering, which proved just as valuable. Especially when it came to not having a worried dog-walker call the cops on you or getting grounded.

Finally, his time arrived. Ten o'clock was too late for any of S.C.Y.T.H.E.'s day workers and still an hour early for the night shift. Jack had slipped into Margaret's stealthiest attire: a black cashmere turtleneck, tweed slacks, and practical flats. He'd selected a purse big enough to hold any paperwork they needed to smuggle out while still tastefully coordinating with his ensemble. He was ready.

Jack and Dale loaded into the Mercedes, the night air crisp against skin hot with anticipation. Jack rolled down the windows as he drove, savoring everything that came with a night like this: the knot of thrill in his gut, the frantic breeze against his cheeks, the plan etched in his mind like a testament from God. Not that God, sure, but a trickster kind of god. There were lots of those, and they always seemed to be on Jack's side.

This was it. This was what it meant to be alive. Okay, he may have had a small bladder leak in his excitement, but he had the appropriate undergarments for the situation. All that mattered now was that Jack McCoy was back, baby.

THE PARKING LOT WAS EMPTY, BUT JACK EASED THE MERCEDES TO A stop by the curb a few blocks away, just in case. Plausible deniability, like timing, was an invaluable asset in situations like this.

Dale gave a whistle as they approached the glass doors that led to the S.C.Y.T.H.E. offices.

"It's like the office from *The Office*," he said, taking in the five stories of gray brick and glass. "I never had you down for a suit-and-tie man, Jackie."

"It's more a dress-and-kitten-heels situation," Jack clarified.

"Didn't really have you down for that either," said Dale. "But you make it work."

Jack slung his purse from his shoulder as they approached the locked doors. He dug around for a minute. These things really needed compartments. Ah. His hand landed on his lock picking kit. A moment later, they were in. He ushered Dale to the basement and swiped his key card for the archives, a little green light signaling their admittance.

"It's back there." Jack jutted his chin down the middle aisle toward the door hidden somewhere in the dark beyond. Then he gestured to the ceiling. "There are cameras every six feet up there, mostly down the center aisle. If we stay to one side we should be fine."

"Can't I just waft over there all ghostlike?" Dale said.

Jack shook his head. "S.C.Y.T.H.E. employees can all see the dead. It's like a job perk or something. You'll need to stick with me."

"Got it."

Jack turned on his phone flashlight and aimed it at the floor, careful to avoid letting its rays creep into the cameras' lines of sight. They slunk in tandem through the cluttered maze of dark shelves until they reached the door waiting patiently at the end. Section 301 D. Jack fished into the pocket of his tweed trousers and pulled out Gerard's key card. The door relented, another little green light flashing agreeably. He stepped inside the room, stark yellow-white light flashing on at the prod of a finger.

Jack crossed to the dusty corner he'd flagged earlier, Dale following just behind.

"You think the list is in there?" Dale asked.

"Doubtful," said Jack. "Someone along the chain of command has to keep tabs on it. But something in this room might tell us who that someone is, and where they keep it."

"Right," said Dale. "I knew that. So what are we looking for, exactly?"

"No idea," Jack admitted. "But I'll know when I've found it."

Dale nodded. Of course he would.

"You guard the door," said Jack.

It wasn't the most glamorous job, to be sure, but Dale didn't really have the requisite tangibility to do much else. Besides, he always guarded the door. He was good at it. Which couldn't be said for many things when it came to Dale.

Dale nodded again and took up his post. Jack, for his part, began to thumb through the boxes in the corner. Most of the books there were old—1970s old, but also old-old, some with covers that suggested hundreds of years of history were bound between them. Jack cracked open one that looked almost textbook-adjacent, with a colorful cover bearing the *March of Progress* illustration, only the monkey-to-human evolution was replaced by figures in cloaks and capes transforming into corporate drones. Inside were diagrams and chapters devoted to the various incarnations of grim reapers through the ages. He thumbed through it long enough to learn about the historical debate regarding the symbolism of farming equipment before closing the book and moving on to the next. And then the next.

In one, bound all in black and with no discernible title, his eye snagged on a paragraph about possession. When he'd first leapt into Margaret, he figured this must be a relatively commonplace occurrence. After all, it hadn't taken much effort, and Jack couldn't imagine anyone actually wanted to stay dead. But according to the *Collections Agent Training Manual*, which he'd read during his first week at S.C.YT.H.E., possession wasn't technically supposed to be possible at all. Yet it was—Jack was reanimated proof of that. For all he knew, there were others, too. And according to the unnamed author of this title-less book, that was a very bad thing. Because, apparently, the one-soul-per-body rule was the sign of a healthy death ecosystem. And, apparently, the existence of possession would be a sign of an ecosystem in collapse. Like dying bees or hot Novembers. A kind of cosmic climate change. He could see why there wasn't anything to identify the writer. Crackpot theorists existed in all areas of life, it seemed. Jack closed the book.

Time was ticking. The night shift would be arriving in less than ten minutes, and Jack still needed to locate what he was looking for and find somewhere to place the key card where Gerard could easily find it and assume he'd dropped it the previous day. It was a delicate operation. Jack's favorite kind. Still, he'd been out of commission for a while now, and he couldn't afford to mess this up.

In a box by his feet, something caught his eye. A depressed-looking leather-bound thing that clearly hadn't been touched in years. Jack scooped it up and scanned the faded gold text on the cover.

S.C.Y.T.H.E: A Comprehensive History

He eased it open, a plume of dust greeting him from the yellowed pages. The index held a rundown of every boring piece of day-to-day corporate logistics within the organization, from modern dress code (no black robes), to affiliated government organizations (the Department of Agriculture, due to an 1871 misunderstanding regarding the use of scythes in reaping). Jack dragged a finger down the index until a heading caught his eye.

"Psst, Jackie!"

Dale's voice wove its way through Jack's distraction. He looked to the door where Dale hovered, slouched and semitransparent.

"Footsteps," Dale hissed.

Shit. Jack checked his watch. Still five whole minutes until the night shift. Someone was clearly hoping for a promotion.

He flipped to page 186 and snapped a quick picture on his phone before carefully replacing everything where he'd found it.

He and Dale bolted up the stairs and into the lobby just in time for the glass doors to expel a middle-aged man in a business suit. Jack froze. Dale froze. The man in the business suit took a half step toward the elevator and, perhaps feeling left out of all the freezing, froze mid-stride. He dragged his back foot forward and righted himself, taking in the elderly woman and the bodiless essence in front of him. He looked from one to the other and then from the other to the first. This wasn't protocol. Essences never came to the S.C.Y.T.H.E. offices. There was probably a whole chapter on that subject in the battered leather book Jack had found.

"I . . . Hello," said the man in the suit to neither of them in particular.

Jack tossed Dale a look. He would do the talking. That's how this worked. If this was going to work, which still very much remained to be seen.

"Hello," said Jack. "You're from the night shift? Good. Very good."

"Is it?" said the man, still looking between Jack and Dale again like he'd just seen a ghost. Which he kind of almost had.

"Yes. I'd been hoping you'd show up soon." The wheels in Jack's head were turning so quickly he wondered if there was visible steam coming from any of his assorted face holes.

"You were?" said the man in the suit.

"Yes," Jack said again. "I'm special ops."

"*You're* special ops?" said the man in the suit.

Had the shock of seeing Jack and Dale there turned this guy into a parrot? Jack decided not to be offended by the disbelief in his voice. Why shouldn't he be special ops? Sure, he was Margaret just now, but he saw no reason why she shouldn't be special ops either, aside from the arthritis and deteriorating eyesight. Besides, all any underling at S.C.Y.T.H.E. knew was that there was a secret agency within the organization tasked with doling out justice to those who toyed with the laws of death. Who they were and how they operated was knowledge disseminated on a need-to-know basis. For all any agent knew, the Department of Special Ops was made up entirely of little old ladies. If Margaret's tidy drawers of paperwork were anything to go by, it would make for a very efficient agency.

"Yes. I'm special ops on a special mission. This is a special soul for reasons I can't disclose. Special reasons."

"Right," said the man in the suit.

Was he buying this? Jack really needed him to buy this. One word to a higher-up that an agent had an essence in the building without clearance, and he was . . . not dead, exactly. It was too late for that. But fired, probably. Or worse; cast out of his host and into the ether with Dale and the other bodiless souls, doomed to a true end of life.

Jack leaned in conspiratorially. He was bringing out the big guns now. "Listen, uh . . ."

"Jack."

"Yes?"

"What?"

"Oh." The Jack who was not the man in the suit gave a nod. "Jack," said Jack. "Listen, Jack. The truth is, you weren't supposed to see me here. My assignment is highly confidential, which is why I timed it between day and night shifts. But you know how these things go. Souls are tricky and things took longer than expected. But you look like a trustworthy man. I can trust you, can't I? Because I would hate to have to take this interaction to the higher-ups and see what they do to make sure you keep this under your hat. My boss is very persuasive when it comes to top secret missions like this."

The other Jack unfroze long enough to take a step backwards. "Right, yes, of course," he sputtered. "If something's top secret, it's top secret. I completely understand."

From over Other Jack's shoulder, Jack spotted two more suited agents walking toward the revolving doors.

"Good," Jack said quickly. "Excellent. I'll be keeping an eye out to make sure you do."

Other Jack began to say something else, but Jack was too busy shuffle-running to the door at top octogenarian speed to hear it. Dale drifted beside him through one of the doors just as the two other night shift agents entered the building, catching just enough of a glimpse of Dale to prompt a momentary creasing of foreheads before they fully vanished inside.

Jack didn't slow his admittedly slow-adjacent pace until he was back in the Mercedes, Dale in the passenger seat, the S.C.Y.T.H.E. offices somewhere behind them in the thick dark of the night.

10

It was useless. Jack had never done exceedingly well in any high school class, but English literature was where his failures really shone. Not that he couldn't have done well if he'd actually applied himself. Every teacher said so. But he'd had better things to apply himself to than untangling metaphors about unrequited love through the symbolism of curtain color. Until now: sitting at Margaret's marble kitchen island with a steaming cup of black coffee, staring down at the flowery late-Victorian bullshit he'd snapped on his phone the night before. Who the hell wrote about mundane office protocol with words like "betwixt"?

All Jack had been able to glean from the chapter entitled "An Information Hierarchy: The Proprietors of Knowledge and How That Knowledge Ought to Be Disseminated for Optimal Efficiency and Confidentiality Among the Ranks" was that folks nearly two hundred years ago used too many words to say very little. And also that he might well be on the right track, if only he could hack through the weeds of convoluted description to figure out exactly where that track was. He skimmed the introductory paragraph for the seventh time that morning:

> *It best behooves both the daily proceedings as well as the covert nature of our organization that the identities of, and facts pertaining to, those who will presently shed their earthly coils be revealed only to those for whom the knowledge is most pertinent. Staff below the rank of Director are to have said knowledge only as it serves the function of their operation. Chairmen and Directors of one or more S.C.Y.T.H.E. facilities may freely access a comprehensive inventory of impending mortality as it is received each month from* The Place *via telegram. This document is to be secured upon receipt in the* Room of Records *of each facility. Entrance to the Room of Records shall be secreted betwixt that which relieves and that which nourishes, for we as arbiters of the afterlife must always remain cognizant of what it is that separates us from our clientele, in order to maintain a wall of indifference between us.*

Okay, so there was a monthly list, though Jack had his doubts as to whether it was still sent by telegram. Regardless, that was the best he could decipher from the jumble of words on his phone screen. He exited out of his photo app and tapped his phone book, his thumb hovering tentatively over Greer's number. She was in. She'd already said she was. And yet there was a sense of unreality to the past few days that left Jack half-sure it was all some weird possession-fueled fever dream, that she'd hang up at the sound of his voice the way she once had. If she even picked up at all.

He forced his thumb to tap the screen. Greer had gone to college for English literature. She'd studied books for fun. She'd be able to untangle the old tome from Section 301 D if anyone could. That was why he was calling. That and that alone.

"Hello?" She'd picked up. That was a start.

"Hey," Jack said, keeping his tone measured, casual. "I need you." Nope. Try again. "For the job," he added quickly. "I need you for the job. There's this book, I think it's what we need, but I can't understand a fucking word of it, and I thought, hey, Greer would be able to understand this, so that's why I called." Great, he'd just become as unnecessarily wordy as the book he was presently mad at.

"All right," said Greer. "I'll be over soon."

That was it. It was that easy. Of course it was. They were working together, just like they used to. Sure, she didn't exactly seem thrilled about it, but she was the one who'd reached out to him, after all. This was on her. She couldn't be mad at him when this was on her.

Jack pocketed his phone and went to join Dale in the living room.

Greer arrived half an hour later in denim capris and a blue-and-yellow-striped polo T-shirt. Jack could have sworn she used to wear that same T-shirt when they were teens, but that couldn't be right. That was decades ago. Decades ago, but this was still Greer.

"Well?"

Jack led her through to the living room, where his phone waited on the coffee table and Dale waited on the couch. He pulled up the picture and held it up to Greer, who took the phone and lowered herself to the couch. Dale shifted to the other cushion just in time to avoid her sitting through him.

"What am I looking at here?" Her eyes lifted to Jack.

"Pretentiousness," said Jack with derision.

"What's the text?" Greer tried again.

"Oh," said Jack. "It's from an old book I found in the S.C.Y.T.H.E. archives about how the company works and stuff."

Greer nodded and dug back into the image, nibbling a nail. "Have you heard of this 'Room of Records'?"

Jack shook his head.

"Well," said Greer, "apparently that's where this Master List is kept, assuming this information is still accurate. How old is the book?"

"It was published in 1887," said Jack.

Greer gave a heavy sigh. "Great."

"But that's like a drop in the bucket when you think about how long death's been around, right?" Jack added quickly. "Plus, S.C.Y.T.H.E. has been in operation since the dawn of civilization, so that's actually pretty modern by the company's standards."

He couldn't tell whether or not that was enough to make Greer feel any more optimistic about the situation, but she went back to the photo all the same.

"Assuming this room still exists, you'll get to it from between the bathroom and the break room."

"Which ones?"

"Which ones what?"

"This branch of S.C.Y.T.H.E. has five floors, and each floor has bathrooms," said Jack. "There're at least three break rooms, too. It doesn't say which ones?"

"It doesn't," said Greer.

"We could go back and check them all out," offered Dale.

Jack shook his head. "You can't come back with me, bud. It's too risky," he said to Dale. "You were already caught once. Besides, I can't go nosing around the other floors without a reason to be there."

"What about office blueprints?" said Greer. "Those should be able to tell us where to look."

Jack tried to blink the hearts out of his eyes at the suggestion. Blueprints. Yes. That was the perfect way to find this hidden room without raising suspicion. If they were anywhere, they'd be in the archives, most likely in Section 301 D. As it happened, Jack already had an easy way in, in the form of an elderly startled lemur. He'd just have to flirt a little harder. He'd wear one of Margaret's most scandalous skirt suits into the office on Monday. Maybe the baby blue one with the tartan print. It hit just below the knee and went perfectly with a pair of brown-and-tan heeled oxfords Jack only pulled out when he really wanted to dazzle. Gerard wouldn't know what hit him.

11

Éclairs

March 2002

The great thing about schools being forever underfunded was that they required students and families to raise money to prevent the cafeteria ceiling from falling down again. That meant coming home with boxes of chocolates or cookies intended for selling but used for eating. Or auctions where covetable Lego sets could mysteriously disappear. Or an annual spring bake sale featuring some of the best and sugariest confections the local parents could dream up. Every year, that bake sale rolled around like clockwork, and every year, each member of the You Again gang was given only enough pocket money to purchase one treat apiece. This was, of course, depressingly inadequate. There were pies in every color and filling Jack could ever hope for. Cakes that had so many layers they nearly reached his chin from the display tables. Cookies with chocolate chips or chocolate chunks or chocolate frosting. Or raisins, but he decided not to think about those. That he had to choose only one option among them was an injustice, and after years of unnecessary suffering, Jack decided to take a stand.

The school bake sale took place on the first Saturday of March. Friday was load-in day, which meant the gym sat empty of people but full of baked goods from school dismissal that afternoon until midmorning the following day, the smells of rubber and sweat and athletic disappointment replaced by vanilla, chocolate, and strawberry. It was now nine p.m. on Load-In Friday, and Jack wore black from head to toe.

Despite the hour and the lingering chill in the air, Fort You Again was warm. Everyone sat shoulder to shoulder as Carter unrolled the school blueprints he'd found in the library: the initial spark that had set this plan alight. The gym was always locked on Load-In Friday after the raccoon incident of '98, which rendered it firmly out of bounds and off Jack's radar, but all it took was one rainy recess stuck indoors and suddenly Mrs. Leigh's Oreo cheesecake was within his grasp. Carter laid the blueprints on the cold earth that acted as the fort floor and pointed to a line among the many other lines that crisscrossed the page.

"That's the air duct that leads directly from Principal Singh's office to the gym. It also goes off to the boys' locker room, so you'll have to stay left, but you'd be able to smell it if you took a wrong turn." This Carter said to Jules, who was by far the smallest of the group in the days before puberty hit, and thus the best suited for duct spelunking. She nodded diligently, pigtails bouncing with her determination.

"Got it."

"The rest of us will be just outside the gym doors," said Jack. "All you have to do is unlock them and we'll nab the goods."

Another nod. She was ready. She always was. Nothing Jack asked of her ever seemed to faze Jules. She was like a hardened military official packaged in pink overalls and nose freckles. At nearly nine, she was the youngest of the group, but it was a fact Jack often forgot.

"Great. Everybody got the gear?"

The others held up the loot sacks they'd smuggled from home: garbage bags, milk crates, pillowcases. This was going to be their most ambitious job yet. Now they just needed to pull it off.

JACK STRAIGHTENED THE TARTAN SKIRT, PULLING IT JUST A LITTLE higher on Margaret's waist so that the hemline scandalously grazed the seam of her knee-high compression socks. He wiggled down the stairs into the archives, willing his stiff hips to sway as he entered the gaping beige room and made his way to the desk at the far end. He'd spent the weekend practicing his elderly lady flirting skills on Dale, which neither found a particularly enjoyable pursuit, but it had definitely taught him what not to do. Lip pursing resulted in a look of distressing constipation. Arm touching only worked on days when Margaret's arthritis wasn't acting up, otherwise it looked like his flirtee was about to be the victim of a talon swipe. Girlish giggles only served to make Margaret look possessed, and since she was, they were best avoided. Instead, Jack had settled on pigeon-related innuendo and the eyelash batting that had been so successful last time.

But when he'd made it to the desk, it wasn't Gerard waiting for him. Instead, a woman stood in his place, hair pulled tight into a severe bun at the nape of her neck, a black turtleneck taut against sharp shoulders. She was the human equivalent of an exclamation point, all harsh lines and intensity.

Jack stopped wiggling.

"Where's Gerard?" He could have started with a "hi," perhaps, but he was too thrown off-balance to remember the word.

"Dead," the woman said as though stating he had gone to the bathroom.

"Oh," said Jack. "What?"

"Last night, I'm told. They brought me in from another branch as an emergency replacement."

"Oh," Jack said again, because what else was he supposed to say? His only date in years was dead, and with him went the key card to Section 301 D. Still, this wasn't the first time his plans had been stymied. He'd had to think on his feet before. After blinking a moment, he found a few other words. "I'm sad." Then some better words. "What I mean is, that's very unfortunate news. He was in the middle of helping me with a work assignment, actually. I know he'd want me to complete it. It was probably even his final wish. I'm wondering if you could help me."

The woman studied him from under sharply arched brows. "And how would I do that?"

"There's something I need from Section 301 D," he said as casually as possible. For a moment he wondered if he should try batting his eyelashes, but something told him that would be less effective on her than it had been on Gerard.

"Very well. I'll need to see your ID, of course, to confirm you have access."

"About that," said Jack. "I'm not a manager. But this is a very special case."

"Do you have written permission to access a prohibited section?"

"Not exactly, but—"

"Then I can't help."

Jack stood there in silence for a long moment. Finally he said, "How do you feel about pigeons?"

Nothing. This was not the audience he'd prepared for. Fuck it, what else did he have to lose? Jack gave his eyelashes a hearty bat. The woman managed to refrain from swooning.

"Are you unwell?" she asked instead.

"No," Jack said. "Just . . . grieving."

"I'm sorry for your loss," said the exclamation point, her tone the very antithesis of the punctuation.

"Thanks," said Jack. He glanced down the middle row of metal shelves, somewhere beyond which stood the door to Section 301 D. And behind it, the information he needed to complete his heist.

He was slipping. There was a time when he'd have been able to weasel his way out of a situation like this. To sweet-talk or bribe or gently manipulate. But in becoming Margaret Chen, it seemed he'd lost a bit of Jack McCoy. With this woman guarding the restricted section of the archives and his skills rusty and dulled by his host, he'd have to find another way.

AT SOME POINT, JACK WOULD HAVE TO CALL GREER AND TELL HER he'd failed. Great. Just what he needed, to look like a fool in her eyes. He'd always been the competent one, the man with the plan. A plan he'd always aced. He hadn't expected it all to start going downhill as soon as he hit his midthirties. Or his early eighties, which he had the unusual opportunity to experience simultaneously. He was on Margaret's white leather couch, feet through Dale's thighs, head propped on three pillows. This was not the way things were supposed to go today.

He'd spent the rest of his workday ruminating over this exotic taste of failure, his focus only occasionally returning to the tasks he was being paid for. By the time he'd returned home, all he wanted was to curl up with some comfort food and a good book. Which was definitely Margaret's influence. When he was fully Jack, he'd have licked his wounds with some beer and a round of pool. Sharing himself like this was not what he'd expected when he body-hopped, but at least it was better than the alternative.

Said alternative was sitting on the other end of the couch, hands awkwardly in his lap, apparently unsure of what to say. Then something like a thought seemed to come over him.

"Hey, Jackie," he said. "What about Carter?"

"What about him?"

"Remember the great bake sale heist of '02?"

Jack did. He could still taste the pies and brownies and cookies and cupcakes, both when he scarfed it all down and when they reappeared later that night. He nodded, now both hungry and nauseous.

"He figured out the school blueprints, right?" Dale continued.

"Yeah, but we actually had blueprints that time."

"Right," said Dale. "But we're not kids now. Carter works in graphics and shit. If we can get him some pictures of the building, he might be able to figure out a place where a secret entrance would make sense, don't you think?"

Jack sat up. Slowly, because it was the only speed his body currently had, but the wheels in his brain were spinning quick.

"Dale, that could work," he said. It could also fail spectacularly, but it was definitely worth a shot. "Only thing is," Jack continued, "Carter wants nothing to do with this."

"Right," said Dale. "That is a thing for sure."

The old Jack McCoy wouldn't worry about such a small detail. The old Jack McCoy would know he could persuade Carter with some clever words and that any issue would be smoothed over without even breaking a sweat. But this new Jack McCoy, the one who was no longer entirely Jack McCoy, felt a slight waver of confidence for the first time in his life. He didn't like it.

"I'll convince him," Jack said, though he wasn't convinced himself.

JACK WAS SENT TO VOICEMAIL FOUR TIMES BEFORE CARTER PICKED up the phone.

"What?" he said by way of greeting.

"It's about Greer," said Jack.

A long pause on the other end, followed by a resigned sigh. "She okay?"

"She's fine, but her kid isn't. We're going ahead with the job. She needs the money."

"Jesus."

"But we've encountered a snag," said Jack.

"Yeah, of course you have. You're trying to steal something from Death, dude, that's going to have snags."

"Thing is, though," said Jack, "we think you might be able to help us get out of it."

"No," said Carter.

"Okay, but—"

"No," he said again.

"Remember the chocolate éclairs?"

Another pause. "The what?"

"You always wanted to try chocolate éclairs but your mother never let you because she hates the French. Remember how good they tasted when we snuck into the gym that night before the bake sale?"

"They were fine."

"Bro, you were practically high off them."

"So?"

"So it wasn't just the éclairs, was it? That night, back at Fort You Again when we stuffed our faces with so many baked goods Eli got the shakes and thought he could see the end of the universe, and we all laughed so much Greer peed herself, it wasn't just the éclairs. We were all together. We did the thing. We won. *That's* what made everything taste so good. That's why you were already asking me what we were on to next while we still had cakes and shit left to eat. You can't just forget what that feels like, man. I know it's still in you somewhere, the taste of it. The taste for it. Under the knitwear and the sellout graphic designer bullshit, it's still there. We can have it again, one last time."

This was it. Jack was back. He hadn't given such a rousing speech since the great convenience store supply truck robbery of '17, which landed him with enough cases of energy drinks to keep him comfortably jittery until just a few months before his death.

A third pause on the line. Carter was thinking. Good. That meant Jack had him. It was just a matter of time before he . . .

Hung up the phone.

Carter had hung up the phone. Shit. Had Jack really lost his touch, just like that? Would this afterlife really be worth living if it meant he had to forfeit all the things he used to be?

Jack turned slack-jawed to Dale, who hovered at his shoulder.

"No Carter?" Dale asked.

"No Carter."

"Jeez, Jackie," said Dale. "Never thought I'd see the day."

Jack swallowed down a lump of something thick and bitter he vaguely recognized as defeat before turning back to his phone. Greer needed to know. Jack had let her down. Everything she was counting on him for, everything he'd promised her, today and always, he couldn't deliver. The lump returned, harder to swallow than the last. Maybe she just . . . wouldn't notice? It probably wouldn't be quite that easy. Greer noticed things. Most things, even. She'd notice that she wasn't any richer. She'd notice that Jack wasn't who she needed him to be anymore. He tapped her number.

Twenty minutes later, Greer was on the white leather couch, staring up at him expectantly. He should probably say something. It was what she seemed to be waiting for. It was what he'd planned to do. But nothing came. Where would he start? Every thought in his head was wrong. This wasn't like him. Was this Margaret creeping in? He couldn't imagine her ever having a moment of uncertainty in her eight decades of life. It seemed to be a new experience for both of them.

"So I went back to the archives this morning," Jack began.

Greer readjusted her hands on her lap. Her hazel gaze weighed heavily on him.

"Slight problem," Jack continued. "The guy who got me into the section with all the secret shit last time is dead now."

"Dead?" Greer repeated, her voice up an octave in alarm. Then a strange look settled over her. "What kind of dead?"

Jack creased his already creased brow.

"Like, you're a kind of dead, right?" said Greer. "And so is Dale."

Dale gave a little wave from where he sat on the ottoman.

"Oh, no," said Jack. "He's the usual kind." The souls of S.C.Y.T.H.E. employees were always collected and moved along quickly. It was a perk, or perhaps a drawback, of the job, depending on who you asked.

"So what does that mean for us?"

Us. Jack tried not to dwell on that last word, even as it echoed in his ears. The time had come. Rip the bandage off. Peel the scab. Get an infection and deal with the pus. There was nothing else he could do.

Except there was a knock at the door. He could answer the door. A couple of Mormons would be a nice change of pace about now.

"Just a sec," he said to Greer, smothering his tone and facial expression in apology. Jack hustled to the door, mentally thanking whoever stood on the other side. A moment later he was face-to-face, or, more accurately, nose-to-chest, with Carter.

"I'm here to help Greer," he said before Jack had time to even think of what to say.

"Good," was what he landed on. "That's good. Thanks."

"Don't thank me," said Carter. "I told you, I'm not here for you, or me, or fucking éclairs. I'm here for Greer."

"Noted," said Jack.

There was a time when Jack could square up to Carter, eye to eye, with only half an inch of height between them. Now that

Carter towered over Jack, the dynamic felt weird. Jack no longer had the upper hand, or even an equal one. Instead, he was half-certain Carter was about to pick him up and toss him through the window like an especially unpleasant and disappointingly sober game of cornhole.

"Carter?"

Jack turned around to find Greer padding toward them over the marble foyer floors in her rubber-ducky socks.

"I thought I heard your voice. What are you doing here?"

Carter looked at Jack from the corner of his eye. He wouldn't say the real reason. The You Again gang didn't do sympathy, at least not out loud.

"Jack needed my help with something," Carter muttered.

"For the job?"

He nodded.

"I thought you were out," said Greer.

"Guaranteed money is hard to pass up."

She studied him for a second before turning back to the living room. Jack and Carter followed in silence. As they all filed in and found a place on the furniture, Jack couldn't help but feel like they'd slipped right back into Fort You Again, to a time when no one understood a life beyond the present moment. Only Eli was absent. And Jules, of course. He'd nearly done it. He'd nearly brought his army back together one last time. Jack McCoy was still as Jack McCoy as ever, even if it took a little longer to feel it. And all that remained to prove it once and for all, to himself and to the world, was to steal that Master List.

12

Jack had just survived another day at the death offices when Carter called to say he was nearly done. A few quick stops later and Dale and Greer were in the car, the trio headed off to see his progress.

Carter held the door open as everyone filed into his house—all except Jack, who was bringing up the rear. Before he had the chance to slip inside, Carter went to push him back by the chest. His palm grazed Margaret's bosom as the new reality of the situation caught up to Carter and he opted for creating a physical barricade with his body instead.

"I need you to promise me that none of this will come back to bite me, Jack," he said, folding his arms across his chest. "I can't have work finding out I'm participating in this."

"Since when does that matter?"

"Since I grew up," Carter said, a sharpness to his words. "Not all of us want to go through life running from responsibility. It's taken me years to get where I am. I'm not sacrificing that. My part in this shit ends here, got it?"

"Got it," said Jack, though he didn't get it. Jack was only as diligent at work as he needed to be to maintain his Margaret disguise. Under normal circumstances he wouldn't be caught dead—literally—much less alive in a corporate office. Why sell your soul—figuratively—when you can spend your life doing the things you love with the people you love, and having those things give you money in the end? But Carter always was the most straight and narrow of the generally crooked and unwieldy group, and Jack needed him on this, so he decided not to ask too many questions.

Inside, the little kitchenette bled into what had probably been a living room at one point but currently served as a makeshift art studio, canvases with paintings in various stages of completion leaning against every wall and propped against easels. Off to one side of the room stood a high-top table strewn with charcoal pencils and pastel crayons. Sprawled across it lay a giant sheet of paper scribbled with lines, pieces of computer paper inked with printer-etched photographs surrounding the central drawn image. Greer and Dale had already gathered around it, studying the details, when Carter ushered Jack over.

"It's done," Carter said to the group at large.

Jack slid beside Carter and Dale and stood on Margaret's tiptoes in order to peer onto the table. The photos he'd spotted from the doorway were of the S.C.Y.T.H.E. offices from various angles, inside and out, bird's-eye and straight-on. Reference photos. Jack may have been artistically impaired, but he knew enough to determine that much. The sketch itself was a little rough. A line drawing of lines. But that was all they needed, really. There were notes scribbled along the side, which Jack recognized from all the layout information he'd given Carter the night before. There was even a key along the top with symbols and short descriptions. Carter always did put his all into everything he did, even when he didn't want to do it.

"All right, I'll break it down," said Carter, his voice a little weaker than it had been at the door. He hated the spotlight, even when it was only his oldest friends in the audience. "Entrance is here. Bathrooms here, here, and here. These are the break rooms. They're all laid out exactly the same on each floor, except that the second-floor break room is about eight feet shorter than the others, going by the window placement. There must be an entrance to this Room of Records thing from somewhere in there, unless there's a door in the hall."

"Who's this little smiling guy?" Jack said, pointing to an image in the key.

"That's a broom. It represents storage closets."

"It's so happy."

"It's not important," Carter nearly snarled. "The point is, your best bet is to try the second-floor break room. Weird placement, but it's an older building, so my guess is they stuck the entrance there before break rooms were a thing."

"Okay," said Jack. "Thanks. Hey, this is really good, you know? You're really good."

"Yeah, that's why they pay me the big bucks."

"They pay you big bucks?"

"They pay me bucks. Consistent bucks."

"You happy?"

Carter shrugged.

"Hard to compete with that broom," Greer said.

That got a small smile from Carter. "I'm not not happy. Graphic design is almost art sometimes, when they let you be creative about it. It's happened once or twice. Anyway, that's my work done. You guys can take it from here."

Greer placed a hand on Carter's arm, her face soft in gratitude without saying a thing. Dale gave him a small salute no one else could see. Jack, for his part, offered a hand that Carter took in a reluctant but firm shake. And as quickly as the group had reassembled, it dissolved again. The three newfound strangers left, pseudo-blueprints in hand, a cool breath from the sigh of lost years settling into steady rhythm between them. Jack found himself wondering, not for the first time, if he could still be Jack McCoy without the people who made him feel most like himself.

MARGARET'S CUBICLE, ALONG WITH THE REST OF THE MURDER DEpartment, was situated on the first floor of the S.C.Y.T.H.E. offices, near its break room. It meant Jack would need a good excuse to use the one on the floor above him. Thankfully, Jack was always full of excuses.

When he'd first taken over Margaret, he'd made a promise to himself, and to the part of her he could still feel hanging out in there beside him, that he'd take care of her things. He'd mostly lived up to that promise, but cleaning out the fridge was something he'd hated doing in life and wasn't keen to spend even a moment doing in his afterlife. He could chalk that up to laziness, or hedonism, but just now he decided it was because he somehow knew he'd eventually have a use for rancid yogurt. It meant sacrificing one of Margaret's designer tote bags, but smuggling the dairy stink bomb into the office incurred far less scrutiny than when he'd attempted a similar feat in an effort to get out of an eighth-grade math test. By ten a.m., the main-floor break room was officially out of commission, forcing a mass lunchtime exodus to the second floor and giving Jack a reason to linger up there without raising too many questions.

Lunch hour eventually came to an end and agents from both the first and second floors slowly trickled out of the break room and back to work. Jack had made a show of blowing on each individual noodle from his microwave chicken penne until no steam or sauce remained, chewing each bite no less than forty-five times and taking a long sip of juice in between. When his last coworker had wrapped the crusts of her ham sandwich back in their tinfoil, he still had a quarter of his meal remaining. He returned the woman's smile as she left the room and then promptly threw the last of the freezer-burned pasta into the trash. Then he shut the door and set to work.

There had been no door in the hallway, which meant that, if it still existed at all, the entrance to the Room of Records had to be in here. Jack had spent the morning trying to imagine what a bunch of corporate Victorians would have dreamed up for a secret door, but given what little he knew about the era, all he could think was that it wouldn't involve sex or smiling in photographs. He'd hoped for one of those bricks you pushed that made all the other bricks around it open up into a doorway, but despite the somewhat mystical nature of this job, he didn't think S.C.Y.T.H.E. operated under cartoon logic.

Jack pulled open every cabinet along the far wall, shifting mugs and cartons of tea in case there was something helpful behind them. In the end, the cabinets turned out to be cabinets, the mugs just mugs, and the tea heavily apple-forward but otherwise unsuspicious. He slid the trash bin away from the wall, crawled under the table, felt around every floor tile. Nothing.

He was still on his hands and knees when the break room door opened. Jack's head whipped up. In the doorway stood the exclamation point of a woman from the archives. She looked down at Jack. Jack looked up at her. They held each other's gaze for longer than was comfortable. Jack's arthritic knees were cramping. His borrowed boobs grazed the floor. He needed to think fast before his whole body remembered how old it was and completely gave up on him. Maybe he could say he dropped his glasses? But Margaret didn't wear any, and that would be pretty evident around the office by now. He could say he was hiding from someone, but who? And why? Every excuse he could think of was something Jack would do, not Margaret. What would bring an eighty-year-old woman to her knees under a break room table? Only absolute filth rose up to answer that question.

Something clicked on somewhere deep down, below Jack's essence, where Margaret still resided.

"Yoga," he said. It felt like a burp. Like something he didn't mean to release but that needed to come out and so it pushed its way into the world. "Under-table yoga. It's supposed to be really good for staying limber. And keeping your floors clean."

The woman narrowed her sharp eyes but didn't ask any follow-up questions. Instead she went to a cabinet and popped an apple-cinnamon tea bag into a mug. Jack wobbled stiffly to his feet. He'd looked everywhere at this point. Where the hell was this entryway? Then he spotted it. The fridge. The only object in the room he hadn't looked behind. But there was no way he could move that thing by himself in this body. He looked over at the woman from the archives, who was currently microwaving her tea in a way that made Margaret squirm from deep down inside their shared shell. The archives woman didn't have much meat on her angular bones, but she also probably didn't suffer from loss of bone density.

"The first-floor break room's pretty gnarly, huh?" said Jack.

The woman took a sip of her tea. "They forgot to warn me."

"Yeah, some asshole—some rascal left an open yogurt in there. It's basically a dairy stink bomb. Someone said it exploded."

The woman scrunched her face, lowering her mug mid-sip.

"Don't think we'll be back in there for a while," Jack continued. "Unfortunately, someone dropped their yogurt behind *this* fridge today, can you believe it?"

"Has maintenance been informed?"

"Yeah, but—you're new here, right? You wouldn't know this, but our janitor has this policy about fridges. He won't move them. They'd let him go, but he's married to one of the manager's sisters, it's a whole thing."

"Nepotism gone mad," said the woman.

Jack hmm-ed his agreement. "We could always move it, I guess. Save this break room from going the way of the first floor. You definitely don't want to have to use the one on four. They're crazy up there. Not enough sunlight or something."

The woman sucked her teeth. "I suppose we could."

"I'll pull if you push."

A few moments later and they were two bread slices in a fridge sandwich. The woman was unexpectedly strong and so, to Jack's great surprise, was Margaret. Maybe there was something to this under-table yoga thing. Within a handful of minutes, the fridge was shifted from its home, a rectangle of grime surrounding the patch of floor on which it had stood like a chalk outline at a crime scene.

"Where's the yogurt?" the woman asked, but Jack wasn't listening. He was too busy staring at a faint etching in the wall behind where the fridge had been.

13

Alone in the break room again, Jack traced his fingers along the brick wall behind the fridge. A crack extended down, up, and across in straight lines: the faint outline of a door. Jack's heart rate picked up as he felt the cool air seeping through from whatever lay on the other side. He hadn't felt this rush of adrenaline since long before he'd died, and part of him had believed he never would again. This wasn't just his standard heist, either: a casual convenience store robbery or restaurant till theft. This was some Indiana Jones shit.

He pushed against the hidden door, but nothing happened. There had to be a way in. He scanned the bricks again, running over each one with his eyes and fingertips until he spotted a tiny, almost imperceptible symbol etched into a brick toward the middle left of the door. A scythe crossed with an arrow pointing upward—S.C.Y.T.H.E.'s logo. Steadying his hand, Jack pressed the brick. Maybe the company really did operate under cartoon logic. Something rumbled from the other side of the wall. Jack held his breath. The bricks didn't magically gape open for him, but the one that he pressed spun away from him and into the inner side of the wall, revealing a brass doorknob circled with a dainty filigree on the other side. Jack tossed a cautious glance behind him, then grabbed the handle and gave a twist.

The door creaked open with an exhale of cold, stale air. The world beyond sat in a heavy sort of darkness that seemed almost annoyed at the disturbance. Jack pulled his phone from his purse and switched on the flashlight, illuminating more bricks that stacked into a narrow passageway surrounding the top of a winding iron staircase. He chanced one more look into the break room, the fluorescent light beyond the dark passageway like the sun during an eclipse. The room remained still and empty. Nothing had changed anywhere except in his perception of this place, which had been relatively bland up until roughly twenty seconds ago. He eased the door closed behind himself and started down the stairs. The steps clanked beneath his heels, the staircase itself trembling slightly at the affront of being used. Jack decided it must be safe all the same. Someone was using it to store and retrieve the Master List every month, after all.

He wound down deeper into the belly of the building. He must have passed the first floor by now. And maybe even the archives. And yet the staircase continued, round and round, down and down, until it came to an abrupt stop on a roughly carved stone floor. The walls around him were of similar stone, jagged and mismatched and yet somehow unmistakably, artfully sturdy. On the wall across from him hung a whiteboard with markers of various colors Velcroed to it. The phrase "Dream it, believe it, achieve it" ran along the top in bubble letters. The main text consisted of dates next to initials scribbled beside them in different hands. Countless colors stained the surface of the whiteboard from years, maybe decades, of use.

On a marble podium in the center of this strange chamber, beneath a dome of glass, sat a hefty skein of paper densely rolled into a scroll. The paper seemed almost to shimmer faintly in the dim light of the single covered lantern strung just above. Jack found himself altered in its presence, almost reverent in a way he didn't know he was capable of. In front of him stood a list of everyone in his branch's jurisdiction who was slated to die over the next thirty days. He imagined that someone so senior Jack didn't even know of their existence would follow the winding staircase down here each month and write the list of names and death information into case files to be delivered to the office's administrative coordinator, who would then divide them up by department and send them off to agents for collection each morning. Send them to him. This was where that whole mysterious cycle began.

Well, not quite where it began. Someone or something had to have the foreknowledge to write that list to begin with, and Jack wasn't sure they'd be working an office gig. But for the workers of S.C.Y.T.H.E., from directors and middle management straight down to his desk, this was the epicenter of forbidden knowledge.

Jack looked over the glass dome. Near the bottom, where the glass met the podium, he spotted a small keyhole molded for a skeleton key in the shape of a scythe. He crouched, pressing an eye to the lock. Inside, it curved and narrowed in strange ways. Jack pulled his lock picking kit from Margaret's purse but, as expected, he hadn't come prepared for this. He'd kept his kit scaled back to only the essentials so it would be easy to transport, but the tools he'd brought were too clunky for such a delicate job. He needed something almost toothpick-thin but sturdy. Which, of course, he had. Just not here.

He checked his watch. He had a pickup scheduled for fifteen minutes from now. Essences grew pretty impatient if you kept them waiting. He could smash the glass, hc considered, but that might damage the list. And that was assuming the dome didn't have some weird booby trap, or that it was even made from the normal kind of smashable glass to begin with. He still had weeks until this list would be replaced with a fresh one for the coming month. Now that Jack knew what he needed, he could return tomorrow, prepared for both the hidden doorway and the lock that kept him from the Master List. It wasn't quite the win he was looking for, but he usually scouted a location prior to a job anyway. The only reason he hadn't this time was because said location was hidden behind a fridge. Besides, he had a recently deceased forty-nine-year-old who'd kicked the bucket Elvis-style waiting for him, and Jack wanted to get the awkwardness of a trip to a stranger's bathroom over with as quickly as possible. The list could wait another day, he decided. And with that decision, he walked back up the winding stairs without a single inkling of the regret to come.

14

The next morning passed as slowly as time usually passes when you're waiting for something. It was a slow day in Murder; Jack's first pickup wasn't until four p.m. A strangulation at the boxing club with a jockstrap as the garrote. He hoped it was at least unused, for both the victim's sake and his own.

In the meantime he had only a small amount of paperwork to catch up on. The report he'd submitted on Dale's collection hadn't been flagged, at least not in a significant enough manner to get back to Jack, which was a relief. He supposed there wasn't much reason for the average agent to lie about a client making it to processing, so cross-referencing the departments probably didn't happen as thoroughly as it should.

He finished up his report on yesterday's case, still unnerved by both the murdered man on the toilet and the inexplicable decision to carpet a bathroom, and looked at his laptop clock. Somehow only an hour had passed since he'd arrived at nine that morning. Eventually the lunch hour came and went, leaving Jack alone in the break room once again. A single-minded focus on lunch and a reticence to move heavy things among Jack's fellow agents meant the fridge's new location went unnoticed, or at least undisturbed. As soon as his last coworker had finished their Tupperware of leftovers and returned to work, Jack was through the hidden door and spiraling down into the office bowels, the most delicate of his lock picking tools stashed snugly in his purse.

The mystique of the Room of Records had faded slightly since the previous day. Now that Jack knew what to expect, the little chamber felt almost like just another room. The walls were just stone. The series of dates and initials on the whiteboard were just routine office scribbles. Even the Master List itself seemed to have lost its faint glimmer, appearing like little more than basic printer paper beneath its dome of glass.

Jack slid his tools into the small lock on the dome, waggling them until he heard a familiar click. With hands made steady by a lifetime of practice, he eased the dome back, revealing the list to the cool air of the room. He carefully removed the scroll from its plinth, grasping the edges delicately in his fingertips. The paper was grainy and thinner than he'd expected. When he unrolled it, just slightly, just a few careful inches, handwritten names greeted him from the page. For a brief moment, the reverence he'd felt the previous day returned. In his hands were countless lives about to end. It was a strange thing, holding the future. He did it a little bit every day, but the deaths he dealt with daily felt more like a foregone conclusion than the information he now held. These people still had days, sometimes weeks of life left. Knowledge of their deaths, in the right hands, meant that maybe they didn't need to die at all. That's what he had here. That's what he was selling. The possibility of rewriting the future. After all, it was only ink on paper. And that was as impermanent and easily altered as life itself.

And it would be worth a fortune. Jack returned to himself. He pulled a padded envelope from his purse and unrolled the piece of paper tucked within. On that paper he scribbled the information from the Master List in a close replica of the handwriting it was inked in before placing the forgery on the pedestal where the original list had been. He then gently placed the true scroll inside a second envelope, sealing it so no air could weather the paper. With careful hands, he lowered the dome over the forged Master List and locked the little hole built for a skeleton key.

He'd done it. No alarms sounded. No paper ripped or smudged. He had the Master List tucked safely away, ready to sell, ready to bring Greer peace. He was Jack McCoy, and nothing, not death, not a new body, could take that away from him.

15

The Master List burned a hole through Margaret's purse. Not literally, of course, though that would have been impressive. But all throughout the rest of the day, through the mind-numbing paperwork and the strangulation pickup, Jack could feel the weight of the list in the bag on his shoulder. This wasn't the usual contraband, this was a mystical object stolen from Death itself. By the time the workday came to a close, Jack worried he might have given poor Margaret an ulcer. Still, the adrenaline coursing through his borrowed veins was intoxicating. He'd forgotten how addictive a rush like this could be.

As soon as he pulled Margaret's Mercedes into the driveway, he dialed Greer. She had to be here for this. To witness his win. To see Jack in his element.

He went inside and eventually found Dale in the backyard, watching intently as two squirrels taunted a yappy Jack Russell on the other side of the fence.

"Honey, I'm home," Jack announced, bosom puffed in triumph. His voice startled the squirrels, sending them darting into a nearby oak tree.

Dale turned around, face brightening. "You have it?"

Jack whipped the envelope from his purse and waved it above his head.

"Can I see?"

"Better not," said Jack as Dale came rushing over. "Can't risk any damage before we sell it."

Dale gave an obedient nod. "Who we selling it to, Jackie?"

"The soon-to-be departed and their families, mostly," said Jack. "I'll start googling the names on this thing and see who's willing to pay. I know I'd have shelled out a ton to know when I was gonna die."

"Same," said Dale.

For a moment, neither had anything to add. They were two dead men holding the means to keep others alive. It was hard to think of much more to say to that. Then the doorbell rang and the moment passed, and Jack skipped inside to bring Greer into the fold.

"You actually did it," Greer said after Jack finished reliving his conquest. He furrowed his brows slightly at the note of disbelief in her voice. Had she not thought he would? Had she forgotten who she was dealing with?

"Of course I did," Jack said.

"Well, thanks," said Greer. "Thank you, Jack."

Jack turned away. "We've got a lot of googling to do and phone calls to make," he said. "If you're up for it."

"Okay," said Greer. "Let's get this thing sold."

THE TROUBLE WITH THE LIVING WAS THEY ALWAYS DOUBTED DEATH. They knew it would come for them, sure, but until it did, they usually struggled to conceive of encountering it. Only goths and your weird aunt believed in ghosts; only the chronically religious and your weird aunt believed in an afterlife; only priests believed in possession, because that one was too weird even for your weird aunt. And yet life, for all its complexities and unknowns, had nothing on the utter strangeness of death, and no one seemed open to hearing as much until it came for them. Jack figured this out after the sixth person in a row hung up on him that evening. Apparently, no one wanted to hear that their loved one was going to die that month and that they could find out who, where, and how, for a perfectly reasonable fee. Jack hadn't expected this process to be quite so difficult, but then, he'd been having an afterlife crisis for long enough now that the idea of predeath foresight seemed like a given to him.

Greer was having no better luck, and between the two of them, she seemed more affected by the lack of success. It had been three hours and her face was already drawn, the puffiness under her eyes thicker, her frown lines deeper. She looked exhausted, defeated. It hurt Jack more than any angry phone call recipient could.

"This isn't going to work," she said at last, the sky behind her darkening in tandem with her mood. "How the hell are we supposed to convince strangers that anything we're saying is true? We sound insane. Fuck. I don't know how I let you convince me this was a good idea."

Jack looked across the couch to Dale, who didn't seem quite so quick to take credit for the plan this time. Greer was right. They wouldn't be able to sell the Master List to just anyone. Their story sounded too far-fetched, which was something Jack would have realized if he were still alive and playing by those rules. But that didn't mean they couldn't sell it at all. There had to be someone out there—someone as full of schemes and mischief as Jack was—who'd take a chance on the list.

"I may have some old contacts who would be interested," Jack said, mentally running through the names of all his former connections as he did so.

"No one's going to believe this," said Greer. "Not even the lunatics you used to know."

"Unless you know someone who specializes in death stuff," Dale offered.

"Nah," said Jack. "Most of my guys were into your basics: money, drugs, lifted merch. Kind of boring, in hindsight. But . . ." Something niggled at him deep in the back of his mind, something from years ago. A nineteen-year-old Eli knocking on the door of Jack's apartment, face drained of color, eyes wide and rimmed with dark circles, hand cut like it had been used for a blood sacrifice in a horror movie. He never came to Jack unless something was very, very bad. This had been. "Greer, does Eli still know that guy with the Cruella De Vil hair and all the chains?"

"I have no idea," said Greer. Jack thought he saw a small shudder run through her. "Why?"

"Just remembering something Eli said a million years ago. Apparently he won't talk to me, but he listens to you. Could you talk to him? See if they're still in touch?"

Greer readjusted her position on the couch. "You really think nothing's changed since we were kids, huh?"

"What does that mean?"

"Eli isn't the same little boy who looks up to his big sister, Jack. And I'm not the same girl who goes along with dumb ideas out of boredom anymore. He and I barely talk these days, and when we do, it inevitably turns into yelling."

Jack took a moment to digest this, and even then, he wasn't sure his stomach acid was sufficient to break down the information he'd just received. Eli had always been sullen and a bit of a prick, but no matter how much he thought he hid it, he worshipped at the altar of Greer with just as much vigor as Jack, albeit in a very different way. Eli and Greer had always been close in a way that was uniquely them, a way that was filled with annoyance and angst and glares and love. At times Jack had even envied it and imagined what it would be like to have a sibling: a built-in teammate to take on the world with for the rest of his life. But something had changed between Eli and Greer, and somehow that built-in teammate thing no longer applied to them, and Jack couldn't quite wrap his head around this new world where the boy who looked at his sister as the only cool authority figure in his life was gone.

"Ah," he said at last.

"Yeah," said Greer.

Jack could feel himself drained of ideas. It felt like running at full speed toward a brick wall. He was about to be pancaked against it like a Looney Tunes character, and there were no thoughts in his head with enough substance to slow him down. He knew this feeling. It had been rare in life, but he'd felt it before, and each time, it had taken days, sometimes longer, to scrape himself off that wall and figure out a way around it. Now the rules were different. Now the friends he'd leaned on were mostly scattered to the wind. Now the stakes were a child's life, not just the thrill of the game. Now Jack wasn't fully convinced he still had what it took to make it around the wall at all. It seemed to loom higher, sturdier than before. This wasn't like him. Jack McCoy didn't do walls.

"Would you try?"

Greer looked at him. "Jack."

"Greer. Would you try?"

"You think that chain guy can help us?"

Jack couldn't be sure. He was basing all this off a sun-bleached memory. He was running straight into a brick wall and Greer's hazel eyes could almost certainly see it. "I do."

Greer took a sharp inhale. "Then I'll try."

16

Eli paced circles on the thread-worn carpet like a tiger in a cage. He ran a hand through unruly curls, flashing looks at Greer and Jack from the corner of his eye. Finally he stopped his circles and planted his feet in front of his unwelcome guests, who sat stiffly on the corduroy couch of apartment 3A.

"This is fucked," he said. Then he homed in on Greer. "For you of all people to fall for this bullshit. It's fucked."

"It's not bullshit," said Jack. "I have the list."

"That's not what I mean. Christ, Greer, I really thought you were above this shit now. You have a family."

"My family is why I'm doing this," Greer snapped. "And that's some very high and mighty talk from the guy who's fresh out of prison. Again."

Eli flinched as if a fist had just sailed by his face. "Fuck you."

Greer turned to Jack. "I told you, it's pointless."

To Jack McCoy, few things were ever actually pointless. A little tricky, sure, but they usually served their purpose in the end. This conversation was beginning to feel like an exception to the rule. Still, he never was one for letting a friend's better judgment stand in the way of a plan. And in this case, and perhaps only ever this case, he also had the greater good on his side.

"She's scared, dude," Jack said to Eli.

Greer's gaze was sharp on him now, but he decided not to feel it.

"This is her kid's life we're talking about. Your niece."

"That's low, McCoy," said Eli. "Even for you."

"It's true, isn't it?"

"And what's in it for you? Money? Thrill? You've never done anything out of the goodness of your heart in your entire miserable life. So don't start pretending that's what's happening here."

Jack stared at Eli for a long moment, mouth agape like a Big Mouth Billy Bass with its batteries taken out. Then, as quickly as his elderly body could manage it, he was on his feet, poking a wrinkled finger at Eli's chest even as Eli towered above him.

"What's in it for me? Seriously? Everything I've ever done has been for you guys. I spent my entire youth providing for the You Agains like a goddamn mother duck. How did you and Greer pay for that overnight field trip to the museum? How did Carter get those art supplies freshman year? You think the jobs we did were just for the thrill? You never got anything out of them?"

"What I got was a criminal record," said Eli.

Greer stood from the couch and made her way to the door. She tipped her head at Jack. "Come on. I'm done here."

Jack looked back up at Eli, whose blunt features were tangled up in a scowl. Behind them, not even that far, Jack could still see the petulant boy who would roll his eyes and bitch and sigh before diving into every scheme with more zeal than anyone, even Jack. It was the zeal that always got Eli caught in the end, but it was also what made him special. Because he cared so much about everything that it made him act as though he cared about nothing at all. But Jack could always see it, the way he cared, and when it had been just the two of them, sometimes Eli wouldn't pretend otherwise.

A sad smile tugged at Jack's lips. His poor little duckling. "It's okay," he said. "I get it." And he did. Even as his old life slipped further from his grasp, he did get it. Because as much as he longed to be Jack McCoy again, even for a moment, Eli was fighting to be less himself, if only to stay on the right side of the law. If only to prevent another incident like . . .

Swimming

July 2005

Eli looked like one of those rats who climbed out of the sewer dragging a week-old pizza crust in its jaw. He was wet, for a start, hair slick to his scalp in places and springing wildly in others. Under one armpit was a plastic bag of belongings: a wallet, a pair of glasses he only wore when Greer yelled at him to, and a pair of tighty-whities that sat at the front like a white flag of surrender.

He gave Jack the crooked smile of a man who was only half on this plane of existence, then barfed on Dale's shoes.

"Gross," said Jules.

"Not again," said Dale, his entire focus on the second pair of his shoes Eli had been sick on that night.

"Hi," said Eli, who had no real focus at all.

Jack had always known it was only a matter of time until someone in the You Again gang would face the strong arm of the law, he'd just never expected that strong arm to be grabbing at a drunk, naked Eli. Still, he'd kept a little nest egg for just such an occasion, and when Eli's bail fees were announced, Jack had been able to pay them without issue.

It wasn't Eli's fault, really. Jack should have known better than to suggest the grad party knowing Marla Liu would be there. Eli never handled crushes well.

But most of the You Agains wouldn't be graduating for a few years yet, and it seemed like as good a time as any to get a sneak peek at the revelries to come. Besides, Greer was off from college for the summer, and despite complaining about the prospect of babysitting a bunch of younger teens for the night, she'd slapped on a blue satin dress and crashed the party with them all the same. Jack could hardly believe his luck. There he was at a high school senior pool party with the most beautiful girl in the world on his arm (or at least occasionally acknowledging his existence), his dearest friends in tow, and his first full beer to himself. Apparently the host of the party had conveniently oblivious parents. Jack's favorite kind.

Then Marla showed up. She wore a halter dress with a chevron pattern, which made her hard to miss no matter how much Eli tried, and before long, he was tossing back contraband alcohol in a way his body was not entirely sure how to handle. Jack had been forced to abandon Greer poolside to talk Eli down from his fourth vodka tonic, but it was too late. When Marla swished by, ignoring Eli's clumsy attempt at a wave, Eli took off one shoe, then a sock, and before Jack could tackle him, Eli was in the pool, naked as a sphinx cat. Jack stripped down to his boxers and dove in after him, hoping this would be enough to take the heat off his naked friend, but the same oblivious parents who didn't notice an underage party flowing with alcohol had called the police at the first sign of a penis, and Eli was hauled away, butt cheeks jiggling a drunken farewell behind him.

It was Eli's first encounter with the law, which helped, as did being a minor, but it was also the moment that solidified in Jack's mind the lengths Eli would go to when he truly cared about something. That was unusual. That was useful. That was dangerous. And now it was up to Jack to make sure things never went this far again.

Dale shuffled out of the barf puddle as Jack and Greer each wrapped an arm around Eli to help him wobble out of the police station and into the misty tendrils of early morning. Eli lolled his head over to Jack's shoulder and whispered, "You think she noticed me?"

Jack gave Eli's back a pat. "I think she did, bud. I really think she did."

This inspired another crooked, half-present smile from Eli. "Good. I felt so shy."

"JACK." HIS NAME CAME FROM BEHIND GRITTED TEETH. IT DIDN'T want to be there, and the mouth that uttered it didn't want the residue on its tongue.

Jack turned from the doorway to face Eli. "Yeah?"

Eli gave his head a shake. A deep exhale. Jack recognized the pattern but tried not to get his hopes too high.

"Why this job?" said Eli.

Jack stared blankly back.

"You come back from the dead as an old lady to do one last job," said Eli. "Why this one?"

Jack fought to keep from sliding any meaningful looks in Greer's direction. It was an art he hadn't had much reason to practice in recent years, but one he'd been forced to hone back in their youth. Eli had known him for too long and knew him too well not to pick up on these things otherwise. Instead Jack kept his eyes steadily locked on Eli's own.

"Because Greer asked me to," he said matter-of-factly. "And I don't let my friends jump in the pool alone."

Another head shake. Jack tried to keep his expression as bland as the undecorated white walls of apartment 3A. He was dealing with a caged tiger, after all. The last thing he needed to do was give him a reason to pounce.

"I'll make a call," he said, then he turned to his sister, who stood half in the hall. "I'll make the call."

Greer bowed her head in thanks and followed Eli's outstretched arm back inside, where she and Jack returned to their previous perch on the couch. Eli slid his phone from his jeans pocket and disappeared into his bedroom, leaving a heavy silence in his wake. Jack looked around the barren room, the very same room where he'd had his little afterlife intervention only a few short days ago. His friends had tried to get him to move on then, or at least to leave them alone. Now they were almost as good as back to the You Again gang. It was funny the difference a few days could make. Funny, but not surprising. Jack was a man who was used to doors opening for him, even the ones that had initially been slammed in his face. When he put his mind to something, it was all only a matter of time and strategy before he had it in his grasp, and the one thing he'd always put his mind to above all else was the people in apartment 3A with him right now. And Dale. And Carter.

And Jules. But some doors were beyond even Jack.

Apartment 3A was one more formerly slammed door that had opened for him.

Three down, one to go.

17

When Jack was alive, he knew everything there was to know about life, because as far as he was concerned, life only existed within eight city blocks. He knew the rules of those blocks, who lived where, what that world would look like at any given time of day. Then he died, and suddenly life was a lot more confusing than he'd realized when he was living it.

Eli hadn't said much after he got off the phone the night before. He'd just handed Jack a piece of paper with an address scribbled on it, his cheeks nearly as ashen as they'd been the night he turned up on Jack's doorstep after first seeing the man with the chains. Turns out, death wasn't only a thing you did when life ended, and neither was encountering a bureaucratic industry made up of suits and copy machines and reports. To those who knew how, death was also a resource worth exploiting. And apparently the people who operated the Bleak Market knew how.

Jack wasn't as surprised by this as he might have been in life. Working for S.C.Y.T.H.E. meant his surprise bar had been raised fairly substantially and now required something in the realm of extraterrestrials or perhaps a very well-trained cat to truly get his eyes widening. Once he'd gained a better handle on the mechanisms of death, it made sense to him that people wired the way he was would find a way to monetize it via less than legal means. Still, while Jack wasn't surprised to learn that an underground trade in afterlife paraphernalia existed, he couldn't help but feel as though the world he thought he knew had never really existed at all.

"You good?" said the man over whose body Jack stood contemplating his grasp on reality.

"Oh, yeah, sorry," Jack said, returning his attention to the backyard where he'd been sent to collect the soul of one Chris Crisp, a man of roughly Jack's age who was both sprawled on the grass with a gunshot wound to the head and hovering just to Jack's right. "It's just . . . you ever feel like there's more going on in this life than you'll ever know?"

Chris Crisp gave a shrug. "I dunno, man. I just got a bullet in my head, you know? I'm kind of still stuck on that."

"Yeah, no, right," said Jack. "I get that."

He took the long way back to the office after dropping Chris at processing, windows down, sunroof open. The world, it turned out, was a very strange yet predictably cash-driven place, and Jack couldn't help but feel glad to have stuck around long enough to find that out, even if he had to do so in someone else's body. Even if it meant that on the next full moon—a detail he found at least a little cliché—he would be venturing into an underground market of death. Even if it killed him a second time.

According to Eli, the monthly Bleak Market operated out of a condemned old factory downtown. Access required a password, speakeasy-style, that only Eli was allowed to learn, which meant he would be along for the ride whether he wanted to be or not. It all seemed best-case scenario to Jack, who always enjoyed a classic touch to a criminal enterprise, and who couldn't help but feel a little triumphant at having dragged Eli back into the fold. The job itself would be straightforward enough: as the morning neared and deals were sealed, an auction of only the highest-ticket items would take place at the market. Jack knew a list of the soon-to-die would fit that bill, so all he and the You Agains had to do was find a buyer with deep pockets. As far as he was concerned, this would be a cakewalk.

He returned to his desk feeling more alive than he had since he was in his own body. Margaret's essence had graciously receded, and Jack was fully back in the driver's seat. His fingers flew across the keyboard as he typed up Chris Crisp's report, humming quietly to himself. The Eagle, Jack's cubicle neighbor, popped a sharp nose over the divide between their desks, but Jack decided not to notice. He wouldn't need to be Margaret forever. Maybe after the Master List sold, he could retire from S.C.Y.T.H.E. and live out the rest of his time in this body in the South of France, the way he'd first imagined. Maybe Greer would join him. Sure, she had a husband, but who had she come to when she needed help? Nothing in life lasted forever, not even life itself. Marriage was no exception. Granted, his current aesthetic might not be to her romantic taste, but they say love is blind, and at least he didn't have acne scars anymore. But he was getting ahead of himself. One thing at a time. First he had to sell the list, and the full moon was still two days away, which meant he should probably press pause on his plans for a European elopement.

The rest of the day passed in the sort of haze that settles over a brain when its focus is weeks and miles away. By the time Jack caught up to himself, he was back at home watching reality TV with Dale. Just above him, the Master List waited patiently on his bedside table. He'd read it over twice on the day he'd brought it home, holding the paper in delicate fingertips, just in case he recognized any names. He couldn't decide whether that would be a bad thing; after all, he was already dead and it had been mostly fine so far. But something about the thought of seeing a loved one's name made him uneasy, and he couldn't help feeling for whoever encountered that scenario once the list was sold. Not everyone got the chance to stick around the way he had. In fact, as far as he knew, he was the only one. For everyone else—and even for Dale once this job was done—death was a pretty permanent deal. All the more reason people would shell out for the list, Jack figured. Having the chance to disrupt death would be worth a pretty penny, there was no question about that. The only question that remained was whether this was what an underground buyer would actually use the list for. Back when he first became Margaret and was in the throes of researching S.C.Y.T.H.E., Jack came across an internal memo about an agent who'd uncovered a secret ring of soul snatchers within the company ranks. They'd been stealing and selling essences to some mad scientist or other. Details were sparse, but the thought of a soul being experimented on made Jack shudder in his borrowed shell. Thankfully it was a thought he didn't hold on to for too long, first because he'd been too busy learning how to be a senior citizen grim reaper, and now because the impending job took up too much space in his mind for much else.

Life faded into a dull sort of background noise over those forty-eight hours leading up to the Bleak Market. Jack accomplished his newfound weekend routine of water aerobics and a trip to the nail salon through little more than muscle memory, his mind too busy with the persistent hum of anticipation to focus on much else. His nights, meanwhile, were spent around Margaret's marble kitchen island with Dale, Eli, and Greer, working through the logistics of their upcoming Bleak Market trip: Would anyone be able to see Dale if he came? Who should they talk to? Who should they avoid? Most of their conversations were built on a foundation of pure speculation. Eli hadn't been given much to go on, and the market didn't exactly have a presence online.

Then, on the evening before the full moon, something unexpected happened. A knock on Margaret's door. Jack opened it to find Carter there, hands in his jeans pockets, head hung.

"Hey," said Jack, allowing a small note of surprise into his voice. This was bordering on well-trained cat levels of unexpected. Carter was not a man to change his mind.

"You're going to get everyone killed," said Carter.

So he hadn't changed his mind. Fine. Surprise revoked. "Wanna come in?"

Jack escorted Carter into the kitchen. Everyone around the island looked up at their entrance, and Jack did his best to repress the chill threatening to run through him. They were all here, gathered together the night before a job. It felt so right. But Carter wasn't gonna make it that easy. Jack would have to win him over.

"Carter," Greer said, pulling herself upright from where she'd been leaning on the marble island. "Are you—"

"Eli told me what you guys are planning to do," said Carter. "It's insane."

"We've done crazier," said Jack.

But Carter didn't look at him. He was gearing up to plead his case, and apparently he'd decided that Jack was off the jury.

"Look, Greer, I know how important this is for you, for your kid, but you're about to walk into a building swarming with people who deal in death. You have no idea what they might be capable of. Hell, until Jack came back from the dead, none of us even knew there was an afterlife. Don't you think you're out of your depth here?"

"Jackie knows what's up, though," said Dale. "His whole job is this shit."

Jack quickly relayed this input to the group. Sure, his day job was death, but that didn't mean he knew much about it. Still, this was just another job, wasn't it? And hadn't he always figured things out as he went? Besides, he bet the Bleak Market was nothing but a bunch of rich goths with more knowledge than was good for them.

Greer barely seemed to hear anyone's arguments. She was too busy looking at Carter, hazel eyes flashing with determination. "It's worth the risk." Then she turned to the others. "For me. But Carter's right, this could be dangerous. The rest of you don't have to do this if you don't want to. The last thing I'd ever want is for anyone else to . . ." She didn't finish her sentence. She didn't have to. Everyone in Margaret's kitchen could finish it for her. It started and ended with Jules, just like so much of their lives had.

"I'm already dead," said Jack.

"Same," said Dale.

"At least the law won't be on my ass for this," Eli said with a shrug.

Greer lowered her eyes, but not before Jack caught the sheen of tears building in them.

Carter looked from one to the other. "You're actually going through with this?"

No one replied, which was enough of a reply for him.

"Fuck," he said.

Jack knew that "fuck." "Yeah?"

Carter's hands were balled into fists. He was fighting himself, but it was a losing battle. As far as Jack was concerned, from the moment he'd entered Margaret's house and seen the group, he'd already lost. "Somebody's got to keep you idiots out of trouble."

Jack swallowed his grin and opted instead for a sage nod. This had always been the way, and as far as he was concerned, it always would be. Jack came up with the schemes, Dale followed enthusiastically, Eli took things too far, Greer talked him down, and Carter smoothed things over. This was the You Again gang, and it always would be. No matter how hard the others might have tried to fight against it.

"Tomorrow night, then," Jack said, trying to keep the thrill from his voice.

Carter's nostrils flared in annoyance, but it was too late. "Tomorrow night, then."

"TOMORROW NIGHT" SLIPPED INTO "TONIGHT" WITH THE EASY flow of a tide pool's still waters peeling back into the reckless sea, and soon the gang was gathered back around the kitchen island as though the hours between the evenings had never occurred. A muted hum filled the room, the bees of anticipation under everyone's skin buzzing just enough to become a palpable note in the air. The preheist jitters had only intensified over the decades, it seemed, an odd sort of stage fright for a performance that, if it all went according to plan, no one but a select few would ever see. Even Jack could feel it. This job was different, after all. It wasn't just a broken bone or a stint in jail at stake here; it was Greer. He forced a steadying breath and scanned the room.

It had been years since Jack had looked over the faces of the You Agains on the evening of a job. Now, as they stood around the kitchen, all he could see were the kids he'd once tackled the world with. The lines drawn across Greer's face had receded, replaced by freckles and heavy eyeliner. Carter's sharp cheeks had plumped. Dale's fullness grew lanky. Eli's curls were untamed. Even Jack, for only a breath, was in his own skin again. He blinked and the mirage faded but didn't fully disappear. It never would. This was who they all were at their core. It was like he could see through to their souls, and no matter the years that passed or the experiences that filled those years, their souls would never change.

"Ready?" he asked no one in particular. Everyone turned to him, expressions ranging from excitement to trepidation to full-on dread. Oh yes, they were ready.

They parked several blocks from their destination, as Eli had been instructed, and filed out of Margaret's Mercedes onto the curb. Despite the apprehension written across everyone's features, Jack was mostly at ease now. His work was almost done. All they had to do was go in there and sell a piece of paper. They could handle that. But that thought wasn't what mattered to him in this moment. What mattered was that everyone was here, together, and soon they'd have one more job under their belts. One *last* job.

The late spring air held a touch of coolness left over from a long and uninspiring winter, but every inhale was perfumed with notes of lilac and freshly mowed grass, while the full moon hung silver and wise in a cloudless purple sky. *This is what being alive feels like*, thought Jack.

He led his merry band of thieves toward the abandoned factory. It took a decent amount of scouring in the dark to find the heavy metal door around the side, on which Eli rapped in a sequence of knocks that might have been Morse code or possibly the opening notes of "(Don't Fear) The Reaper" by Blue Öyster Cult, or maybe both. A slat in the door slid open, revealing a set of bronze-brown eyes framed by heavy brows. Whoever the eyes belonged to greeted Jack and his friends with a grunt. Eli leaned in and whispered something that seemed too long to be a password and was more of a pass-sentence or even a pass-paragraph, gauging by the amount of time Eli was over there. The whole process was unnecessarily dramatic and secretive and reminiscent of criminal underworlds of old, all of which Jack couldn't help but be a little impressed by. Another grunt preceded the clicking of metal, and the door swung open. The owner of the bronze eyes was taller than anyone in the group, bald-headed, and pierced along his left ear.

"You'll be here for Cyrus, then," said the man. "Third floor, second room on the left. Stairs are at the end of the hall."

Eli nodded his thanks and took the lead, guiding the group toward the stairs and giving Jack the freedom to take in his surroundings for a moment, which he was grateful for, because he'd never been surrounded by anything quite like this.

Ceilings strung with metal fixtures loomed high above, propped up by walls of chipping white-painted brick. Small windows rimming the uppermost level cast delicate white moonlight onto the cement floors in little rectangles, but otherwise the space sat in a moody sort of darkness, air chill and damp and tinged with the scent of disuse. Along the walls were little white tents, each marked with strange symbols, presumably to identify the vendors or the nature of the wares inside. Hushed voices filled the musty air as buyers and sellers of the intangible negotiated for things neither should know existed.

The flap of a nearby tent opened and Jack caught a glimpse inside: a table full of odd-looking eyeglasses he couldn't begin to imagine the use for. Then, just as quickly as the tent's innards appeared, they were back beneath the secretive white flesh of tarp.

A winding metal staircase greeted the group at the far end of the factory, sprouting from the cement floor like a fairy-tale beanstalk. Jack took the rear as they climbed, twisting upward, the Master List secure in his purse. They reached the third floor and turned left to the room containing some guy named Cyrus, who they were apparently here for. Once again, it was Eli who knocked on the door.

This time they were greeted not by eyes, much less the entirety of a person. Instead, a voice on the other side said, "Come in," and so they did.

The room was lit only by a vintage green desk lamp, spilling yellow onto stacks of papers and oddities including an amulet holding a rich red stone, books as old as anything Jack had seen in the S.C.Y.T.H.E. archives, and no fewer than three human skulls.

Behind the desk and the collection of death tchotchkes stood a thin man in a pinstripe suit and itty-bitty wire-rimmed glasses.

His shoulder-length hair—half jet-black and half whiter than the moon beyond the window—dusted the collar of his suit, and his long, skinny fingers were in the middle of skittering over the papers on the desk as the group entered. This was Cyrus, Jack supposed. Also, unfortunately, this was the man with the chains. He was older now, and there were no chains in sight, but it was unmistakably him.

"Ah, Eli and friends, excellent." Cyrus's fingers stopped skittering and found one another in his lap as he lowered himself into the leather chair behind the desk. He looked to be in his early forties by Jack's best estimate, though for all he knew, the man was actually some kind of ancient vampire. Nothing seemed off the table these days. All Jack properly knew about him, besides the recent development that his name was Cyrus, was that he'd done something that thoroughly freaked out Eli back in the day and now he worked for an underground marketplace of death merchants. The combination of these facts didn't do much to endear Cyrus to Jack, if he was honest.

"Please, sit." Cyrus waved a spidery hand at the two chairs in front of the desk without paying any mind to the fact that four people and one disembodied spirit stood across from him. Jack supposed math didn't matter much to someone who dwelled in the hinterland between life and death, but even a dead man like Jack still employed basic arithmetic from time to time. Eli, whose cheeks had grown white again in Cyrus's presence, took one of the chairs without further prompting. The rest, apparently unsure of how to navigate this without ending up in one another's laps, opted to stand.

"It's been a while." Cyrus flashed a toothy grin at Eli, who didn't seem to have enough blood flow to reply. "May I?" He reached forward and scooped up one of Eli's hands, unfurling the clutched fingers and revealing a line etched into Eli's palm from where he'd cut it all those years ago. Cyrus gave a small chuckle. "God, we were dumb back then." He held his own palm out to Eli, revealing a matching scar. Then he shook his head, still chuckling, and returned to his seat. "Now, I believe you have something for me?"

Jack dug into his purse and pulled out the envelope that held the Master List. He began to extend it toward Cyrus, but something inside him made him stop mid-reach. At first he wondered if it was Margaret, but she still felt distant. No, it was something else, something from Jack. A conscience? Inconvenient timing if so. But the memory of that soul-snatching memo in the S.C.Y.T.H.E. archives crept back into his thoughts, the black ink stark and foreboding.

"It's all right," said Cyrus. "I just need to appraise it so we know what to start the bidding at."

Jack could feel the names of everyone scribbled across the list pressing against his fingertips. He quite literally held their lives, or at least their afterlives, in his hands. Could he truly trust the man who scared even Eli to do right by them?

Before he could decide, Greer slid the envelope from his grasp and placed it in Cyrus's outstretched hand. Cyrus eased the list out and held it gingerly in front of his face, pale blue eyes heavy with reverence. "I've heard rumors about this existing for years, but I never thought . . ." He took a deep breath. "I won't be long, if you wouldn't mind waiting downstairs. You'll stay for the auction, of course, as my guests."

Eli rose and everyone turned to leave, but Jack couldn't quite bring himself to move just yet.

"What'll happen to them?"

"To who?" asked Cyrus.

"The names on the list. The people."

"That depends on who buys it, of course," said Cyrus.

"Of course," said Jack.

Greer took him by the arthritic wrist. "Come on."

Jack reluctantly allowed himself to be dragged from the room, his mind still on the list. If the look on Cyrus's face was any indication, it was worth a fortune, but at what cost? Not that that mattered, of course. His job was nearly done. He reminded himself of this fact on repeat as they spiraled back down the iron staircase to the main floor.

Downstairs, he slowly returned to his senses. Sure, they'd initially set out to sell the information to the people on the list or their loved ones, who'd most benefit from the foreknowledge of impending death, but that hadn't panned out, so they'd had no choice but to pivot. There was no use fighting it. And the very same was true of death. The soon-to-die and their loved ones were no worse off than if Jack had never found the Master List to begin with, surely.

Jack had never experienced cold feet before, in all his years of schemes, and he wasn't about to start now.

He offered a gentle elbow to Eli's side. "You good?"

Eli was staring off into the distance. "Fine."

"I'm looking forward to getting the fuck out of here, I'll tell you what," said Carter.

"Dude, it's fine. Nothing bad's happened, right?" said Jack. At least, nothing to any of them.

"This whole place has a messed-up vibe," said Carter.

"Well, yeah," said Jack. "It's an underground criminal enterprise dealing in death. It's not gonna feel like Disney World, dude."

"I feel fine," said Dale on a shrug.

But Greer said nothing. She stood a few paces behind the others, arms wrapped around each other in what would have been a hug if there was anyone in between them.

"Greer?" Jack pulled away from the group and closed the gap between them. "What's up?"

"This is going to work, right?" Her gaze never left the floor.

"You heard what that Cyrus guy said," said Jack. "The list has only been a rumor until now. That makes it rare, and rare is expensive. This is going to work."

Greer nodded but still didn't look up. "It has to work, Jack."

"For your daughter, I know," Jack said, voice soft.

Greer's hazel gaze lifted for just a second, as if his words surprised her, before it fell back to the floor. "Exactly. For my daughter."

Before Jack could say anything else, something grazed his elbow. He turned to find Cyrus just behind him, a strange look on his face. Cyrus pressed the list to Jack's chest with more force than was strictly necessary, pale blue eyes aflame. "Get out."

Jack slid a quick look at Greer as the others gathered behind him.

"What's up?" Jack tried to say, but he'd barely finished the first syllable when Eli cut in, snarling, "Jack, what the fuck did you do?"

Cyrus beckoned the bald man by the door with a curl of the finger. "This is a forgery."

Jack grabbed the paper and ran a frantic eye over it. This definitely wasn't the copy he'd made from the original; the handwriting wasn't his, and he'd taken every precaution to keep the authentic list and the copy separate. But the paper he held in his hands was of the same type as the scroll beneath the glass dome in the Room of Records at S.C.Y.T.H.E.

"That's impossible," said Jack.

"*If* the Scroll of Souls exists," said Cyrus, "it's written in the first ink invented in ancient China, just as it has been for as long as paper-based writing has existed. This is *ballpoint pen*."

Jack peered at the list. Cyrus was right. The names did seem to be written in the streaky blue ink of the Bic pens lying around the office, something Jack hadn't given a second thought to until now.

The man from the door appeared in front of them, face hard, and with a quick nod from Cyrus, he escorted the You Agains from the factory with one meaty hand on Jack's bony shoulder and another on Eli's. Greer kept her eyes on Jack the whole walk to the door, a pleading look scribbled like ballpoint ink across her features. He could feel himself stumble under the weight of it, but there was nothing he could do. Not now, not as puzzle pieces he hadn't even known were missing slotted into place.

The night air brushed his cheeks as he staggered out the door with a measured shove from the bald man, the metal click of a lock reverberating behind them. Jack hopped a step or two, regaining his balance as the others gathered around.

"Well, shit," said Jack, closing his fist hard over the forgery of the list he'd forged. "Looks like someone beat us to it."

18

There was a cunning thief lurking within the corporate beige walls of the S.C.Y.T.H.E. offices, and Jack couldn't believe it wasn't him. Someone else had snuck into the Room of Records and taken the Master List before he had ever had the chance, but for the afterlife of him, Jack couldn't imagine who, or why. His coworkers all struck him as fairly corporate beige themselves. Stealing a priceless death list didn't really seem like the kind of thing Linda from Accounts or Arnold over in Natural Causes would get up to in their free time. But someone had. And whoever it was had to be high enough up to know of both the Master List's existence and its location. That would narrow down the suspects, but truth be told, lowly agents like Jack only ever dealt with their immediate supervisors, the department managers. Anyone above that rank seemed to rarely step foot in the office, and if they did, he'd certainly never been introduced to them.

Still, at least the department managers offered him a place to start. After being manhandled out of the goth flea market the night before, Jack and the others had gathered back at Margaret's, the buzz of earlier in the evening replaced by the weight of defeat. It wasn't the first time they'd botched a job. That went with the territory. But this time it wasn't a math test score or a night in the slammer at stake, it was Greer's daughter. It was Jack's second chance.

From the moment Jack had taken in the ballpoint scribbles on the paper he'd stolen, he knew. There was no question in his mind that someone—someone *else*—at S.C.Y.T.H.E. had taken the list. There wasn't any use trying to convince Cyrus of the authenticity of its contents; if the list was forged, there was no reason for him to believe Jack that the information it contained was true. What he needed now was to discover who had the real thing and get it to the Bleak Market. He'd have to work quick: Dale needed to cross over within forty-five days of his death to avoid becoming a ghost, and while Jack didn't know how imminent things were with Greer's daughter, her desperation made him decide it would be better to get this done sooner rather than later. But Jack McCoy never shied away from a challenge.

From the expensive austerity of Margaret's living room, surrounded by the people who mattered most, Jack explained the situation. He was met with more pushback than he'd anticipated, Eli and Carter ready to abandon the job altogether, but Dale was undeterred, and Greer, well, Greer didn't have the luxury of giving up. So it was decided: Jack would return to work in the morning and find out what he could about the heads of each department so the group could recalibrate and formulate a new plan. Someone at his office had the Master List in their possession, and Jack needed to sniff them out so he could take what was rightfully his. Or at least, what was no more wrongfully his than it was for whoever had taken it.

The Murder department of Jack's branch of S.C.Y.T.H.E. was headed by a woman named Brenda Wahl. Brenda shared a rough age bracket with Margaret and stood only a few inches taller than Jack's borrowed height of five feet. The photo app on Margaret's phone suggested she and Brenda had something of a friendship outside of the office, with pictures of the women on the golf course or at upscale cocktail bars scattered among images of Wesley and one photo Jack had initially taken as risqué but that turned out to be medical in nature.

Margaret's friendship with Brenda meant Jack just had to play the part convincingly enough to suss her out. A quick knock on her office door and he was ushered inside with a singsong greeting from within. Jack poked his head around the door and Brenda's dyed-brown bob lifted from where she'd been craned over her desk, reading through files.

"Oh, Margie, come in!" She closed the files and propped her chin in the bridge formed by her clasped hands, her elbows resting on the desk.

Jack took the chair across from her and carefully crossed one leg over the other. He'd practiced this move many times over the past few months. Not having anything at risk of getting caught between his legs certainly made the maneuver easier, but he still hadn't fully adjusted to sitting so demurely. He straightened his plum pencil skirt and tried to imagine how these two geriatric gal pals talked to each other. This was probably not a "what's crackin', home slice?" situation. Though situations rarely were these days.

Before he had the chance to try his elderly lingo, Brenda spoke. "This isn't about dinner at the Honeysuckle, is it? Sorry again, Margie. I've been so swamped lately, but Roger and I would still love to go at some point."

"Oh," said Jack. "No, that's cool." And it was, because Jack had no idea what the Honeysuckle was or who Roger happened to be. But his words elicited a furrowed brow from Brenda. "I mean," he added quickly, "I completely understand. There's a lot going on, murder-wise. You've got your hands full."

"If people could just stop killing each other for a few weeks," Brenda tutted. "Or at least stick with one victim at a time. We had three agents at one scene on Wednesday. The paperwork is a nightmare."

Jack gave a sympathetic nod. "Speaking of paperwork," he said, tone as casual as possible, "I was just thinking about my list of clients for the day, and it occurred to me that I have no idea where those names come from. But you must, right? Being a manager and all."

Brenda snorted at this, the sound a stark contrast to her manicured appearance. "Oh, you're cute. You know they don't tell us shit."

"None of you?" Jack asked, unable to smother the surprise in his voice. Sure, department managers weren't at the top of the death industry pecking order, but they were a full rung above Jack and his colleagues, so he assumed they must know more than agents were allowed to. "You don't know where we get our case files from?"

"We get them from the higher-ups." Brenda's voice was a shrug. "Where *they* get them from is anyone's guess."

Anyone but Jack's. He knew exactly where they got them from. What he didn't know was— "Who are the higher-ups?"

The question was out before Jack could stop it. Before he could assess whether or not this was something he should know. But Brenda's expression only shifted to a thoughtful glance into the middle distance. "Now, let's see," she said. "You'd have met Mr. Bajwa at the company baseball game last summer, though he didn't stay long and doesn't leave much of an impression. Ms. Summers works almost exclusively from another branch and is, if you'll forgive me, terrifying. Then there's Ms. Cook and Mr. . . . gosh, something with an *F*. I've only ever seen either of them a handful of times around the office. The only one I ever see with any regularity is Ian—that is, Mr. Grant. He'll pop his head into my office every once in a while. Cute tush. The rest only show their faces on Teams meetings for the most part, or for quarterly reviews. Though rumor has it they're in here when the rest of us aren't. If I'm honest, Margie, I barely even know what they do, but I know they can fire me, so I don't go around asking."

Jack forced Margaret's face into what he hoped was an engaged expression, but his mind was too busy cataloging names to be sure he didn't just look constipated. In truth, he was also that, but neither were his main focus just now. He muttered something in commiseration with Brenda that, in hindsight, was probably a verbatim lyric from "9 to 5" before rising creakily to his feet.

"Manicures next week?" Brenda asked, examining the vivid pink on her nails. "I'm thinking it's time for something bold."

"Me too," said Jack, and then he left the office.

19

Bajwa. Summers. Cook. F. Ian Grant.

Bajwa. Summers. Cook. F. Ian Grant.

Bajwa. Summers. Cook. F. Ian Grant.

Jack repeated the names over and over to himself as he made his way back to his desk. BullShit Crap Fucking Idiot Goldfish. There were a depressing lack of cuss words beginning with *g* in the English language, Jack realized, but it didn't matter. The mnemonic device did its job. If he was right, he wouldn't need to remember the entirety of the higher-ups' names anyway, just their initials, but he wouldn't be able to test that theory until lunchtime, and it was only nine-thirty a.m.

He dropped into Margaret's chair and wheeled himself up to the desk, rummaging through drawers until he found a pad of lined paper. He plucked a pen from the neat little porcelain holder on the desk and scribbled down the names. Bajwa. Summers. Cook. F. Ian Grant. B S C F I G. BullShit Crap Fucking Idiot Goldfish. The ink curving through each letter was a faded blue.

When he looked up from the notepad, he found The Eagle's eyes sharp on him. Jack quickly ripped the page from the pad, folded it, and slipped it down his bra without breaking eye contact with The Eagle. Of all the inconvenient times for his nosy cubicle neighbor to be spying on him, this ranked up there with the first time he'd tried wearing one of Margaret's designer thongs to work. The Eagle slunk back into his nest as soon as Jack stopped being interesting, and time slowed its pace to something between a crawl and a gentle creep as Jack turned his full attention to the little clock at the top of his laptop screen. Finally, the office began filling with the sound of squeaky chair wheels rolling back from desks and business casual shoes on linoleum floors. Lunchtime had arrived.

The yogurt stink bomb had been subdued, which meant everyone had returned to eating on their designated floors, but Jack wasn't concerned. By this point he'd spent enough of his lunch hours on the second floor to know that no one up there really left their desks after they'd finished the last of their reheated lasagna. He just needed to keep his head down and he'd be fine.

The fact that his coworkers in the Murder department brought tuna sandwiches for lunch utterly baffled him. Had they learned nothing about the motives of workplace homicide from their jobs? Still, the hour passed odorously but otherwise without issue, and Jack was climbing the stairs to the second floor by 1:05 p.m. The upstairs break room stood still and dark, a distinctly microwavable ramen smell still clinging to the air. Jack made his way back through the hidden door and down the winding staircase to the Room of Records, the temperature dropping as he spiraled down, making him regret not bringing the tasteful dusty rose cardigan he'd left at his desk.

The secret chamber looked as it had the last time he'd snuck in, except the glass dome now lay empty of its doubly forged contents. Jack's gaze lingered on that empty space, as if he could somehow stare long enough to conjure a play-by-play recap of everything that had happened to it over the past few days. Unfortunately the glass revealed nothing, which Jack decided was fair, and so he shifted his focus to the whiteboard on the wall. He plucked the piece of paper from his bra and scanned the marker scribbles in front of him. Beside the dates written down the center column were the initials he'd spotted last time. Now, paper full of names in hand, he examined each set. GS. OB. JF. IG. PC.

Ms. G. Summers.
Mr. O. Bajwa.
Mr. J.F.
Mr. Ian Grant.
Ms. P. Cook.

The paper trembled in Jack's hands, his palms suddenly moist. Every one of the higher-ups Brenda mentioned had access to this room, to the Master List. One of these sets of scribbled initials must belong to the thief. This was now his list of suspects for the crime he should've been the one committing. BullShit Crap Fucking Idiot Goldfish. The only question remaining was which one had beaten him to the list, and why.

Jack took a shallow inhale, every nerve in his elderly body alive and tingling with electricity. He hadn't experienced an adrenaline rush like this since he and the You Agains had stolen an Xbox from the local Walmart, and this time he didn't even have to outrun a burly store security guard to get his heart racing.

He followed the initials down to the bottom of the whiteboard, where they stopped beside the most recent date. The last letters inked in dry-erase marker were PC, making Ms. Cook the last documented employee in the Room of Records. That gave Jack a place to start, though tracking her down wouldn't be easy. He only had a surname to go by, and S.C.Y.T.H.E. didn't exactly have a website listing its employees. As far as the World Wide Web was concerned, outside of the darkest and most conspiracy-based parts of it, at least, the company didn't exist. Still, documentation of S.C.Y.T.H.E. staff had to exist somewhere, if only for the sake of the employee payroll. The archives were his best bet, but with the Exclamation Mark in charge, access would be tricky. What he needed was a way around the archivist, but when she wasn't there, the archives were securely locked, and Jack could no longer flirt his way into a key card.

This would require something more complex. This would require strategy. This would require bugs.

20

Prom

May 2006

Jules never cared about being popular. Greer pretended she didn't, and Jack tried not to care, and Dale thought he was, and Carter and Eli, well, they actually were, but Jules, she just wanted to be Jules. And she was good at it. All through elementary school, no one ever batted an eye at how Jules walked through the world, often in mismatched shoes, always with several bows holding back her dark hair. She was perpetually covered in poetry and doodles, her skin just a canvas for haikus about her hatred of artichokes or a badly drawn homage to her pet frogs. Until puberty, that kind of thing was allowed. But when she finally joined the others in high school, the rules changed and no one had informed Jules. Frankly, she wouldn't have done anything different if they had, but still, it would probably have been nice to know.

The bullying was relentless. Between her eccentricities and

the weight she'd gained through puberty, Jules never stood a chance. Jack and the You Agains were already juniors by that point with the exception of Greer, who'd already graduated. That gave them a small modicum of clout, which they used to protect Jules to the best of their abilities, but what went on when she was alone was beyond even Jack's reach. It wasn't even the other freshmen causing Jules the most torment. For reasons Jack still couldn't wrap his head around, it was mostly popular seniors on the verge of graduation who decided to devote their high school legacy to making Jules's life a living hell.

Jules never wavered in her inherent Julesness. She never starved herself to fit into skinny jeans when she was perfectly comfortable in her size 12 cargos. She never wore makeup unless it was purple. She never shied away from asking a question in class, even if the bell had just rung and everyone, even the teacher, wanted to leave. But behind Jules's fierce onyx eyes, Jack could see her light beginning to dim as the year wore on.

This simply could not stand.

Jack kept Jules by his side at every lunch hour, daring anyone who looked their way to try anything with a well-honed glare. Greer brought her up to her college campus on weekends for some quality girl time filled with kickboxing classes and *CSI* binges. Eli even ended up suspended for a week after getting into a fistfight with one of the guys on the football team after he'd shoved Jules into a locker. But it wasn't enough. As the end of the school year rolled around, and with it the giddy anticipation of Senior Prom buzzing through the high school hallways, Jack knew exactly what he needed to do.

The night before the fairy tale–themed soirée, Jack dropped a glittery handmade invitation on Jules's doorstep. Sure, technically he and the others were only going as guests of the seniors they'd managed to finagle dates out of, but he wasn't about to let Jules miss this.

He'd spent three hours hopping around thrift stores until he found a suit that fit; the fact that it was orange, ruffled, and smelled like mothballs and cat pee was really neither here nor there. His date, Sara Hornbeck, had texted him a list of prom criteria including a dress code, and while this would break most of the rules on the list, it did qualify as something a fairy-tale character would wear. That character just happened to be a hobgoblin, but really, this was on her for not specifying. Besides, he wasn't going because he actually cared about prom, and Sara was only going with him because she had a crush on Carter but was too shy to make a move, so her eye roll when he showed up felt a little unwarranted.

The school gym filled up with girls in princess dresses and boys who looked itchy, and by eight p.m., the party was in full swing. Jack kept his eyes on the door as he and Sara attempted an awkward, arm's-length sway on the free throw line of the gym basketball court. Finally Jules slunk in, hair in four bows, wearing a purple sequined tube top and the pants of a tux clearly borrowed from her father or brother, tied with a scarf around the waist to make them fit. Jack's face broke into a smile and he pulled away from Sara, who seemed relieved to have her toes out of stomping range. He made a beeline to Jules as the others caught sight of her and joined them by the door.

"Why am I here?" Jules asked by way of greeting.

Jack tipped his head at Dale, Eli, and Carter, who promptly disappeared, before he turned back to Jules. "End of year present for you."

"Prom?" Jules practically gagged on the word.

"Kind of," said Jack. It was then that he caught Jules's eyes flicking away from him, their movements like a hummingbird. Jack followed them with his own. The You Agains weren't the only ones who'd spotted Jules's arrival. Her bullies had also taken note, and were whispering among themselves, pointing in her direction and giggling. Jack could feel the blood surge into his cheeks, his fists clenching hard enough for his nails to bite into his palms. He released one fist and slipped Jules's hand into his.

"Come on," he said from between clenched teeth, guiding Jules across the gym to a corner set up with folding tables topped with bowls of chips and soda. He pulled some chairs out from one of the tables and Jules, still half-distracted by her tormentors, moved to sit down, but Jack quickly stopped her. This caught her full attention, one of her heavy black brows quirking.

Jack smiled again and hoisted himself up so he was standing on one of the chairs. Now Jules cocked her head. She was fully back with Jack, fully distracted by his antics. Good. The bullies didn't deserve her focus. He held out a hand and motioned to the chair beside his. Jules hesitated a beat, examining the outstretched hand with a scrunched face. She'd only just gotten over the concept that boys had cooties a few years back, and sometimes she still wasn't convinced they didn't. But with a giggle bubbling from her lips, she eventually accepted the hand and stepped onto the other chair just as Dale, Eli, and Carter returned, walking over with devious smiles. Then they, too, hopped onto chairs as Jack held his breath in anticipation.

The first scream came a moment later, from somewhere deep in the throng of teens at the center of the gym. Then another. Jules looked from one You Again to another for explanation, but it didn't take her long to understand. A little brown rat snuck away from the crowd of seniors and scampered past them. Another slunk over a polished dress shoe, and a third was climbing a nearby tablecloth on an unwavering mission for chips.

Jules's giggle turned into a laugh, and then, as more rats emerged and more teens ran screaming from the gym, it became full-blown hysterics. Even the teachers and chaperones on site gave in to their fight-or-flight instincts and fled the room, the drama teacher and two of the dads pushing students out of the way as they raced for the door. Before long, all that remained in the gym were the You Agains and a bustling pack of rats who seemed delighted by both the privacy and the abandoned snacks. At some point Jack would need to pack them back up and get them safely returned to the dumpsters he'd collected them from, but for now he wasn't able to do much; his own laughter had him doubled over, tears streaming down his face, as he and the others succumbed to the absurdity of the situation. By the time they'd all returned to themselves, the light behind Jules's eyes shone more luminously than Jack had ever seen it. She would be okay. He would always make sure of that.

21

Jack could feel the pocket of his designer slacks wriggling against his mid-thigh. He could also feel Margaret wriggling in her own right from somewhere beside his soul, her disapproval at this abuse of fashion more evident than it had been at any of Jack's breaches of S.C.Y.T.H.E. policies. It was okay, he mentally reassured her, this wouldn't take long.

The Exclamation Mark stood at attention behind a standing desk that hadn't been there before. Great, she was making herself at home. She hadn't noticed Jack yet, her attention firmly locked on the company-issued desktop suspended at chin height. Still, Jack wasn't taking any chances. He bent down as low as his arthritic knees would allow and feigned retying one of Margaret's navy snakeskin oxfords with one hand, while his other worked to empty his left trouser pocket as subtly as possible. The wriggling ceased both externally and internally, and Jack righted himself with a few pops and creaks before making his way over to the desk. Margaret's vocal joints had done the job of attracting the interim archivist's attention, and she was already in the middle of a terse "Can I help you?" by the time Jack reached her.

"Yeah," said Jack. "I need the case files for a guy called Duncan Finch, died 1997." Uncle Duncan held the record for second-dumbest death in Jack's family, meeting his end after a night of heavy drinking led to accepting a dare to lick his friend's pet newt. Apparently, the newt, named Petunia, tasted like beef and cinnamon, which may have been due in part to the quantity of poison her skin contained. Jack knew all the gory details—hell, they were near legend at this point—but S.C.Y.T.H.E. agents had access to archived case files, which meant that requesting one would give him a reason for being down there without raising any eyebrows.

The archivist gave a nod and let her fingers do their necessary dance across the keyboard as she plugged in Uncle Duncan's information, her hand movements as sharp and measured as an Irish dancer's legs. She'd been given her name badge for this branch of S.C.Y.T.H.E., Jack noticed, "Greta" etched in the silver metal pinned to her crisply tailored midnight blue blouse. Jack tapped his manicure against the handle of his purse as he waited.

"Thanks, Greta, dear," he said, infusing syrupy warmth into his voice. He was a little old lady now, and that was something worth taking advantage of. Greta, for her part, didn't let a single flake melt off her icy demeanor. "That color looks so lovely on you," Jack tried. "Really brings out the blue in your . . ." Shit. Her eyes flicked up just long enough to reveal them as a cold gray. "Uh, veins." Another eye flick. Okay, no buttering up, then. He'd just have to get straight to the point. "Say, Greta, is that . . . ?"

With a gasp that would have knocked Meryl Streep out of Oscar contention, Jack staggered back against the desk and pointed frantically at one of the cockroaches he'd loosed not five minutes before as it skittered down one of the aisles. Two more crossed in front of the desk, bumping into each other and changing direction as yet another came into view. Jack waited for the shriek, for the expletives, for the frenzied run from the room, but when he chanced a look over his shoulder, Greta was as ramrod straight and stone-faced as she'd been throughout their entire interaction.

"How inconvenient," was all she said, capping her words off with a disappointed tut.

Jack stared at her for a moment, trying to make sense of her complete lack of panic. That was not part of the plan. She looked back at her computer screen and addressed Jack as though there wasn't a cockroach currently clambering up the side of her standing desk.

"Row forty-eight," she said. Then, as Jack wandered slowly in the direction she indicated, Greta picked up the landline on her desk.

Jack slipped into the aisles, putting on a big show of scanning shelves but actually looking for any security cameras pointed in his direction as Greta made her call.

"I need an exterminator at 1162 Millgrove Avenue. Yes. Wednesday at nine a.m., then. How long will I need to be out of the office?"

Her last sentence crawled up Jack's leg like a cockroach, scuttling across his torso and wiggling its way into his skull until it transformed into a thought and then into an idea. Greta the Exclamation Point would be out of the archives on Wednesday morning. Jack needed to be in the office when she wasn't there. Of course, the reason she'd be gone was because, presumably, a group of exterminators would be there instead, filling the space with the kind of toxic fumes that might impede Jack's mission to keep his current body alive. Unless they weren't.

Jack grabbed a decoy file from a nearby shelf and hustled back past the desk, giving Greta a tip of the head as she carried on her phone call and he carried on out the door, up the stairs, and away from the archives.

Back at his desk, Jack dug his phone out from the bottom of Margaret's purse and opened his texts, tapping Carter's name.

JACK: does your cousin still keep bees?

A few minutes of staring at a blank laptop screen passed before his phone buzzed.

CARTER: yeah, why?

JACK: we need to borrow her suits. And a van. Know anyone with a van?

CARTER: . . .

JACK: ???

CARTER: how fucked up is this gonna be?

JACK: medium

JACK: but i think im onto something here

JACK: i think i know how to track the list down

JACK: for Greer

Jack watched Carter's little speech bubble appear and disappear twice. After a third time, the text followed through.

CARTER: I'll make some calls.

Jack leaned back in his chair, hands resting behind his head, satisfaction coursing through him like rushing blood. By the time he left the office that evening, his plan had solidified into an almost tangible thing, and Dale would be the first to behold it, just as he always had been. As soon as he got home, Jack sat Dale on the leather sofa and regaled him with his untempered genius, the unspooling of his scheme eliciting the hushed awe it deserved from his audience. That was the thing about Dale: he wasn't the brains or the brawn, but he was always the first to remind Jack of his brilliance, and a guy needed that from time to time.

After a satisfactory amount of oohing and ahhing, Jack left Dale to the TV and called the others. There was a time when this conversation would have taken place between the flimsily connected branches of Fort You Again, or over questionable coffee in a booth at Billy's Diner, but FaceTime would have to work in a pinch. The faces of his friends soon encircled his own on his phone screen.

"Yeah?" Eli was the first to speak, his phone camera partially masked by steam as he cooked something on the stove.

"You gonna tell me why you need Cousin Angie's beekeeping suits?" Carter said.

"Beekeeping suits?" Greer piped in.

"And a van," Carter added.

"Shit," said Eli. "Jack, what are you dragging us into now?"

"What are you all up to Wednesday morning?"

The answer to that question, after more negotiations and reassurances and explanations than Jack felt were strictly necessary, was meeting him at the S.C.Y.T.H.E. offices. When Wednesday morning dredged itself out from the misty tendrils of the night before, everything was in place. Jack was in the parking lot just as Greta came marching out the front doors to meet the incoming exterminators. He intercepted her with more energy than any octogenarian should have first thing in the morning, barreling toward her with a cacophony of inane questions primed on his tongue. She was too caught off guard by the chipper accosting to resist at first, but that wouldn't last long. Soon she'd come to her senses and shake Jack off to complete her mission. He shot a look down the parking lot. The others would have to work quickly. Very quickly, actually, now that the exterminator van had driven into view.

Jack kept the barrage of senseless words coming, but his hold was beginning to break. Greta's inadvertently given attention was fading. Where were they?

A second, unmarked van entered the lot, swooping past the first and parking just in front of it, so the majority of the first van was hidden from view. Carter hopped out of the driver's seat in a puffy white suit that made him look like he'd dressed for a Pillsbury Doughboy convention. Greer exited the passenger side in the same uniform and made for the driver of the original van.

"I can't help you without my computer," Greta said in response to a question Jack only half realized he was asking. "For the last time: all the information is there. You'll have to wait until I'm back in the office later today." She made to turn, at which point she would have witnessed an unexpected face-off between two men in tasteful khaki boiler suits and three roughly human-shaped marshmallows, so Jack screamed. This was enough to pull the woman's focus back to him, which meant, much to his own displeasure, that he now had to follow through.

After a quick mental run-through of all possible elderly ailments in his repertoire, he settled on a classic, grabbing his left arm with his right hand and gurgling slightly. Then he clutched his chest, pulling frantically at the silk fabric of his salmon blouse. Greta's face remained stiff, but something that might have almost passed for concern flashed very briefly behind her eyes, though whether that was for Margaret or the silk blouse, Jack couldn't be sure. Behind her, the first van pulled away and the marshmallows piled back into the second. Jack quickly straightened and caught his breath.

"Are you quite well, Ms. Chen?" Greta said, though her tone suggested she wasn't overly invested in the answer. "Should I call an ambulance?"

Jack shook his head. "Sorry, dear, when you get to be my age, every little twinge feels like you're at death's door." He paused and glanced at the glass double doors beside him, which led into an office staffed by grim reapers. "Just indigestion, I think."

Greta gave a sharp blink as the unmarked van drove up and parked near the front of the building. Everyone filed back out of the van again, slamming doors as they did so and dragging Greta's eyes their way. She gave a tight head tilt goodbye to Jack and strode over to greet the impostor exterminators. For his part, Jack slipped back inside and stood behind a plastic Dracaena by the window. Outside, Carter was using broad gestures, which meant he was trying to make Greta laugh, despite it being a wholly futile and unscientific pursuit. A few minutes later, Greta was leading the others up to the building. Jack shrank harder against the plant as the procession passed. Only Eli, who trailed the others, noticed Jack and offered him a nod as they all disappeared into the stairwell. Jack slipped out from his hiding place and paced the office lobby until the stairwell door creaked open again, this time revealing only Greta. Jack pressed his phone to his ear and pretended to be in the middle of a Very Important Phone Call as Greta swept past, giving him only a quick glance before disappearing back out the front doors. Cut off from the archives, there wouldn't be much for her to do on-site until later in the day, which meant she was presumably off to do whatever it was a woman like her did in her spare time, like yelling at children or perhaps shaking her head disapprovingly at small puppies.

Jack quickly padded down the stairs and into the cool, sterile cavern of the archives. The others were already at work by the time he got down there, Eli and Greer scanning shelves, Carter rounding up cockroaches and placing them gently into a shoebox with carefully poked holes in the lid. The You Agains had a policy of nonviolent crime, and that covered violence against potential victims of any size, and with any number of legs.

"She gave you the key card?" Jack asked no one in particular as the door swung shut behind him.

Greer popped her head out of a nearby aisle. "I have it."

"Good. They wouldn't leave employee info out here where just anyone could access it," Jack said. "We'll have to check Section 301 D."

He led the way to the back of the room and Greer tapped Greta's key card, a little light beside it flashing green in response.

Jack opened the door and ushered the others inside, making his way directly over to the little pile in the corner. He'd already scoured it before, but he'd been looking for information about the Master List then. He likely wouldn't have noticed if there was anything in there about the higher-ups. The others spread out across the meager shelves scattered around the small room. The box of books felt smaller than it had when Jack had done his first round of rummaging, and the contents all seemed too old to contain anything pertaining to current employees.

A small pamphlet caught his eye from where it lay wedged between two dusty tomes, its glossy finish a starkly modern contrast to the books' leather bindings. He slid it out.

A Condensed History of S.C.Y.T.H.E. for the Modern Agent

The first incarnation of S.C.Y.T.H.E. was formed in roughly 4000 BCE. Its original name is lost to time, though it is believed to have been called something very different, as acronyms had yet to be invented. The organization began as a community of deeply wise and spiritual people who were charged with the caretaking of souls recently shed from their bodies.

Over the millennia, this community grew and spread to different countries across the world, but it wasn't until the Black Plague that a collective within the community felt the need to organize on a more formal level. Those who carried out the duties of modern agents donned black cloaks to signify their role in society and were dubbed Reapers because they collected souls in a manner similar to the way a farmer har-

vests wheat: with care, duty, and sometimes more manure present than one would hope.

By the end of the nineteenth century, S.C.Y.T.H.E. had completed its evolution from loosely connected individuals carrying out the same secret task to the thriving company you know and love today. During this period, S.C.Y.T.H.E. faced backlash for a few small, new-business hiccups in which the mishandling of cases resulted in the production of several hundred ghosts. As a responsible purveyor of afterlife care, S.C.Y.T.H.E. reevaluated its systems and processes, hiring some of the most exciting minds to invent new ways for our employees to best serve their clients, with everything from name badges that grant near invisibility to a color-coded filing system emerging from this era.

Today, agents have shed their tarnished Reaper label and the robes of yore in order to uphold our nationwide company with world-class skill, setting the standard for similar agencies across the planet. You, agent, are an integral cog in this machine we call the circle of life.

Jack had never been a cog before. He'd always been the wheel. But there was someone else setting things spinning now, and he didn't like it. Add to that the fact that his predecessors apparently got to wear cool robes while he was stuck in an itchy skirt suit and he all but tossed the pamphlet back into the dusty box.

He looked up. The others were mostly standing around now, occasionally poking at a book on a nearby shelf.

"Nothing?" he asked.

Eli shook his head.

"You really think there's going to be details about current employees in these ancient books?" Greer said, echoing Jack's own earlier thoughts.

In truth, he knew there wouldn't be, but he couldn't think of where else to look. This was the only section everyday agents didn't have access to, and he couldn't imagine information about the mysterious higher-ups being kept anywhere his fellow cogs could get at.

Greer cut into his thoughts. "What about the computer?"

"What computer?"

"The one on the standing desk by the front."

Jack's mind flashed back to his half-focused interrogation of Greta in the parking lot. He'd asked her questions about everything from previous cases to other branches of S.C.Y.T.H.E. And what was it that she'd kept repeating? She couldn't help him until she was back in front of the computer. Because all the information was there.

He quirked a smile, catching Greer's hazel eyes and holding them tenderly with his own gaze. "You're a genius."

22

Well, 'genius' may have been overselling it," Eli said as he tried yet another password on the desktop, the little S.C.Y.T.H.E. logo jiggling like a head shake at their failure.

"What does she like?" Greer asked. "That Greta woman. That might give us something."

"Sweet of you to think she likes anything," said Jack. "Besides, this is a company laptop. The company IT department might have set the password."

"Death1234?" Carter suggested. He held the cockroach-infested shoebox delicately under one arm to prevent its residents from being too heavily jostled.

"If the company set it, it's probably wordplay," Greer said.

Jack cocked his head at her. "How do you mean?"

"The company is literally called 'scythe.'"

"Yeah, it's an acronym," said Jack.

"Right, and it's also the symbol most associated with grim reapers. Clearly whoever's in charge of naming things around here can't resist playing with words. Even the login request is for your 'ideathification.'" She rolled her eyes at this, but Jack knew

Greer too well. Words had been her favorite things to play with growing up: not toys, not boys' hearts. She'd been on the honor roll as an English lit major and likely would have gone on to be a teacher or even a writer had she not left college and started a family before the end of her junior year.

"Think you can crack it?" he asked, but it wasn't a question, it was an offer, and as much as Greer tried to hide her pleasure at the thought of taking it, she pushed her brother aside and stepped in front of the computer with enough force to reveal her eagerness. This time Jack swallowed his smile. She didn't want to let that part of her show, so he would act like he couldn't see it. If that was what made her happy, he would do it without question, just like he always had. But the truth of it was that he could see, and that was enough to make him happy too.

Where Greta's fingers had Irish-danced stiffly over the keyboard only a few days ago, Greer's pecked like a hungry chicken at scattered corn. This was not a performance, this was a game. Her hazel eyes took on a glow, a subconscious smirk pulling one lip slightly higher on her face. Jack watched with careful appreciation as her mind worked, its thoughts reflected in her eyes as they poured through her fingers. Reluctantly, he peeled his gaze away long enough to glance at the delicate gold watch on his thin, liver-spotted wrist. They'd already taken more time than he'd realized in Section 301 D, and while he'd overheard Greta on the phone telling the actual exterminators she'd be out of the office for the morning, he wasn't sure if that meant the entire morning or just an hour or two.

"How's it coming?" he asked.

"Don't rush me," said Greer.

He'd expected that.

"Eli," he said, "stand guard at the top of the stairwell."

"So when the ice queen comes back, I'm the one who gets in the shit?"

Before Jack could counter this, Carter gave Eli a fraternal clap on the back. "I've got it," he said, then gave Jack a look Jack couldn't interpret for the life of him. Carter disappeared to the stairs and Jack allowed himself the luxury of moving closer to Greer if only so he could peer over her shoulder at her progress. Just now she was trying "MourningPerson123," though even she seemed disappointed by that one.

She tilted her head at Jack. "I'm running out of ideas," she said.

"You've got this." It was as much a hope as a vote of confidence, but a few taps later and the lock screen disappeared, replaced by an immaculately organized home screen.

"You did it," Jack practically yodeled. "How did you do it?"

Greer almost seemed to shrink at this.

"How bad was it?" Eli asked.

On a sharp inhale, Greer said, "The password was 'Passedword.' I don't want to talk about it."

"Harrowing," said Eli. He gently shouldered his sister out of the way and took the mouse from her, scanning through documents on the computer's desktop. Eli's reluctance to play lookout aside, everyone in the You Agains knew their roles and slid into them without a second thought. Eli, for all his erratic moods and extreme actions, had a surprising knack for technology, both using it and stealing it.

"All right, what've we got," Eli said, absently chewing his bottom lip. The screen's reflection danced in the lenses of his wire-rimmed glasses as he bounced around different folders on the home screen. "Well, well, well." He tapped an icon and a document popped open, revealing a color-coded spreadsheet. Along the bottom columns, highlighted in yellow, was Margaret Chen's name, along with the rest of the agents in her department. Above it was a list of Accidental Deaths agents in blue, and above that still was the Natural Causes department in green. Then came the department managers in pink, and above that, in a column marked "directors," was a collection of names whose initials he recognized.

A thunder of footsteps on the stairs.

Carter skidded into the archives, chest heaving slightly from his speed. "She's coming."

Jack's head swiveled between Carter and the computer. He needed those names. Then he needed to disappear, and quick.

THE DICKENS PROTOCOL WAS FIRST ENACTED BACK IN FRESHMAN year, when Mrs. Holloway returned in the middle of an otherwise flawlessly executed heist of the answers to an upcoming quiz on *A Tale of Two Cities*. The protocol was built around three principal components:

1. Distract.
2. Confuse.
3. Run the fuck away before anyone's the wiser.

As the rhythmic tap of ballet flats echoed in the stairwell leading toward the S.C.Y.T.H.E. archives, the You Agains readied the protocol.

1. (then): When Mrs. Holloway reentered her classroom half an hour after the final bell rang, she found Carter by the door, pulling her attention away from Eli, who was crouched beneath the teacher's desk, clutching the answer sheet to his chest.

1. (now): When Greta reached the archives, she found Greer and Eli by the door, pulling her attention away from Jack, who was crouched behind the standing desk, and Carter, who clutched the box of cockroaches to his chest.

2. (then): Carter told Mrs. Holloway he was sure he'd left his jacket in class that afternoon, prompting Mrs. Holloway to lead him to the back of the class, where she kept a lost-and-found box overflowing with water bottles and at least one inexplicably forgotten shoe.

2. (now): Greer told Greta they'd found the source of the cockroach infestation and led her to the back of the archives, where nothing particularly infestation-related waited for them.

3. (then): With the teacher distracted, Eli raced for the open window and handed the answer sheet off to Jack, who waited in the bushes just below. Jack then handed the sheet to Dale, who ran it across campus to ensure no one would be caught red-handed with the evidence. As soon as the coast was clear, Eli flung himself out the same window and he and Jack rounded the school to meet Carter,

who came sauntering out the front with a newly acquired jacket.

3. (now): With Greta distracted, Jack snapped a picture of the spreadsheet on his phone and logged out of the computer as Carter handed the shoebox off to Eli, who was hovering by the door. As soon as the logout was completed, Jack raced over to the stairwell and grabbed the box from Eli before barreling up the stairs as fast as his elderly legs would take him.

Back upstairs, he paused for a second at the top of the stairwell to catch his breath. From below, he could hear a puzzled Greta trying to make sense of this crew of exterminators who'd gone into an infested area without any equipment and yet still seemed to have succeeded in their mission. Part two of the Dickens Protocol—confuse—often lingered on into part three. Jack allowed himself a smile before making his way out into the office lobby and then out onto the pavement beyond the glass double doors. A few moments later the others joined him, still in their marshmallow suits, as Jack crouched as low to the ground as he was able to, releasing the shoebox's residents into the concrete wilderness.

"Well?" he asked, easing himself back upright.

"She seemed a bit suspicious, but it's hard to argue with our efficiency," said Carter.

"You found the names?" Greer asked.

Jack held up the photo of the computer screen on his phone. "I've got a pickup in an hour and then I'll head home. Since this Cook woman was the last one in the Room of Records, we'll start with her. Can someone stop by Margaret's place and let Dale know where we're at with everything? I always feel bad when I have to leave him home alone for a full day."

"He's not a dog, you know," said Greer.

"I know," said Jack. "Plus I always make sure to leave him with lots of enrichment activities."

"I'll go," said Eli.

"Thanks," said Jack. "See you all there at around six?"

Everyone nodded their agreement and dispersed to the van as Jack turned to make his way back inside, but something caught his eye, forcing him to pause. A silhouette in the window, watching the events unfolding just beyond: ramrod straight and sharp as an exclamation mark.

23

Murder was exhausting. The souls his department collected were always the least cooperative and most full of complaints:

"It wasn't supposed to happen like that."

"I need revenge on that motherfucker."

"A ladle is such an embarrassing thing to be killed with."

Just once, Jack would have loved a simple car accident or heart attack, something without much to complain about. But it was not to be. That afternoon it was a drunken stabbing, and the spirit was still too wasted to make for an easy collection. Jack had to explain the situation no fewer than seven times before the man understood that the body he kept jokingly air humping was his own. That sobered him up enough to elicit a slew of expletives aimed at someone called "Dirty Steve," and a repeated complaint about how his butt looked from the angle he'd fallen.

By the time Jack parked Margaret's Mercedes in her driveway, he wanted nothing more than to crack open a beer and watch the latest episode of *Love Island*, but his car wasn't the only one in front of the house. The other You Agains were already waiting for him inside, snapping Jack back into his own life.

Everyone gathered around the kitchen island as Jack airdropped the photo he'd taken from his phone to his laptop. The branch directors' names were scattered around the top of the spreadsheet, interspersed with details like other branches they were affiliated with and their ratio of in-person versus work-from-home days. Jack had to zoom in on the sheet, in part because his eyesight was currently that of an eighty-something, but mostly because the amount of information on the page meant the text was frustratingly small. Still, it didn't take him long to find Pamela Cook, and with her full name finally known to the group, Eli took over and searched for her online.

It took sifting through the Facebook pages and LinkedIn profiles of a surprising number of middle-aged blond women before Eli tracked down the correct middle-aged blond woman through an entry on her LinkedIn for a job as director of a transportation firm, 1998–present. "Transportation" had been used as code in the soul-ferrying industry for decades, and in many ways it was a pretty accurate assessment of the gig. After all, most of Jack's newfound job was just driving essences around, like a cab driver without the tips.

Pamela lived in an apartment in the same upscale neighborhood as Margaret, with her husband, Barry, and two Maltese dogs, according to a thorough review of her social media accounts. She looked to be pushing sixty, which made her practically a youth by Margaret's standards. They'd have to approach her accordingly, which likely meant leaving Carter and his biceps and Eli and his attitude behind. Not taking Dale was a given. If

Pamela was a higher-up at S.C.Y.T.H.E., she'd be able to see him, and since he wasn't supposed to be still wafting around days after his death, that would only end badly.

That meant it would just be Jack and Greer going to sniff Pamela out, which Jack had no complaints about. It also meant they'd need a convincing backstory to get access to Pamela's apartment, and the only backstory he could dream up to fit the bill was one he absolutely did have complaints about; enough complaints to put any drunk stabbing victim to shame. As he and Greer made their way to his car, he looked up at her, half in quiet reverence and half in dread of the words he was about to utter.

"So, you're my daughter," he said, swallowing a gag.

WISTERIA LOFTS PIERCED THE SKY LIKE A WHITE BRICK NEEDLE, each unit jutting a small cement balcony into the ether, the collection of which encircled the building in loosely connected rings. The lawn leading to the main entrance boasted well-tended shrubs in geometric shapes, a few bunches of pastel flowers artfully scattered between them. The building doors stood locked. Jack moved to press a random buzzer on the wall beside the doors when a man no more than six months younger than Margaret walked up behind them, key in hand. Jack gave a well-honed bat of his lashes at the man, who may have blushed, though his cheeks were too hollow to be sure. The man propped the door open with spindly arms and ushered Jack and Greer in ahead of him, knocking one problem off Jack's list.

Inside, the tiled lobby reeked of chlorine thanks to a marble fountain in the middle of the space that was likely the height of taste at one point but currently reminded Jack of an elaborate urinal. He pushed through a sad moment, during which he wrestled with the fact that he'd never use one of those again, and made his way to the elevator. Eli had already scoped out Pamela's unit number. She lived on the ninth floor, apartment 907. It was only a little after seven p.m., and with any luck, she'd be inside.

A cacophony of yaps erupted in response to Jack's tap on the unit door, followed by a singsong voice cooing at the yappers. A moment later, the door opened and Pamela poked a middle-aged blond head out. Her headshot must have been a few years old by now, her hair infused with strands of gray left untouched by dye, though it was set in the same elaborately styled coif as in the photos Jack had seen.

"Can I help you?" she asked, scooping one small dog under each arm.

"I believe so," said Jack, procrastinating the next part of that sentence with a long smile. "My daughter"—gross—"was born in this apartment. To me, her mother."—awful—"We're back in the neighborhood for the first time in years and were wondering if we could have a look inside. I'm very old and will probably die soon, so this might be our last chance."

Pamela's brows dropped. "That's odd, the apartment was just built not long before I moved in. I didn't think anyone lived here before me and my husband."

Shit.

"No," Jack agreed. "We didn't live here."

"But you had your daughter here?"

"I—uh . . ." Double shit. Why hadn't Eli warned him about this? His brain whirled. He could say they'd been squatting there while the building was vacant, but that probably wouldn't do much to endear them to this woman. Mistaken location? But then there was no way they'd get an invitation inside.

"No, of course we didn't actually live here." Greer stepped into both the conversation and Jack's thoughts, squishing his utterly futile ideas like unhelpful ants. "But the story my dear mother"—disgusting—"always told me was that she and Dad, rest his soul, were looking at renting this very apartment when she went into labor. It all happened so fast that she didn't have a chance to get to the hospital before I came out into the world, and into this unit. Isn't that right, Mom?"

And there it was. There *she* was. Perfect and clever and one step ahead of even Jack at all times. He took a breath to steady himself, his heart beating a song it only ever played for her.

"That's right," he said.

"Oh my word." Pamela bounced her little dogs under her arms. "The miracle of life, right here in my apartment. Please, come in, come in. What room did your water break in? The guest room? We always wondered about that stain."

Jack and Greer followed her into the apartment. It was dated in color, the walls a salmon pink with aqua accents in the decor, and Jack couldn't help but wonder whether it had looked like this for as long as the urinal fountain had dribbled downstairs. Pamela walked them through a narrow hallway lined with framed family photos and into a floral-forward primary bedroom, complete with a plush, leaf-shaped headboard. Aside from the early '90s time warp, the space was tidy and nondescript. It didn't appear to be the bedroom of a thief, but if there was one thing Jack knew by now, it was that appearances could be deceiving.

Pamela continued the tour in the guest room, its walls a

faded peach. Sure enough, the beige carpet did hold an unidentifiable stain in roughly the shape of Australia. Pamela's face brightened as they walked in, her gaze resting expectantly on Jack.

"Yup, this is where the magic happened," he said, as out of his element as he had been in the ladies' lingerie department the first time he needed to buy a new bra for Margaret's G cup.

"It must have been a very quick labor if you couldn't even get to the hospital," Pamela said.

"Yeah, you know how it goes," said Jack, who didn't.

Pamela's smile faded at this. "I'm afraid I don't. It had always been a dream, but Barry and I were never able to . . ." She turned her face to the window, leaving Jack in the echo of an increasingly uncomfortable conversation.

"They aren't usually that fast," Greer said, voice softening. "Mom had it easy with me. I've had two births, myself. With the second I was in labor for thirty-six hours. Nearly needed a C-section by the end of it."

"But it's all worth it in the end, isn't it?" Pamela brought herself back from the window, landing a sad smile on Greer.

"I wouldn't have changed a thing," Greer said, the tenderness of her words striking Jack over the head like a baseball bat swung at full force. Her youngest, the child she'd spent thirty-six hours in pain to bring into the world, was sick, and it was up to Jack to help make her better. The weight of his mission landed heavily on his shoulders in that moment, more heavily than Greer's hazel eyes ever had. She continued, "Do you have any kids in your life?"

"Three nieces," said Pamela. "All grown now. The oldest two have their own children. They were just here on the weekend."

Greer gave Pamela's arm a gentle pat. "The photos in the hall?"

Pamela nodded.

"You have a beautiful family."

They looked at each other for a moment, something unspoken passing between them, then Pamela spoke. "Come, sit down for a bit, won't you? I'll make us some tea."

She led the way back to the living room and offered a garish floral sofa for her guests to sit on, scooting up across from them on a rusty orange La-Z-Boy that looked as though it had had to fight for its place among the retro pastels. "Tell me," she said, crossing one leg over the other and leaning forward, "where are you living these days?"

This conversation was going to take a while, Jack could feel it, and what it felt like was a waste of time. He needed to see if there was anything in this apartment to indicate that Pamela had the Master List in her possession, and he couldn't get that done by regaling her with a fictional life story.

"Actually, I have to pee," he said. "Sorry, bladder's not what it used to be." Which was true; it used to be a thirty-four-year-old man's until only very recently. "Bathroom?"

"Down the hall, just past the guest room," Pamela said with a finger pointed in the direction they'd just come from.

Jack gave a grateful smile and hurried off to do his business, which just now was snooping, though in truth he actually could use a bathroom. He so often could these days, which made him very grateful for the stash of Depends in Margaret's upstairs bathroom.

Back in the primary bedroom, Jack carefully eased open the drawers of the teal bedside tables, finding nothing more than reading glasses and stacks of old *Time* magazines. A small family of dust bunnies greeted him from under the bed, and the dressers boasted only socks, underwear, and an unexpected hot pink lace bra.

The guest room yielded little more than a closet of empty hangers. Eventually Jack made his way to the bathroom he was meant to visit in the first place, finding hemorrhoid ointment and contact lenses in the medicine cabinet but otherwise nothing of note. With a pang of mild defeat, Jack allowed himself a commiseration pee before returning to the living room.

Greer caught his eye as soon as he walked in, and Jack tossed her a subtle headshake in answer to the question she didn't need to ask.

"Well, it's been lovely chatting with you," Greer said to Pamela as she rose. "You've been so kind to let us have a little tour of your beautiful home."

"Of course, of course, anytime," Pamela enthused, flashing a warm smile over her guests. She and the little white dogs walked Jack and Greer to the door, where she offered each a hug, nearly smooshing the dogs, who were back under either arm.

As they made their way back to Margaret's car, Jack recounted to Greer the nothing he'd found in Pamela's apartment.

"So it wasn't her," Greer said.

"I doubt it," said Jack. "She may have been the last one down in the Room of Records, but all the directors knew where to find the list, and they'd all have access. It could've been any of them."

"So we rule her out and look into the other ones?"

"That's what I'm thinking."

"It's weird, right?"

Jack tilted his head up at her.

"It's just, we're usually the ones who have people trying to track us down for theft. I'm not used to being on this side of things."

"No, I feel you," said Jack. "But I seem to be going through a big trying-new-things phase at the moment." He gestured to Margaret's body with a wave of his hand.

For a brief second he thought he saw a crack of laughter flash behind Greer's eyes before her trademark steely determination smothered it.

"Who's next?"

24

Next on the spreadsheet was the answer to the "something with an *F*" Brenda had mentioned a few mornings ago. One Mr. Joaquín Flores primarily worked out of the branch one town over, but also did the hiring for Jack's office. In fact, there was a good chance he'd given Margaret the job Jack had now, which meant it was very possible the two knew, or at least had met, each other.

Jack tossed around ways to use this to his advantage as Eli fed him information from his semilegal web searches. He also tossed around a tennis ball as he lay on his back across the leather couch in the living room, the ball soaring to the second-floor balcony before returning to Jack's palm. Dale sat on the ottoman in the middle of the room, watching the ball on its exploration of gravity like a cat watching a laser.

"Divorced, two kids," Eli continued. "Boys. Ages fifteen and twelve."

"Good ages," Jack said. In many ways he was pretty sure he was still somewhere in that general bracket himself.

"Anything in there you can use?" Greer asked from the kitchen island, where she sat perched beside her brother.

"I'm working on it," said Jack. *Working* on it. *Working.* Wait. He sat up, the airborne ball forgotten just long enough to come down directly into his lap. For the first time since his death, Jack found himself grateful for the new arrangement of body parts. "What time does Carter get off work?"

"He said he'd be here by seven," said Greer.

Jack checked his watch. It was just past six-thirty.

"What is it? What's the plan?" Dale asked.

"This guy's in charge of hiring, right?"

Eli nodded.

"Maybe Margaret has an ideal candidate in mind for the Natural Causes department. When I was up there for lunch a while back, they were complaining about being short-staffed."

"And you're thinking Carter?"

"He's the only one who has a steady work history and no criminal record," said Jack. "No offense, Eli."

This garnered no response from the Eli in question beyond the subtle twitch of the muscles in his jaw.

"I'm thinking we get Carter into his office and see what he can find," Jack finished triumphantly, letting his brilliance hang in the air until it was inevitably swept away by the adulation of his friends. Dale was already offering an enthusiastic head nod, but as the silence stretched, no one else seemed particularly eager to fill it. Was it his new voice? It didn't have quite the gravitas of his old one, sure, but there was something to be said for a bit of rasp, even despite the nasal quality that came with it. Or maybe it was hard to see authority in someone a full toddler shorter than anyone else in the group. He decided to chalk it up to pure and simple ageism in the end, which he'd have to take up with them at some point. After all, he'd be very old for the rest of the foreseeable future, and it felt pertinent to stick up for his newfound community.

Carter arrived a short while later, arms full of Chinese takeout bags from the order Jack had placed online. The You Agains filled the plush high-backed chairs around the glass dining table Jack had never seen fit to use before now, and beneath a geometric chandelier, Eli and Greer laid out an array of biodegradable containers stuffed with glistening meats and noodles in various shades of brown. It made for quite the leap from their days of eating instant ramen in Eli and Greer's basement while Jack cooked up the kind of schemes that promised something with a side of fries on their future table.

Jack forked a wedge of beef onto his swirl of chow mein and looked over the You Agains from the head of the table. Carter had a steady job, Greer a family, and Eli was back in his apartment with a mission to stay out of jail. Even Dale, who joined the others at the table despite no longer having a body that needed sustenance, had made it work with Savannah for going on seven years when he died. It was a strange thing, seeing them all together again, just as they always had been and nothing like they once were. Jack couldn't quite understand it, the way the kids he'd known had grown into adults with responsibilities to worry about and less enthusiasm than was warranted for their old way of life. He couldn't help but wonder if Jules would have been the same: grown into something familiar yet barely recognizable. If only she'd had the chance. If only Jack . . . He pushed the thought aside, just as he always had. Just as he always had to.

But as Eli and Carter fought over the last egg roll, and Greer gave Jack an eye roll before stealing it for herself, he knew deep down in the soul that was all that remained of him that nothing had really changed, not where it mattered. Not among those he had left.

By the end of the meal, Carter had come around to the new plan and the others were too full of fried foods to maintain any level of grownup decorum, the high ceilings ricocheting old inside jokes and laughter back to them in tones that had been locked away in a time capsule until now. Jack cleared the table by himself, unwilling to let the others move from their trance and lose the moment. When he sat back down, Eli pelted him with a plastic-wrapped fortune cookie. The rest of the group had theirs open in front of them, little paper rectangles scattered across the glass table like confetti.

"Wait, will the fortune be for Jack or for Margaret?" Greer half teased.

"Depends whether or not he likes it," said Carter.

"I should probably get two," Jack shot back.

"You can have mine," said Dale, sliding a hand through the cookie placed in front of his seat. "I never really liked them anyway."

"Open the damn thing," said Eli.

Jack cracked open the cookie and unfurled the little paper inside.

That which we hold on to most tightly will ultimately hold us back.

Jack looked down at the weathered body enabling his continued life, a lump forming in the throat that wasn't his. Fortune cookies had always seemed as believable to him as horoscopes and haunted houses. But, in a sense, he was little more than a ghost haunting someone else's body. And he was definitely a Capricorn. Being dead made the concept of believability a lot more fluid. Still, he'd never been one to listen too intently to baked goods, and he wasn't about to start now. Jack folded the paper and stuffed it into his bra.

"Well?" Greer prompted.

"Something about living life to the fullest," said Jack.

"Trade you for a 'bad news is on its way,'" said Carter.

"Do they mean for you specifically, or in general?" Greer asked. "Because I just uninstalled my news app."

"No idea," said Carter. "But my lucky numbers are 32, 27, 11, 5, 8, and 18, so it all probably balances out."

"Thank god for that," said Eli.

"Nothing to worry about, then," Dale said on a chuckle.

Jack patted the breast harboring his own fortune. "No, nothing to worry about."

25

Jack wanted nothing more than to make the call to Mr. Flores as soon as he arrived at work that morning, but unfortunately work had other plans. The first file on his desk stated a collection time of 9:47 a.m., which meant he'd barely had time to sit down before he was back in the car and heading across town. Morning murders were something of a rarity. Before noon, there wasn't usually enough alcohol or pent-up rage to inspire violence, but every so often, someone would be just unlucky enough to get on the wrong side of somebody who hadn't yet had their first coffee of the day, and then blood was shed.

In this case, it was shed from a fifty-four-year-old man named Hank who had a habit of telling his wife of thirty years where she could go and with whom. That morning he'd apparently forbade her from going out to garden in a tank top despite the heat, and the straw that broke the camel's back became a shovel to the head.

When Jack pulled up, Hank's wife was calmly weeding her hydrangeas in the deadly tank top, humming contentedly to herself and blissfully unaware of her husband's disembodied soul screaming something unintelligible at her from the driveway where his corpse lay, tucked just out of view of the sidewalk by the couple's SUV. Jack had to shout to be heard over Hank's ranting, but when he finally got the spirit's attention, it was another battle to get him to the car. The gender of Jack's borrowed body didn't help much. Apparently this guy didn't enjoy taking direction from a woman, and for a very brief moment, Jack let himself wonder whether that wasn't the reason his friends had responded so indifferently to his plan the night before. But he quickly dismissed it when he remembered all the times Greer or Jules had taken the helm unquestioned. No, this was clearly a Hank problem, and Jack decided he didn't like it much.

Sure, Jack had seen this kind of bullshit impact his female friends, but even in his time as Margaret, he hadn't fully experienced just how obnoxious it could be before this guy came along.

"Hey," he said, prompting a brief pause in Hank's ranting, "you're kind of an asshole, huh?"

This caused a longer pause. Hank appeared to have forgotten to close his mouth.

"Huh?" Hank said at last.

"Your garden looks nice," Jack said. "Now, you coming or what?"

Hank's mouth seemed to be working through a variety of options, not quite landing on anything for long enough for Jack to grow bored. He shrugged and trundled back to the car. A moment later, Hank whipped a "Hey, wait up" at Jack's back before hurrying to catch up with him.

Back at the office, Jack quickly typed up the report for Hank's collection and then made his way to the single-stall accessibility bathroom on the first floor. He really didn't need The Eagle poking his beak over the dividing wall while he made this call.

Mr. Flores answered on the second ring, his voice rich and deep as it tumbled down the line. It was definitely the kind of voice that carried gravitas, Jack decided.

"Mr. Flores?" Jack said in a voice that carried the remnants of being a smoker in the '70s. "I'm not sure if you'd remember me."

AS IT TURNED OUT, MR. FLORES DID REMEMBER MARGARET, THOUGH she'd been on staff too long for him to have hired her. Still, they'd crossed paths from time to time over the years, apparently, and while Eli's intel that Mr. Flores was the primary hiring authority for this branch of S.C.Y.T.H.E. was outdated, Mr. Flores was looking for someone for Accidental over at the branch he did most of his work out of and was willing to consider any referrals from current employees. In fact, that was one of the main S.C.Y.T.H.E. hiring practices. Because of the secretive nature of the company, most new hires came from referrals or headhunting, the latter of which had been the case for Margaret, who'd been a travel agent for years when she got the call for an interview. At least, that was the best Jack could piece together from the information he'd been accumulating over the past few months. In many ways, S.C.Y.T.H.E. employees were travel agents in their own right, really, only it was very much a one-way trip and no one really knew what the final destination was.

After twenty minutes of fiddling, Jack figured out how the fax machine worked and sent Carter's résumé along to Mr. Flores, and after forty minutes, Mr. Flores called back to let Jack know he would be reaching out to Carter for an interview. Carter himself called Jack just after lunch. Apparently the interview had already been set for the next day, which meant Jack had the hazy hours between work's end and the next morning to prep him on everything he might need to know about the organization.

It wasn't their first cram session together. In fact, the You Agains had spent all of high school holed up in one bedroom or another, limbs jittering from a diet primarily consisting of the main three all-nighter food groups—energy drinks, Diet Coke, and candy bars—while they pored over Greer's diligently kept notes from several years before. Granted, actually paying attention in class might have mitigated the need for most of these sleepless nights spent trying to memorize the twelve systems of the human body while actively assaulting several of their own, but it always seemed to pay off in the end. No one ever walked away with lower than a D, and that was a rousing success to Jack.

This time, though, the test at the end of the cramming would be worth more than grades. Carter needed to convincingly portray someone Margaret considered a good candidate for S.C.Y.T.H.E., and Jack wasn't even sure *he* was doing a good job, despite already having the gig.

The best way he could think of to attack the situation was with a mock interview. He always preferred a hands-on approach where he could swing it. By the time Carter arrived at Margaret's after work that night, Jack had transformed the living room into a stand-in office. The couch had been too heavy for his elderly body to shift alone, and Dale, despite his best efforts, wasn't able to be much help, so he set up the TV tables he'd found in the kitchen cabinet a few feet in front of the couch and placed a kitchen chair on either side. Then, since he still had some time to spare, he collected an assortment of papers, a stapler, an antique lamp, and his laptop and arranged them on top of the table just so. If you ignored the couch on one side and the TV on the other, and maybe squinted a little, you could almost buy this as an office.

Jack guided Carter over to the faux office and pulled out the other chair for Dale, who was standing in as Mr. Flores for the dry run. Then Jack made his way over to the couch, which he decided was the "backstage" area, so he could observe, translate from spirit to living for Dale, and offer notes.

"Is this really necessary?" Carter asked, mindlessly fiddling with the edges of the paper on the table.

The honest answer here was a solid "maybe." Since no one was really supposed to know about S.C.Y.T.H.E. or its goings-on outside of those who already worked for it or those utilizing its services, Jack imagined prep work for an interview probably didn't involve too much foreknowledge about the organization. That said, those being interviewed were selected for a reason: they were physically nondescript and had a small social circle, or they had a skill set connected to the main causes of death in the department they were interviewing for. He'd even read about one instance where someone died on the operating table and ended up networking with an agent who was at the hospital on a different collection before being revived and offered the job. But Carter had none of these things going for him. He was a handsome, reasonably social graphic designer who had never come closer to dying than when he was put under anesthetic to have his wisdom teeth out. That meant he'd need to fake the rest.

"It is necessary," Jack decided. "All right, let's get this party started. Dale?"

"Right." Dale cleared his throat, puffing himself up a bit in his seat and looking down at the list of questions Jack had left on the TV table for him. Jack didn't know what Mr. Flores would ask, but based on all the research he'd done when he first slipped into Margaret's life, he'd made some educated guesses. "Mr. King, thanks for coming in." Dale glanced over his shoulder to gauge Jack's response to this little flourish before carrying on, forgetting Jack would have to relay it all for Carter regardless. "First of all, it looks like you're a graphic designer. Can you tell me a little about how you think that experience would help you in your role at our organization? Bearing in mind this is a customer-facing position and will require a lot of driving and paperwork, and a strong stomach."

Carter blinked as Jack finished reiterating Dale's words and slipped back into observer mode. "Uh . . ." Then he looked at Jack. "What should I say here? I'm not supposed to know what the actual job is, right?"

"Correct," Jack said, punctuating the word with a sage nod. "Say you've got really strong attention to detail. They're fucking animals for attention to detail. Every report I turn in, it's always 'we need more attention to detail.'"

"Okay . . ." Carter slid back into the mock interview. "I've got really good attention to detail."

Another sage nod from Jack as Dale carried on with the list of questions. "Great. And how are you with severed body parts?"

STAYING UP ALL NIGHT IN YOUR TEENS WAS A BREEZE. YOU COULD bounce back enough to make it through a full day of school, including gym class, and still have enough energy left over at the end of the day to steal the novelty boxers off Mr. Bianchi's washing line. Staying up all night in your thirties meant a fairly groggy next day fueled by no less than three to five coffees before three p.m. Staying up late in your eighties, it turned out, felt like the kind of hangover a dormouse might experience after a night of drinking with the Russian navy.

Jack dragged himself into the office on legs of lead, landing on his desk chair as if he'd been dropped by a giant. He cracked open his laptop and flipped through the thin stack of files waiting for him on his desk, his brain filled with fog too thick for names and dates to penetrate. Carter's interview was set for eleven that morning, and with any luck, the hours spent cramming until the first scratches of dawn etched pastels across the night sky would pay off.

It was a little after eleven-thirty when the call came, and Jack once again sequestered himself in the single-stall bathroom to take it. Carter didn't bother with pleasantries, but it seemed to be more down to an eagerness to share his news than anything.

"Okay," he said as soon as he heard Jack inhale in preparation for a "hello." "So this Flores guy can't be our guy."

"Did you remember to talk about your attention to detail?" Jack asked, hoping Carter's proclamation wasn't the result of him being caught out.

"Yeah, yeah, and he really liked that thing about work-life balance. Whatever. Not the point. The guy was out of town with his kids the week the list was stolen."

"You're sure?"

"Yeah, I asked for a water when he offered a drink, and I checked the calendar on his computer while he was out of the office. He had 'Jamaica with kids' blocking out the whole week, as well as check-in info for his Airbnb."

Jack pulled out the paper on which he'd scribbled down the list of branch director surnames and crossed out "F." That meant they were down two. Three more to go.

"Nice work, man," Jack said as he circled the next name on the list. Ms. G. Summers.

A pause from the other end of the line. Then, in a smaller voice than had been there before, one from decades in the past, "Thanks, Jack."

Jack hung up a few moments later. Apparently the job was Carter's if he wanted, which he didn't, but the offer was flattering nonetheless. Flores, in Carter's words, was a friendly if no-nonsense guy who had little to say when Carter had tried to subtly inquire about the higher-ups in the nearby branches.

With the only pickup on his docket done shortly after lunch, Jack spent the remainder of his working hours napping with his chin propped in his hand so it just looked like he was concentrating very intently on his laptop screen to anyone passing by. The all-nighter had resulted in a whittling down of his culprit list, and when he returned home that night, he'd hunt down Ms. G. Summers's information on the spreadsheet and vet her next. Everything was going exactly as he'd expected, which was exactly as he liked it. This job, while a little unorthodox, had no real surprises to worry about. Of that he was sure. And of that he was grossly mistaken.

26

Jack had always known Fort You Again wouldn't hold forever. It had been cobbled together by discarded elements of nature, and it was only a matter of time before nature reclaimed them. Eventually the kids who'd built the fort became teens who could barely fit in it, and branches that had once seemed like trunks became little more than twigs rotting their way back into the earth they'd once grown from. It hurt to say goodbye. The wind in those woods whispered with their secrets and plans. The leaves rustled with their laughter. That forest was theirs. But as long as Jack had the You Agains, he could plant his roots anywhere.

Billy's All-Day Diner became the next logical hub. Billy himself ensured every booth was a confessional, and their apple pie was impossible to top. High school was merely an often avoidable obstacle between evenings at the diner, the six of them crammed onto ripped upholstery as they plotted or schemed or gossiped or, very occasionally, did homework. The grime on the walls and the scuffs on the tables made sense to Jack the way the sunrise in the mornings and the jingle of his mother's keys at night made sense.

The world had a rhythm and its patterns were etched on every coffee-stained cup placed in front of him.

That rhythm carried him through the decades, until one day he died, and the rhythm no longer seemed quite so smooth anymore. Suddenly his greasy diner had been replaced by the marble tabletop of Margaret's kitchen island in a house worth more than Jack's organs had been before they were buried, but Jack didn't really notice much. As long as he had the You Agains, he could plant roots anywhere. And as everyone gathered in what had now been solidified as their usual spots, he could feel those roots taking anchor, even through this strange trunk that wasn't his. Because, in some ways, it was becoming easy to forget. He was Jack McCoy, after all, and that felt just as true now, in this new old shell, as it had in his old but comparatively new one. It was something Jack had always been good at, finding himself no matter where he found himself, and he would do anything, even cheat death, to keep from losing that. Not after last time death came for the You Agains and he'd lost everything.

Eli was back behind his laptop as Carter unpacked his interview to the others and Jack listened on with his eyes closed, ostensibly to better absorb the story but mostly because it meant he could doze a little through the bits he'd already heard.

At some point Eli's voice replaced Carter's through Jack's sleepy haze, though he let most of the words run off him like water until one broke away from the stream. Jack's eyes flew open.

"Say again?"

"You needed the info on that Ms. G. Summers person, right?" Eli said. "Well, that's her."

"Right," said Jack. "But her name. What did you say her name was?"

Eli poorly stifled a grunt. "You could at least pretend you were paying attention. I said it's some chick named Greta. Greta Summers."

Jack's thoughts raced back to his conversation with Brenda when she'd reeled off all the directors' names: "*Ms. Summers works almost exclusively from another branch and is, if you'll forgive me, terrifying.*"

The new archivist certainly fit the bill for terrifying, and she'd transferred over from another branch after Jack's would-be date Gerard died, but would a higher-up at S.C.Y.T.H.E. work what was, as far as Jack could tell, a mid-level job in conjunction with a position at the top? It didn't make sense, really. Unless, of course, she'd come to Jack's branch with the sole purpose of stealing the Master List. She'd have had one at her own branch perfectly primed for stealing, but maybe the Room of Records was easier to access here. Maybe the names would be worth more for some reason. Jack couldn't be sure. All he knew was that, if his suspicions were correct, the human exclamation mark in his office basement wasn't who she seemed, and Jack knew a thing or two about what that was like. Which meant he'd have the upper hand in finding out the truth.

27

Twins

September 2000

Julia Nguyen transferred to Jack's school two weeks after term started, which was not an ideal way to set a third grader up for success, but at least she had her twin, Martha, to commiserate with. Jules was quiet, infamously weird, and could also be a bit of a biter. Martha, on the other hand, was bubbly and dangerously unafraid of confrontation. By the end of their first week, even the fifth graders like Jack had taken notice of these strange specimens. Opinions were divided into three camps: Team Jules, Team Martha, and Team Both Suck, with the latter two garnering the most votes among the student body. Everyone noticed the way Jules spent most of her time mumbling to herself alone. Everyone noticed how Martha could silence the whole cafeteria with an applause-inspiring burp. What none of the other kids seemed to notice, but what Jack picked up within days, was that he'd yet to see the twins together.

Thursday of that first week, Dale, Carter, Eli, and Greer met at Fort You Again for a debrief. Greer, who was a freshman in high school, deemed the whole drama totally lame. Ashley Robinson had been caught with weed and expelled, which seemed way more interesting to her for reasons Jack simply could not fathom.

"My mom said they never call Martha's name during class attendance," said Carter, whose mother was a teacher at their school and thus got the juiciest intel from the teacher's lounge.

"Because there is no Martha," Jack said matter-of-factly.

"But I've seen her," Dale said in a rare instance of disagreement with Jack's opinion. "She always wears that denim headband."

"Yep, and Jules always wears braided pigtails with ribbons and feathers. It's smart," said Jack.

"What's smart?" Greer's tone was an eye roll.

"To give Martha and Jules different looks."

"I don't get it," said Eli.

"Jules is Martha," said Jack. "Martha is Jules."

Everyone stared at him for a long moment, tendrils of late summer sun poking through the branches of the fort.

"But why?" Greer asked at last.

"Because nobody's on Team Jules," said Jack.

"Wait," said Greer. "There are teams?"

Jack shrugged. "You haven't been in elementary school in a while, huh?"

"Teams are mean." Greer's cheeks colored with the pink of righteous indignation. She could never bear cruelty. It was one of the main reasons why, when the You Agains officially formed the year before, one of their core tenets became "menace without harm, unless they really deserve it." It was one of Jack's favorite things about her, the way she cared. It made him care more too, and he needed that, because sometimes he forgot to.

"Well, we have to do something," Greer said, hazel eyes burning with determination, and Jack decided in that moment that whatever that something was, he would do it without question.

The next day at recess, he and the others—except for Greer, who, as a high school student, no longer knew the sweet joy of recess—made their way across the schoolyard to a shaded little corner where Jules was sitting on her own, holding a snail. She was so intently glued to its slimy progress across her index finger that she only looked up when they stood directly in front of her, their shadows falling across her face.

"Oh," she said when she finally noticed them.

"Hi," said Jack. "Are you Jules or Martha today?"

Jules froze, a surge of fear mixed with defiance flaring behind her dark eyes.

"It's okay," said Jack. "I just wanted you to meet my twins."

He waved a hand at the others: olive-skinned, curly-haired Eli, squat Dale, and Carter, who was Black. Jack, for his part, was in a lanky growth spurt, with a constellation of freckles across his pink cheeks.

This obvious lie prompted a glare from Jules, who placed the snail onto a nearby leaf and started to skulk away.

"Hold up," said Jack, hurrying after her. "Okay, so they're not my twins, but they are my brothers, basically. And if you want some siblings, they'll be yours too; we all will. You don't have to be alone here."

"You don't mean that," said Jules as she wiped the snail slime on her cargos.

"Sure we do," said Jack. "Heck, you're smart enough to fool half the school into thinking you're two people. We could use a brain like that."

"For what?" asked Jules.

"Whatever we want," said Dale.

"As long as we don't harm anybody," said Carter.

"Unless they really deserve it," said Eli.

Jack nodded at all of this. "We call ourselves the You Agains, because that's what the teachers say whenever we get detention."

"And we get detention a lot," said Dale.

"Especially Eli," said Carter.

"There's Greer, too," said Jack. "She's cool, I guess, if you don't mind annoying teenagers."

"She's my sister, so we're stuck with her," said Eli.

"But she's cool," Jack said again quickly, then added. "She knows someone who got expelled for weed."

"Whoa," said Jules. She gave her chin a scratch, contemplating. "Well, if you need me, I guess," she said at last. "I could use some brothers."

Jack felt his chin rise slightly at this.

"And it wouldn't be twins," Jules added. "There's four of you, so it would be quadruplets."

"Right," said Jack. "I knew that."

Martha never came back to school after that, and eventually the voting and interest in the twins stopped, but the You Again family had grown by one sister.

THE HEAVY GLASS FRONT DOORS OF THE OFFICE SWUNG CLOSED BEhind Jack, shutting out a muggy spring morning heaving with allergens he hadn't previously been aware of. In his old body, Jack typically avoided spicy foods and dairy to prevent an evening on the toilet, but otherwise he was able to handle most of life without consequence. In Margaret's skin, though, he quickly realized that sometimes air could make your nose stuffy. The idea of newfound allergies hadn't even occurred to him until the late spring pollen began tickling his sinuses, and suddenly he found himself very grateful he hadn't learned this lesson after munching on peanut butter or shellfish.

The Eagle watched Jack walk past his desk like he'd spotted an elephant on safari. Jack plopped his laptop down and tried to shake the feeling of eyes on his back with a tight shoulder shrug. He needed to talk to Brenda, but he'd have to wait out the attention of his neighbor. As much as Margaret and Brenda seemed to be friends, and a workday visit might not seem out of the ordinary, he didn't want to rouse any suspicion just in case. Someone in this office had a secret to protect, and they might have allies.

He rifled through the two files left for him that morning, putting on a show of deep interest in the details of a bludgeoning case slated for pickup just after lunch. After what felt like an appropriate amount of time had passed for a pee to brew in an elderly bladder, Jack got up and made as if he was walking toward the bathroom before changing directions just out of view of his row of cubicles and knocking on Brenda's office door instead.

Last time, Brenda had said Greta Summers was terrifying, which meant they'd met, which meant she might have information about her that could be useful. It also meant she'd be able to recognize her as an interloper and confirm Jack's theory. Of course, he couldn't exactly ask her outright. He needed to get that information in a subtle way. A way that wouldn't raise any eyebrows. A way that felt natural to Margaret and Brenda's existing dynamic. It seemed a safer option than confronting Greta herself, who didn't seem keen to talk under the best of circumstances. All he had to do was approach this the way he'd approached gossip growing up. He'd seen Greer do it a thousand times. It seemed easy enough.

"Bren!" Jack swung the door open with a flourish and pranced inside as gracefully as his creaking bones would allow. "Hey, girlie. What's the hot goss?"

Brenda looked up from her paperwork with a blank expression. She pushed her glasses lower on her nose bridge and blinked up at Jack in what he realized was growing concern. "Margie? You okay, hun?"

He slipped into the seat across from her and tried again. "Yes, thanks, doll. I'm great. It's just been a while since we've had a proper gossip."

Brenda leaned in over the desk. "You've got something juicy for me?"

"Oh," said Jack. "Uh. Yeah. Did you hear they had to get exterminators into the archives? Roaches, apparently. Poor Gerard dies and now this."

"Roaches!" Brenda shuddered. "Gosh, tell me they got them all. If any make it up here, I'll end up on the collection roster myself."

"Uh-huh," said Jack. "So the archives, huh? Always something going on down there. Like, have you met the new archivist?"

Brenda shook her head. "I don't get down there much, I'm afraid. I'm actually surprised to hear you've been lately. Agents really only use it for particularly difficult cases, in my experience."

"Right," said Jack. "Sure. I had a real humdinger last week."

"Which one?" Brenda's concern returned, this time not for Margaret's well-being, it seemed, but for her job. Which made sense. If Jack had actually had a particularly hard case, he'd have been expected to talk it over with his superior, who happened to be Brenda. And if he didn't talk it over with her, then at the very least, any challenges would have been reflected in his report, which she would have read. But, of course, she didn't, because, of course, there hadn't been any challenges to report.

He could lie to her, say he'd had a tricky case but was able to figure it out in the end and didn't want to trouble Brenda with anything to worry about, even in the report. But admitting to withholding information in his paperwork could get him into proper trouble, which was the very thing he'd always done his best to avoid. He could try to convince her there *had* been a report about a case warranting a trip to the archives, but something told him Brenda was too thorough to be tricked into believing she was the one who'd dropped the ball here. He racked his brain for every pickup he'd had the previous week on the off chance any of them actually had given him any trouble, but by that point the silence had begun to seep across the desk between them and Brenda was readjusting her glasses at an increasingly alarming rate.

Finally Jack decided to open his mouth and commit to whatever half-baked story came out of it, but the first sound to fill the room was that of a knock. For a very brief moment Jack found himself wondering how he'd managed to make the noise, but then the door opened and a man in his midthirties with slick brown hair poked his head into the office.

"Whoops, sorry, didn't realize you had company," said the

man. "Just wanted to drop you these." He emerged from the doorway in a black puffer vest and beige chinos, crossed the little gray room, and placed a small bag of saltwater taffy on Brenda's desk. There was something familiar in his clean-shaven face, but Jack couldn't place it. "I'll leave you to it." The man gave a wink and left the office just as quickly as he'd come, an expensive aftershave clinging to the air in his wake.

"Goodness me," said Brenda, when the door was closed again. "I seem to have forgotten where we were."

For that alone, and a little bit for the intoxicating aftershave, Jack could have kissed the man. He abandoned his attempts at an explanation for his archival forays, taking full advantage of Brenda's swoon to pivot the conversation anywhere but where it had been.

"Who was that?"

Brenda recovered and returned her attention to Jack. "Did you see that tush?" She gave her neck a small fan with her hand. "That, my dear Margaret, was Ian Grant."

Jack's handwritten list of higher-ups flashed through his mind. "As in one of our directors?"

Brenda gave a nod and ripped into her saltwater taffy, offering the selection to Jack. He took a piece, forgetting the partial dentures he currently rocked, and quickly regretted his decision.

"Nice of him to bring you these," Jack said as he tried to readjust the dentures with his tongue.

"Oh, he's the best."

"But not all of them are so great, right?" said Jack, getting them back on track. "You said one was terrifying?"

"Oh, Ms. Summers." Brenda nodded. "You'd never see her bringing us sweets."

"What's so scary about her?"

Brenda shook her head. "The woman is a good thirty years my junior and I can't have a single conversation with her without it feeling like I'm about to be sent to the principal's office."

That certainly tracked for the woman in the archives, Jack thought.

"And she's ruthless," Brenda added. "I mean *ruthless.* Had the old Accidental department manager fired for asking too many questions about the company. That man had been here longer than me and all he wanted was a better understanding of how things actually work around here. Well, I've certainly learned to keep my mouth shut since, I'll tell you what."

And there it was, as close to a confirmation as Jack could hope to get. Why would someone go so far as to fire someone for asking questions unless the answers were something they wanted to keep for themselves? Jack was never supposed to know about the Master List, but he did, and he was after it. For someone else who thought like him, that knowledge would be worth almost as much as the list itself, and they'd do what they had to in order to keep others from finding out.

28

Since his most recent jail stint, Eli had taken a job in construction. He'd never struck Jack as the type for manual labor—when Eli and Greer's parents had taken Jack along to their family cottage one summer, Eli wouldn't even join the sandcastle building competition because he hated the feeling of grit under his nails. But it was a job that didn't mind a criminal record, it kept a roof over his head, and Eli had the kind of determined disposition that meant he could excel at even the things he hated.

Digging into Greta Summers had proved to be just that. Jack found Eli on his laptop at Margaret's kitchen island that night. Eli was still wearing a high-vis vest and a coat of cement dust from the condos he and his team had been steadily accosting the skyline with earlier in the day. Jack had definitely locked the door before leaving and had left the extra key under one of the many flowerpots out front without telling anyone, so there was a very good chance Eli had picked the lock to get in.

"The woman's a ghost," Eli said as soon as Jack walked in. He shot a look in the general direction of where Jack had indicated Dale was lounging on the couch. "Figuratively."

"Not finding anything?" Jack asked, sinking down onto the stool beside Eli.

"The only Greta Summers in the area with a web presence is this chick," said Eli, swinging his computer around to face Jack. On the screen was the image of a woman in her mid-to-late forties, her coarse curls a gradient of gray. "But you said your archivist is blond and scary."

"I didn't say 'scary,'" Jack corrected. "I said 'terrifying.' So no, that's not her."

"You sure there aren't two Gretas?" Dale asked.

Jack tried to keep the condescension from his tone. "What's more likely, bud? That there's two terrifying women named Greta who just happen to be working for the same branch of S.C.Y.T.H.E., or that there's only the one?"

"Right, no, of course," Dale said quickly. "Just the one, probably. That makes sense."

"Anyway." Jack swung back around on his seat to face Eli. "Keep at it. Meanwhile one of the bigwigs popped into the office today. Ian Grant. He was wearing chinos, so I'm thinking we look into him next. Are the others coming?"

"Greer's at soccer with her girls, but Carter should be here soon."

Jack tucked his disappointment behind a noncommittal smile. The last little while, he'd mostly been allowed to forget that Greer had a whole life he wasn't a part of. At moments, he'd even forgotten anything had changed at all since their feral years growing up together. Still, he took a little solace in hearing that if she had to be away, it was because her kids were getting to be kids, especially with one so sick.

"Wait, you said Ian Grant?" Carter asked over a slice of pizza an hour later. The Great Anchovies on Pizza debate of 2006 had nearly rendered the You Agains irreparably at odds. Harsh words were spoken on all sides, but in the end a truce had been declared and all further pizza orders included one small, controversially topped pie for those rogue enough to partake.

"Why does that name sound familiar?" Dale asked from the couch. He'd been firmly against the anchovies-topped pizza because Jack was, but any pizza was tempting to someone who could no longer eat, and so he'd opted to keep his distance.

Eli hadn't closed his laptop despite the sagging triangle of grease in his hand. He was still hyper-fixated on tracking down Greta Summers, but enough of him remained present to prompt a quick shift in focus, and a few keystrokes later Eli was fully back in Margaret's kitchen. "Yo, we went to school with this guy. He was in biology with me and Dale junior year."

"Oh shit, yeah," Dale chimed in. "The kid with the really rich parents, right? Rich Ian?"

"Oh god, Rich Ian?" Carter said, echoing Dale without realizing it. "His parents owned a casino, didn't they? The one downtown. I think it's an art gallery now."

"Rich Ian, the guy who was in love with Greer?" Jack sputtered before he could stop himself.

"Yeah, well, it doesn't look like Rich Ian is all that rich anymore," Eli said, his eyes flicking quickly over something on his computer screen. "Apparently his old man went to prison for embezzlement a year or two after grad and most of the casino's earnings went to lawyer fees."

"So Rich Ian is now Financially Unstable Ian?" said Jack, trying and failing to paint over the shades of glee tinting his voice.

"All I'm finding is that he bounced around jobs for most of his twenties. Doesn't look like he could find much with his dad's reputation hanging over him. Then LinkedIn has him in 'transportation' from 2019 to about three years ago, when he was promoted to branch director."

Jack lifted his gaze to the chandelier above him. To the tastefully appointed yet obviously luxurious furniture that filled the clean, cavernous space surrounding the You Agains as they sat in the adjoining living room–dining room of Margaret's home. Based on the paychecks he'd collected in his time at S.C.Y.T.H.E., all signs pointed to a financially beneficial marriage on Margaret's part rather than the cushy job that being a Collections Agent simply wasn't. Jack had his doubts that even a director at the company would be living the high life. But Rich Ian had grown up accustomed to being, well, rich. None of the jobs he'd taken over the years would earn him enough to get that nickname back again. So, Jack thought, pressing the words to the roof of his mouth in order to taste them, there was every reason for him to *steal* it back. He flicked an anchovy off his slice of pizza, narrowly missing his target of Carter's plate.

"Sounds like the makings of a thief to me."

"So we pivot from Greta?" Carter asked. "It's not like Eli's finding anything on her anyway."

Eli glowered at this. "I'll find her."

"I don't doubt it," said Jack, who doubted it. "But Formerly Rich Ian seems like our guy anyway. Now we just need to see if we're right. Think you can get us a home address?"

"Already looking," said Eli, his pizza now long forgotten.

Dale sat up on the couch, eyes glistening. “How are you gonna get in, Jackie?”

Jack had already asked himself that question, and he was decidedly less than thrilled by the answer that rolled to the top of his mind like the cobalt triangle in a Magic 8 Ball. He looked to the empty chair beside Carter across the table, an overabundance of bread and cheese churning in a stomach better suited to prunes. This, much like his first attempt at putting on control-top pantyhose, was not going to be pretty.

29

The next day crept in on tiptoes, the late-morning sun caressing Jack awake through the crack between the dusty rose curtains of Margaret's bedroom. No alarm screaming at him meant it was the weekend, which hopefully also meant the You Agains would have the free time to make some more progress on everything they'd put into motion the night before.

Jack rolled over and unwrapped the floral duvet from where it wound around his torso, freeing an arm to blindly search the bedside table for his phone. Greer's name lit up the screen, indicating a missed alert. She would just be responding to his text. His mind knew this, but he'd forgotten to inform his heart of the utilitarian nature of the message and it gave a merry skip despite his best efforts to notify it now.

GREER: Can meet at noon. Billy's?

Now Jack was fighting his lips as well as his heart and was losing on both fronts. He felt a smile tug the lower half of his face upward against his will. He'd received this exact text so many times before. High school consisted of four straight years of this text with some classes scattered in between.

For the first time since he'd become Margaret, nothing in her closet seemed fit for the occasion. She had sectioned the walk-in into clothes for every conceivable scenario: work, formal wear, semiformal wear, spa days, exercise, brunch. And yet there was no section for meeting Greer at Billy's, nothing that said, "I'm a cool guy who's going to save your child and win your heart," and that felt like a real oversight. In his old body, Jack would be tossing on his best blue jeans, maybe a clean white T-shirt under a plaid button-up. He'd probably change a time or two. Greer liked him in blue; she'd let that slip once when they both had to get dressed up for Dale's mom's second wedding and he borrowed his uncle's navy suit. He'd taken her words to heart, thrifting an ocean of garments in the years since. But his new shell didn't quite lend itself to the easy, casual style he'd once worn.

Eventually Jack settled on a pair of well-tailored tan capris and a ruffled teal blouse that made him feel like a pirate. It was as close as Margaret had to "casual" in her wardrobe and, with any luck, Greer still liked him in blue despite the physical changes. She was already waiting in their usual booth when he arrived at Billy's, a half-eaten muffin on the plate in front of her and a faraway glaze shimmering over her hazel eyes. Jack slid across from her and Greer blinked herself back into the booth.

"Eli said you have a new target," she said in place of greeting.

Jack gave a nod. No chitchat, then. He adjusted his blouse ruffles. "Do you remember Rich Ian from high school?"

"Barely," said Greer. Which Jack decided was fair. Ian was two years younger than Greer, though after failing a few classes, he had to repeat ninth grade, putting him in the same year as

Jack and the others. Although Ian and Greer had only been in high school together for two short semesters, that didn't stop a crush from developing, and the next year, when Ian found out Eli was Greer's brother, he'd tried weaseling his way into the You Agains to get closer to her. Thankfully Eli had put a stop to this before Jack had to, and Ian had no choice but to move on. Of course, that was all decades ago, but you didn't just get over a girl like Greer. Jack knew that better than anyone.

"Turns out he's my boss's boss now," Jack continued.

Greer cocked a brow. "Small world," she said. "And you think he's the thief?"

"Could be," said Jack. He gave the abridged version of Ian's descent from the nickname of his youth as Greer finished her muffin.

"So what's the plan?" She dabbed at the remaining crumbs on her plate and nibbled them off her finger.

Jack's leg gave a nervous bounce, but he held her gaze. A few short days ago, he'd thought posing as Greer's mother would be the most uncomfortable moment of his life. He had been so young then, so naïve.

"Remember Operation Sports Banquet?"

The way Greer's face dropped suggested she very much did.

"Absolutely not," she said.

"We need to get into his house to look for the list."

"Okay, and we can't just break in because . . . ?"

Jack had to smile at that. There was a time when a harmless little break-and-enter would require some proper arm-twisting to get Greer on board. In the years since she'd run off and started a family, Jack was half-convinced she'd have reverted back. But here she was, more keen to break the law than he was.

“The guy grew up in a casino. Odds are good he has some kind of home security.” Technology had gone too far for Jack’s tastes. Everyone had a video doorbell these days, which was very inconvenient for his former way of life. It was, he supposed, one of the few benefits of the steady nine-to-five he now found himself in.

Greer stared hard at Jack. Jack stared hard at Greer. Her gaze may have weighed a ton, but he’d spent years training to lift it. He wasn’t backing down that easily.

Greer blinked first.

“You’re such a buttmunch,” she said.

“I know,” said Jack. “Believe me, I wouldn’t ask you to do this if I didn’t have to. I really, really wouldn’t.”

Greer let out a long exhale, her shoulders sagging in defeat. “Operation Sports Banquet,” she agreed.

30

Operation Sports Banquet

May 2003

The Winston brothers were infamous in Jack's neighborhood long before Jack knew what the word "infamous" meant. It was nepotism, Jack decided when he eventually learned what *that* word meant. Their father had been a small-time mobster and the boys inherited his ruthlessness and utter lack of charm. One was in Greer's grade, the other the year above her, and both were unholy terrors around their school and the town at large. When the You Agains formed, despite their mandate to menace without harm, the Winstons immediately viewed them as a threat. They were all operating on the same territory, sometimes with the same end goal, and though their methods, ages, and sizes may have been different, they had just enough in common to piss the brothers off.

The You Agains kept their heads down for the first while. The Winstons were already in high school, which meant only Greer had to contend with them, and she wasn't exactly shouting from the rooftops about her involvement in a group of preteen outlaws. It kept them all out of trouble with the brothers for the most part. That all changed when Jack's classmates started turning up to school shaken and occasionally bruised. It didn't take him long to discover the reason: kids whose family had a little extra in the bank had become targets of the Winston brothers. Through intimidation and physical force, the kids had been made to turn over allowance money, cell phones, even gaming devices.

Normally Jack was all for a Robin Hood approach to crime, but these kids were traumatized after being roughed up by two six-foot teenagers with meaty fists. After witnessing the first black eye, Jack decided it was time to make some changes around here. This wasn't going to be easy. There might be strength in numbers, but there was even more strength in the Winstons' wrestling-honed shoulders, and besides, Jack didn't want to put his friends in danger.

If he couldn't be stronger than the brothers, though, he knew he could definitely be smarter. Inside the makeshift walls of Fort You Again one late spring afternoon, Greer was in the middle of venting about all the end-of-year events her high school would be hosting.

"Everyone's taking a date," she said about Homecoming and the big class trip and Prom and at least three different sporting events she didn't participate in. "Not like I care. It's just all dumb, is what I'm saying. That's too many things. How do you even get a date for that many things?"

Jack had an answer to that question but decided it was best to keep it to himself. Instead he asked one back. "You said there's a sports banquet?"

"Yeah," said Greer. "Which is so lame. I mean, why are we celebrating people just because they can run fast or kick a ball? Have they ever created something at once beautiful and profound? Does their jumping around challenge the status quo?"

Everyone looked at one another as though someone else in the fort might actually know the proper response to that.

"N-no?" Jules said at last.

"Exactly!" said Greer. "No."

Everyone collectively exhaled their relief.

"Anyway," said Jack. "That means the Winstons will be there, right?"

Greer scrunched up her face. "Yeah, Roy's being honored for his 'contributions to wrestling,' which just means he's good at beating people up with teachers' approval. It's barbaric. I can't wait to be anywhere but there."

"I need you to go with him," said Jack.

Greer stared at him for a long moment before saying, "What?"

"As his date," Jack clarified, as if that was the part she was most confused about.

"Why the hell would I do that?"

"So the rest of us can sneak into their garage and take back everything they've been stealing from everyone."

"You've got to be kidding me," said Greer. "I'd literally rather eat a shoe."

"You can do that too if you want," said Jack. "But if you go and keep the Winstons distracted long enough, we should be able to make this work."

Greer's expression was hard but she said nothing. Jack had her. He knew he did. She could argue with many things—she was a teenaged girl, after all—but she couldn't argue with the facts.

Besides, she was as upset about the injustice of the Winstons' crimes as anyone.

"What makes you think he'd even say yes if I asked him? Everyone knows he's into Jenny Michaels and I'm not exactly a big catch."

Jack had to actively do battle with his tongue in response to that. Whatever came out of his mouth next had to be chill and nonchalant. Or at least one of the two.

"Bullshit," he practically shouted, effectively achieving neither. Okay, round two. He mentally scolded his tongue and tried again. "I mean, he'd totally say yes."

"What makes you so sure?"

"Because everyone else is too scared of the Winstons to date them. And besides, you're a girl; that's definitely more than enough for Roy."

"You sure know how to charm a girl," Greer said, forcing an immediate blood rush to Jack's cheeks. He'd pivoted too far in the opposite direction and now those hazel eyes looked at him with scorn. Why did no one ever warn him love was hard?

The other boys had nodded along with Jack in agreement, but Jules rolled her eyes.

"Don't be such a buttmunch," Jules snapped. "Greer, Roy's gonna totally flip his lid over you. You're too cool for him but he's too dumb to notice."

"That's what I was trying to say!" Jack said, but all this got was another eye roll.

"They're all a little dumb, I think," Jules added to Greer in an exaggerated stage whisper. Greer couldn't help but leak a giggle at this.

"Ugh, fine," she relented. "Just because I'm sick of those assholes bullying everyone and acting like they run this town. But I'm not wearing some tacky formal dress."

"Deal," said Jack.

GREER'S DRESS WAS SEQUINED ALONG THE BODICE AND FEATURED A short but garish train. When her mom found out she was actually going to a high school event instead of sulking in her room or plotting in the forest with children, she insisted on a shopping spree that nearly ended in an emergency family therapy session. Jack and the others swung by just in time to see her wiggle awkwardly down the stairs looking like a particularly peevish clown fish. The only accessory she wore was a frown. Her sandy hair was pulled forward, side-swept bangs covering her left eye, and her shoes were the combat boots she'd all but superglued to her feet the day she'd brought them home. Jack had never seen anyone look so beautiful.

It took a moment of blatant gaping to collect himself, at which point he forced his brain on to the task at hand. "So," he said, then cleared his throat and pushed his voice down an octave. "So, we'll need you to keep the Winstons busy for at least an hour. There's some big stuff in that garage. At least two computers that I know of. It'll take a while to clear it all out."

"How the hell am I supposed to keep them busy that long?" Greer said, a hint of something frantic in her voice. "Jack, I'm not kissing Roy."

"Good," said Jack, matching her urgency with his own at the mental image. "Definitely don't do that. Just, I don't know, talk to him."

"About what? The proper angle to pull a wedgie?"

"Maybe," said Jack. "Probably not, though. You'll think of something."

"You've got one hour," said Greer, adjusting her dress so it sat higher on her chest. "Then I'm getting the hell out of there."

They shook on it, and Jack wore Greer's candy apple body spray for the rest of the night.

Breaking into the Winstons' garage was a relatively straightforward affair. As Jack had suspected, the adults of the household had taken advantage of their boys being out on a Friday night, and the two-story sandstone was vacant as a result. Eli and Carter had brought wagons from home and Dale stood watch while the others loaded up. Jack had spent much of the previous day's recess creating an inventory from all the kids at his school who'd had something taken from them by the Winstons, and Jules perched herself on a stack of winter tires and read off items as they went to ensure the group only took back what had actually been stolen.

Half an hour in, Carter's wagon was fully loaded with loot and Eli's held no fewer than three in-box Tamagotchis and a thirteen-inch TV. It hadn't been easy, digging through the rusty car parts and boxes of tools and miscellany in the garage, but Jules had already checked off two-thirds of the list.

Eli's jeans started blaring Blink-182. Everyone froze. Their breathing, the shifting of cardboard on cement, and Jules's steady roll call of items had been the only sounds in the garage since they'd arrived. They all turned to Eli, who quickly dug through his pocket and excavated his cell phone. Well, technically it was Greer's phone, but since she was the only one in the group who had one, and since she'd be somewhere with access to a pay phone, Eli got the coveted technology privileges for the night.

"Yo," he said down the line. "Shit. When? Shit."

He hung up, everyone's eyes still on him.

"Greer?" Jack asked breathlessly.

"Yeah. Apparently Roy got handsy, so she kicked him in the nuts."

"Buttmunch," said Jules.

"Totally," said Carter.

"I'll kill him dead," said Jack.

"Me first," said Eli.

The stale garage air filled with angst as everyone stewed in their emotions. None had yet hit an age when the idea of handsiness seemed remotely appealing, and the thought of it coming from someone as gross as a Winston, especially when it was unwanted, was completely egregious. So much so, it took a breath for Eli to relay the rest of Greer's message.

"They're on their way back," he said, finally snapping out of his brotherly rage. "Greer said they left ten minutes ago on their bikes."

That was enough to force Jack out of his own murderous thoughts. "But they only live like three miles away from the high school."

"Which means they'll be here any second," said Carter.

Jack leapt upright, abandoning the box he'd been crouched beside. As leader of the You Agains, it was up to him to keep his men safe, even the ones who weren't men, and even if it meant changing plans.

"We're moving on to phase two," he ordered, prompting the others to their feet. Carter grabbed his wagon by the handle, trying to yank its heft out onto the driveway, but it was too heavy for him to pull alone. Jack nodded at Dale, who got behind the wagon and pushed as the two maneuvered it out of the garage, down the small, sloping driveway, and onto the sidewalk before vanishing into the night.

Eli grabbed for his own wagon, but before he'd made it over the garage's threshold, the night air tick-tick-ticked with the sound of spinning bike spokes. Eli cast wild eyes over at Jack. Jack knew that look. It wasn't the fear of being caught in his friend's expression, it was the look of a boy who was about to do something reckless.

"Dude, no," Jack hissed as two pairs of heavy footsteps approached the garage.

"That bastard freaked out Greer," Eli growled. He didn't turn to look at Jack even as Jack's hand grabbed his shoulder. To Eli, Jack knew, there was no one else there but him and, at any moment, Roy Winston, grabber of sisters. If their years of friendship were any indication, this was about to end very badly, mostly for Eli. Roy would pummel him to within an inch of his life, leaving a curly-haired pulp stain on the garage floor. It wasn't that Eli couldn't fight, it was just that the Winston brothers would require a tag team of Stone Cold Steve Austin and The Rock before they could accurately be described as picking on someone their own size.

The garage door, which had only been left half-open as the You Agains found it, creaked upward. Jack could feel the muscles in Eli's sinewy shoulder tensing as he began to pull away, primed to dart headfirst into the meaty fists of danger. But before he had a chance, something bolted past them. Like a purple-and-khaki-clad bullet, Jules shot across the garage and out the steadily opening door, barreling directly between the Winstons and sprinting down the road, the whole while shrieking a battle cry that verged on a yodel. The brothers, still oblivious to the existence of anyone else in their garage, took off after her on foot, and with only a look between them, Jack and Eli hopped on the discarded bikes, Jack quickly fastening the handle of the second wagon to the bicycle seat with a stray piece of rope from one of the boxes in the garage, and they were off.

It took them only minutes to catch up to Jules, who ran track, and the Winstons, who were as muscled as they were lumbering. They bypassed the brothers and Jack slowed down just enough for Jules to hop into the wagon before they sailed on to their final destination, as per phase two of the plan, losing the brothers in the loose gravel kicked up by the tires of the stolen bikes.

Jack and Eli parked in a ditch just down from the park. Jules hopped out of the wagon and untied it from the bike, and together the trio climbed the little hill to the playground at the top. Despite the late hour and the indigo sky, the park was overrun with kids. Carter and Dale stood atop the slide like kings, having somehow dragged their wagon onto the climbing structure. Jack and the others ascended the ladder and joined them as the assembled kids swarmed closer. Toward the back of the crowd, a sandy-blond head bobbed above the others, making its way through the throng.

Dale stepped aside and ushered Jack to the makeshift stage at the top of the slide. "My fellow students of West District Middle School," Jack declared over the chattering crowd. "We have your shit."

Everyone erupted in applause as Carter and Eli rolled the wagons forward. Jules dug the lined paper with the list of stolen goods out of one of her cargo pants pockets and began reading the items aloud. It was like an auction, if an auction was held on a playground and no one actually spent any money. Jules would announce a stolen good, someone would raise their hand, and Dale would send it down the slide to be collected by its rightful owner. Jack looked on as the fruits of his labor unfolded before him, kids leaping over each other, occasionally in tears, as they clutched beloved toys and games to their chests. But despite his best efforts, his eyes kept being pulled back to the gawky teenager in the sparkly dress standing at the front of the crowd, looking up at him with, if he let himself believe it, something akin to admiration.

Eventually the park cleared out and all that remained were the You Agains and their empty wagons. Jack and the others slid down to meet Greer in the Band-Aid- and candy-wrapper-littered sand encircling the play structure.

"You okay?" he asked Greer as soon as he'd landed in front of her. "Did Roy hurt you?"

"He touched my knee," Greer said. "And wouldn't move his stupid sweaty hand when I told him to."

"I should've bitten him when I had the chance," Jules rued.

"It's fine." Greer lifted her dress just enough to reveal the combat boots peeking out under the hem. "These did the trick."

"Think the Winstons will know it was us that took the stuff?" Carter said.

The Winston brothers were many things, but clever wasn't on the list, and without seeing the faces of their adversaries, Jack had his doubts. "We'll just have to make sure we stay out of their way from now on," he said.

Dale nodded. "No worries there. If I never see another Winston in my whole life, I'll die happy."

31

Formerly Rich Ian lived in a tasteful beige town house with a salmon pink garage door and freshly mowed lawn. It was the kind of place Jack had cycled past on his hand-me-down bike many times growing up, knowing he'd never see the inside by legal means. Of course, he had never expected to end up in a house like Margaret's. Or in a body like Margaret's. But there was still a part of him that felt out of place in this tastefully beige neighborhood, and he couldn't wait to get out of here and back to the mini mansion that, at the very least, his soul's new home felt at home in.

Greer shifted from foot to foot on the front step. She tossed a look toward the side of the house, where Jack and Carter waited for her to gain entry. Carter had already examined the house's blueprints as well as the layout on Google Street View, finding a dog door leading from the kitchen to the fenced backyard. Once Greer had Ian distracted, she'd peek out the living room window facing the side of the house, ostensibly to take in the breathtaking views of suburbia. This was the signal that set the rest of the plan in motion. From there, Jack would use his newfound diminutive size to crawl through the dog door before unlocking the back door for Carter. From the kitchen, it was a straight shot down the hall and up the stairs to the primary bedroom and home office, where anything worth hiding was likely kept. The plan was simple. Foolproof, even. Jack could have done it in his sleep.

He gave Greer a double thumbs-up from his hiding spot, but the look on her face told him that any hesitation she had on that doorstep didn't come from waiting for the official go-ahead. After Operation Sports Banquet, Jack had promised Greer he'd never use her as a honeypot again. She hated being reduced to a pretty distraction, and Jack hated using her as one. And until now he'd been true to his word, even going so far as to dress in drag in a failed attempt to honeypot himself during senior year. He'd make this up to her by getting the money she needed for her daughter; that was the whole point of all this. They both just needed to get through the next twenty, maybe thirty minutes.

Jack offered an apologetic smile and Greer deflated in a sigh. She readjusted her tank top so it sat a little lower on her chest, looking appalled with herself, and then she knocked. A few more foot shifts later and the door clicked open. Jack couldn't see past the front step, but Ian's voice seeped out of the house just loud enough to catch.

"Can I help you?"

"I— Wait, is that Ian Grant?" Greer was all surprise and forced cleavage. When it came down to it, this was what Greer did best. Not the cleavage part, she usually kept that out of the equation, but from the day she'd burst into tears on Mrs. Sullivan's doorstep the first time they met, Greer was forever locked in Jack's heart as the girl who could play any role. In another life, he was convinced she'd be a movie star, but he preferred her in this one, where her stage was sticky club floors or police station lobbies, and her biggest fan was him.

"Holy shit, Greer? Greer Abrams?"

"Yeah, hey! This is crazy. I had no idea you lived around here. My car broke down just over there." She gestured an arm toward a strategic parking job by the curb. "And my cell's dead. I've been knocking on doors trying to find someone who wouldn't mind letting me use their phone, but people really take the whole 'stranger danger' thing to heart around here."

"Well, good thing I'm not a stranger," came Ian's reply in a tone that made Jack want to gag. "Please, come in. Mi teléfono es su teléfono. It's been too long. If you're not in a rush, I'd love to catch up."

"You're a hero," Greer cooed, and Jack did gag a little.

Greer disappeared from the doorstep and Jack shifted focus to the window, allowing time for the gracious host to fetch some sort of beverage from the kitchen. It was the very least of what Jack would do if Greer showed up on his doorstep after all those years. Unfortunately for him, he'd been forced into an afterlife intervention before he'd had the chance.

A few moments later, Greer's upper half appeared in the window. She was talking about something Jack couldn't hear, giggling a laugh Jack didn't need to be in earshot of for it to play like a music box tune in his mind. She looked down at Jack and Carter without letting her jovial expression shift, giving an almost imperceptible nod to her team before disappearing back into the living room.

Jack and Carter rounded the house, opening the metal gate with a muffled snap of the lock. The backyard was a compact affair, longer than it was wide and featuring only a well-kept rectangle of grass and a little shed toward the very back of the space. The dog door looked smaller than it had online, clearly built for a pet of appropriate town house size rather than something more comparable to Margaret in stature as they'd hoped: perhaps a rottweiler or a recently groomed chow chow.

"I'm not sure Margaret's done enough yoga for this," Jack hissed over his shoulder at Carter, who loomed over him from Jack's position on all fours. His joints popped and creaked as he attempted to contort the arthritic body wrapping around him, knees and shoulders and spine alternating their aches. Finally he slunk headfirst into the kitchen, feeling not completely unlike he'd just been given birth to. The floor tiles were cool beneath his palms as he crawled the last of his lower half out of the dog door.

Something tip-tap tip-tapped into the room. Jack looked up just in time to catch sight of a drooling brown-and-white bulldog sliding into the kitchen doorway, jowls swinging with wild abandon. It locked eyes with the intruder on the floor and immediately burst into a series of guttural barks as it barreled toward Jack at full speed.

Jack had never been much of a dog person in life, and this wasn't helping their cause. The creature reached him before he could pull himself to his feet, forcing Jack to roll out of the way of the slobbery security system. For its part, the dog seemed to interpret the move as an invitation to play, and now, instead of facing a protective attack, Jack had fifty pounds of unadulterated K-9 bounding at him with unbridled enthusiasm. Jack continued to roll across the floor as the dog landed on him with heavy paws.

His back thwacked hard against a row of cabinets under the sink. The dog skidded across the floor and raced after him. Jack pulled the cabinets open behind him, fumbling around until he found the one housing the garbage can. He felt through the can, eyes locked on the dog, his fingers wrapping around a discarded toast crust just as the animal reached him.

Jack held the crust up before the dog, wincing in preparation for another lunge in his direction. Instead the dog froze, staring up at the crust as though it held all the wisdom of the universe. Jack hurled the crust across the room, sending the dog after it in a sliding tizzy. He slumped back against the counter, catching his breath. The crust would only buy him seconds, and he needed that time to hoist his aching body upright and unlock the door for Carter. But just as he began to ease himself to his feet, footsteps sounded from the hallway.

"Sorry, he's not usually like this." Ian's voice floated into the kitchen as the hardwood floor creaked under his weight just beyond.

Jack froze.

The dog was just finishing its whole wheat distraction. It would be running back to Jack any second now. Probably around the same any second that its owner would be walking into the kitchen, only to find the little old woman from work plopped on the floor. Jack was not a fan of that second. His hand was still on the door of the cabinet containing the garbage can. He looked down at the body he'd taken: the spindly arms, the generous bosom, the soft middle, the legs that ended not far from where they began. The thought wouldn't have even crossed his mind a few short months ago. It simply wouldn't have been possible. But as the footsteps grew nearer and the dog swallowed its last bite of crust, Jack knew he didn't have a choice. Without a second thought, he shoved the bin to one side and hurled himself backward into the garbage cabinet, closing the door behind him.

In the dark of the cabinet, Jack couldn't see the knees he'd pulled to his chest, but he sure could feel them. His back, now hunched into a letter *C*, might never straighten again if the way each vertebra seemed to lock was any indication. Something wet came snuffling at the crack in the cabinet door. The dog, seeking another trash treat.

"Bentley." Ian's voice, now just beyond the door. "What is it, boy?" Footsteps drawing nearer.

All it would take was that cabinet door opening and Jack would be fully exposed to the world. He pulled his knees closer, smooshing his bust, as if he could make himself so small he wouldn't be spotted.

"Ian?" Greer's voice, distant but distinctly hers. "Everything okay?"

A shift in the footsteps directly in front of the cabinet. A beat, during which Jack failed to breathe. Then, "Yeah, coming!"

The footsteps, human and dog, receded. Jack waited until the silence held for ten Mississippis before cracking the door. The kitchen stood empty again, only a small collection of breadcrumbs offering proof he hadn't always been alone. Jack eased one foot out of the cabinet and then the other, feeling like a piece of origami being unfolded by a particularly rough-handed child. Every bend left a cramp in his muscles, a twinge in his joints.

Finally fully unfolded, Jack hobbled over to the back door and unlocked it, poking his head out and signaling to Carter, who hovered just to the side of the door.

"What took you so long?" Carter whispered as he sauntered over.

Jack, who was still trying to remember how to inhale and exhale in proper rhythm, just shook his head and ushered Carter inside.

They snuck through the hallway and up the stairs, separating at the top. Jack took the office, Carter the bedroom. The taupe office walls were lined with shelves of books about finance and cryptocurrency and manifestation, wedged between busts of great thinkers and marble globes. A mahogany desk sat just under the window, holding only a computer and a plastic plant. Jack pried open the desk drawers and rifled through the loose sheets of paper within, finding little more than old employee evaluations and notes on budgeting.

Jack took each book off the shelves and shook them out one by one in case Ian had secreted the Master List between their pages, but all that fell out was an old receipt for contact lenses used in place of a bookmark. Despite his cramping joints, he crouched to the floor and peered under every piece of furniture on the off chance the list had been stashed underneath, but came up empty-handed.

Footsteps in the hallway. Jack hurried to his feet and scrambled for something to hide behind or—thanks to his cabinet adventures—inside of, when Carter materialized in the doorway. He shook his head at Jack. So no luck there, either. That didn't mean Ian was in the clear, of course, but they couldn't risk taking more time than they already had. With any luck, Greer would have taken the opportunity to sniff out the main floor when Ian went to the kitchen. She might have found something they hadn't.

All that remained was to creep downstairs and give Greer the signal that it was time to go. As the newly minted lightest You Again, that job fell to Jack, being that he was now the least likely to make the hardwood creak. Carter made his way out the back door while Jack slipped down the hall toward the living room, where Greer and Ian's voices tripped over each other in friendly conversation. He padded closer until he was near enough to use the marble in his pocket. It was the same one he'd always used in situations like this, a cat's-eye he'd won on the playground in third grade. But this time something was different. Just as he reached into his pocket, the words drifting out of the living room took shape, shifting from the loose fog of distant voices into comprehensible conversation.

"Two girls, wow. I'm sure you're an amazing mom," came Ian's voice. "And this is the same guy you met in college, right?" There was a note of disappointment in his tone. Jack had begged Greer to play single for this, but she'd insisted that once she'd made it inside, she'd be able to stall Ian with or without a ring on her finger.

"Yeah, the same guy," said Greer. "We're coming up on twenty years."

"Well, congrats." Ian's voice was flat for that, but it seemed to perk up a bit as he said, "Sorry to hear he's so sick, though."

"Thanks. The treatment he needs is expensive, but we're hoping to be able to get it for him very soon." Greer's own voice flared with determination. Jack knew that tone as well as he knew his own reflection. When Greer wanted something, she'd do whatever it took to get it, and many times that meant convincing Jack to help. Only this time Jack suddenly found himself in the dark on what she actually wanted help with. She'd always been direct and up-front. Greer wasn't one to pull punches, especially not with him. Her words to Ian hit Jack across the chin like a right hook. She'd lied to him. It wasn't her daughter who was sick, it was her husband. She wouldn't be misleading Ian about this; she had no reason to. But what reason did she have to lie to Jack?

Jack pulled the marble out with an unsteady hand. He'd grown used to mild tremors by now, but this was something different. This wasn't age. This was something he couldn't put a name to.

Absently, he crouched and let the marble roll silently past the living room doorframe. Instead of immediately making her excuses to leave the way she always did at the signal, Greer fell silent for a second. It wasn't long enough for just anyone to notice, but Jack wasn't just anyone. That silence meant Greer hadn't expected Jack to be there in that moment, that she wasn't prepared for him to overhear her.

"Well, it's been so nice catching up," Greer said after the barely perceptible beat, her voice tight.

Jack slunk toward the back door as a couch creaked behind him and footsteps moved to the hallway. He joined Carter in the backyard, half in a daze, and together they made their way to the front of the house just as the door clicked shut.

Greer padded down the front steps and they all reached the car a moment later.

"How'd it go?" Carter asked Greer.

"Nothing downstairs, you?"

"Nada."

"Damn," said Greer, her tone distant. She wouldn't meet Jack's eye, and he found himself relieved by that. He wasn't sure he could handle that hazel stare he'd always known as piercingly honest. Those eyes felt like strangers to him now.

Greer wedged a hand in her jeans pocket and pulled the marble out. Without raising her eyes, she placed it gently in Jack's palm, her fingertips quickly grazing his creased skin before she pulled away, as if he were made of fire. "Here. Told Ian I had to tie my shoe so I could grab it for you. He didn't notice they're slip-ons."

Jack said nothing. There was nothing to say. Or maybe there was too much.

For the first time since they'd met, Greer had lied to him, and suddenly everything he'd been risking his afterlife for was a lie as well.

32

Married

November 2007

Jack and Greer had different ideas about what information was worth sharing. Greer didn't tell Jack when her grandmother died, or when she didn't get into her dream college, or when her parents separated. The shadows cast over her world only became known to Jack through Eli. It was as if, by not addressing them herself, Greer could trick herself into believing there was only light. But the good things? Those she brought to him like fireflies trapped in her hand, only too eager to share the glow. Which was why it didn't make sense that Jack didn't hear it from her. That he didn't even see her again after the police closed the case. After Jules's funeral.

It had been three months since the You Agains had sat together on that hard wooden pew, black-clad and hollow. Jack had just turned eighteen, and so far adulthood had only stung. After the night that stole his friend, the police had been and gone and been again. Jack had only been spared from legal ramifications because he'd been a minor at the time. But for the first time in a life filled with the ability to inexplicably get away with everything, Jack would have almost preferred the punishment. At least it would have been something that made sense in a world where nothing seemed to anymore.

Lying there on his single bed still draped in the outer space–themed bedspread, feet nearly dangling off the end, he should have felt like a giant in that shoebox of a room, but somehow he'd never felt smaller. Someone knocked on the door and then pushed it open without waiting for a response.

Eli filled the doorframe, all frantic curls and dark circles under his eyes. He'd changed since his first full night in jail three months ago. He'd changed since everything that happened that summer night. They all had. For Eli, it meant a new level of recklessness, as though nothing mattered anymore, as though whatever underused pause button keeping him partly in check had busted, leaving him entirely on fast-forward.

"Hey." He barely lifted his wave.

Jack raised his chin in something he hoped resembled a nod of greeting.

"Greer's home for the weekend," Eli said, feeling through his words with a level of caution Jack didn't recognize in him. But Jack was too distracted to analyze that. As soon as Greer's name was spoken, he bolted upright, shuffling off the bed, his thoughts consumed with nothing beyond seeing her.

Eli was at the bed in three long strides, a hand on Jack's shoulder, pressing him back down. The role reversal brought Jack back into the room in a way Eli's careful speech hadn't. He had held Eli back from his own heedlessness with the same gesture too many times throughout the years. Was that what Eli was doing now?

Eli eased himself onto the mattress beside Jack.

"She doesn't want to see you," he said. "Or anybody," he added quickly.

"Okay," said Jack, swallowing his disappointment in a single gulp. She'd be back again for another visit soon enough. After more than two years of Greer's college career, Jack had grown accustomed to her rhythms. He existed for long weekends and holidays, when Greer drove the two hours back to spend time with family and see her friends. She'd been gone for a longer stretch than usual this time, but under the circumstances, Jack could understand that. Her semester would be ending in less than a month and she'd be home for the winter holidays. He could wait. The last two years had taught him patience even as they taught Greer the ins and outs of literary analysis or whatever it was she did on campus all day.

"Jack," Eli said, and Jack's skin prickled at the way Eli hit the sharp consonants in his name, holding on to them just a bit too long.

"Yeah?"

Eli picked at a scab on his knuckle. Jack tried to remember which fight it was from, but in truth, he'd lost track by now.

"She got married."

Jack looked over at Eli, searching his face for the hint of a prank or a joke, even though neither would have made any more sense coming from Eli than the words he'd just uttered.

The absurdity of it tickled Jack deep in his belly, spreading like the brush of a feather up his chest until it burst out of his throat in a bellowing laugh. He couldn't stop it. The laughter overtook him, ripping through him, and soon he was doubled over in hysterics, tears ripping loose from his eyes and tracing a chaotic path down his cheeks. Eli stiffened beside him, shifting himself away from the cackling lunatic on the bed.

"You don't get it, dumbass, she's leaving." Eli's words cut through the laughter just enough to reach Jack's ears. It took effort, but he sobered up and wiped his face with the sleeve of his T-shirt.

"Huh?"

"She's just back to introduce us to the guy and then they're moving out of state."

Whatever bewildered laughter was left in Jack's stomach escaped through a gasp as the thought of Greer leaving punched into his gut.

"No," was all Jack had left in him to say.

"Just thought you should know," said Eli, sliding to his feet.

"Who?" Jack was still stuck on single syllables, the rest of his vocabulary locked in a box somewhere in the back of his mind, which was now too cluttered to dig through.

"I dunno," said Eli. "Some guy she met last year. One of her TAs, apparently. He just got a job in New Hampshire, so that's where they're going."

A few more words wrestled themselves out of the clutter. "I didn't think she was seeing anyone."

"Yeah. She said it wasn't serious. And then I guess it was."

Eli's hand grazed the bedroom door handle.

"Why?" It was what Jack had really wanted to ask all along, but that little question felt as though it was a root from which an ancient oak grew, and he was afraid he wouldn't be brave enough to climb it.

Eli shrugged. "Love, I guess. Greer wouldn't leave her studies for anything less. Except. Well . . ."

"Everything," Jack finished for him. "She's leaving because of everything. She's leaving everything." She was leaving him.

"Maybe." Another shrug. "She says it's time to move on."

Eli gave one more look at Jack over his shoulder before disappearing into the hall. And then Jack was alone.

Greer did move on. For ten long years, she lived away from the You Agains, building a life of domesticity that the Greer Jack knew would have scoffed at. When she and her family moved back to town, Jack learned that news from Eli too, and he promised himself that until he learned it from her, he would continue to live as if she'd never come back. For her sake, he told himself, if that's what she'd wanted. But in truth, it was mostly for him. Because knowing she was so close and yet, in many ways, so far away from him was worse than her not being there at all.

Greer never told Jack about the shadows cast over her world, and she never told him she'd eloped, and to Jack, that pattern meant something about this new life she chose, something he could never shake.

33

Margaret's front door was unlocked again when they got back, but Jack didn't have it in him to take Eli to task for picking it. It didn't feel like he had much in him at all right then. It felt as though someone had scooped out his innards like a jack-o'-lantern, leaving him hollow.

Greer hadn't said a word since they'd left Ian's, leaving Carter to do the heavy conversational lifting on the drive home. As they entered the foyer, Dale wafted in from the living room to greet them like a dog who'd been left to its own devices all day. By the look on his face, Jack wouldn't have been surprised to find a shredded roll of toilet paper on the rug.

"How'd it go, Jackie?" he all but barked.

"No dice," said Jack without breaking stride. All he wanted was to throw himself on Margaret's bed and let his weathered bones melt into the mattress. Everything hurt. Everything that was Margaret's and everything that was left of him. And for the first time in his afterlife, he found himself wondering what the point of it all was. He was in this shell to stay alive, because life held everyone he cared about, everyone worth dying for. But in the course of an afternoon, of seconds, really, life stopped feeling worth the fight.

"Can we talk?" Greer's voice was an echo ricocheting off the foyer's high ceilings, bouncing back at Jack like a choir of strangers.

"Sure," he said, though he didn't know why. There was nothing to say, and no energy left with which to say it.

Greer gave a tight smile and led the way up to the second floor and into Margaret's bedroom, easing the door shut behind them. How many times had Jack dreamed of a moment like this? In another time. In another body. In another life.

"Jack," she started, then stopped, then tried again. "When you came downstairs at Ian's . . ."

"It's your husband," Jack said so she didn't have to. Somehow he couldn't bring himself to hear it from her lips again. "That's who the money's for. Right?"

Greer's gaze sank to her feet.

"Your kids are fine. It was always your husband."

"Yeah."

"Why?"

That pulled her focus back to his face.

"Why didn't you tell me?" A forest of roots grew from each word, increasingly dense and insurmountable. Whatever Greer said in reply would require a chainsaw to clear through, but he couldn't stop himself. Nothing seemed to matter anymore, so why should this?

"I needed you, Jack."

That alone would have been enough to bring Jack back to life once. It should have freed a swarm of butterflies in his stomach. It should have set his mind racing. It should have turned his knees to Jell-O. But it didn't, because it couldn't, because he was too empty for there to be anything left inside to respond to that sentence.

"Why didn't you tell me?" he said again. Then, "About him."

"I just . . ."

"All those years ago, when you got married, why didn't *you* tell me?"

The question seemed to catch Greer off guard.

"What?" she said at last.

"I had to hear it from Eli."

Greer gave her head a shake and all Jack could see was the brazen teenager in a sundress and combat boots. "There was a lot going on, Jack. There was too much."

"So you decided to add an elopement to it all?"

"That was a million years ago."

"Why?"

"Jack."

He looked down from the top of the highest oak, braced to fall. "Why did you marry him?"

Greer shook her head again. A wet rim lined her hazel eyes before they flicked away from him. "Look, I just wanted to clear the air about what you heard at Ian's, but . . . I should go."

"Greer." He moved forward, but the gesture sent her stepping back, further away, further from him than she'd ever been before.

"I should go," she said again, and then she was gone.

WORK SEEMED ESPECIALLY POINTLESS THE NEXT MORNING. JACK couldn't bring himself to pursue any more leads on the Master

List after everything that had happened the night before. Instead, he found himself coasting mindlessly through the motions of his job: tapping words on his keyboard, driving to addresses listed in the files on his desk, dropping souls off to whatever passed for the great beyond.

He'd only sought out the Master List in the first place in order to reclaim his rightful place in the world and in Greer's life as Jack McCoy. But as he sat at this desk that wasn't his, hips stiff and fingers aching with arthritis, he could feel Jack McCoy fading away again. It felt like death, the kind you couldn't scheme your way back from.

Lunch hour snuck up on him, heralded by shuffling feet and squeaking desk chairs. Jack rose and stretched, eyes strained from a morning spent staring at a glowing screen. He made his way to the edge of the cubicle just as The Eagle's sharp features appeared above the wall dividing their adjoining workspaces. Jack stopped in his tracks, trying to remember how to act casual. He was midway through positioning himself into a nonchalant lean when he realized he actually wasn't doing anything questionable for once. He straightened, shaking off his evasive reflexes, and was about to carry on toward the break room when The Eagle hissed at him.

"Psst, you there."

Jack just stared back blankly, at a loss.

"Come with me," whispered The Eagle.

"Uh, no thank you," said Jack.

"I have intel."

Jack shifted in his kitten heels, trying to make sense of the whole situation. It wasn't every day, or even most days, that his nosiest colleague popped a head over the cubicle and muttered cryptic phrases at him. In fact, despite all the nosing, The Eagle rarely said much of anything at all.

"Intel?" Jack whispered back.

"Come with me," The Eagle repeated.

Jack contemplated the ham sandwich in his bag. He'd grabbed it from the grocery store on his way in that morning and it already looked as though it had seen a good handful of previous mornings before he'd purchased it. Was a clandestine meeting with his mysterious coworker the more appealing option of the two? He looked back up at The Eagle and decided that, by a very narrow margin, maybe.

The Eagle led Jack into the same accessible toilet Jack had used as a soundproof booth for his secret phone calls and Jack found himself hoping this guy wasn't looking for a little bit of workplace romance. The Eagle clicked the door lock and let his bony shoulders relax.

"You've been hiding something," he said, his words indicating that, while he may not have been expecting a fling after all, Jack might very well still be screwed.

"I have?" Jack swallowed hard. If anyone in the office might be onto the fact that Margaret wasn't really Margaret these days, it would be The Eagle. Had Jack let something slip? Something his office neighbor's unnervingly sharp hearing could have picked up? Was the whole "intel" thing a ruse to trap Jack into a confrontation? He'd spent all morning wondering if it was even worth holding on to this second life, but now, faced with the possibility of having it taken away, he knew he wasn't done yet.

"You have," said The Eagle. "But I know what's going on here."

Jack took stock of his options. The Eagle stood a solid foot and a half taller than Jack's borrowed body, opening up the possibility of a good head ram to the stomach. He could strike out, knock The Eagle to the floor, and flee. He'd have to leave the city, maybe even the state, but he could start over again, a third life in a second body. The You Agains could come with him. They didn't have anything keeping them here. Carter could find another job somewhere else, and Eli could start fresh. Greer—well, Greer would never have run away with him even if she didn't have a family, would she? After last night, he didn't feel he could say much about her for certain.

He braced, ready to strike.

"You've been asking around about the archivist," The Eagle continued.

Jack unbraced just a little.

"Uh, yeah," he said. What did that have to do with anything?

"It's an important job," said The Eagle. "One of the most important at each branch. The information keepers. So why did they replace ours in such a hurry?"

"Because Gerard died," Jack said, trying to catch up to this new conversational direction.

The Eagle tutted. "Investigate the archivist, then you'll have your answers."

"My answers to what?" Jack tried. Why couldn't the man just speak plainly?

"You'll know when you find them."

"This is weird," said Jack. "You see this is weird, right? Why can't you just tell me what you know?"

"Because I value my job," said The Eagle. "But I also value the truth. You're seeking it already, I'm just doing my part to help you find it."

Jack chewed his lip, mind still a few steps behind wherever they'd landed in this bizarre discussion.

"Okay, but—"

"The archivist," The Eagle said again. Then, with what might have been a salute, he shuffled out of the bathroom, leaving Jack with a head full of swirling questions and the bashful hope that no one in the office had seen them go in there together.

34

Jack stopped mid-step halfway up the concrete path from the driveway to Margaret's house. Someone sat hunched on the front stoop, just in front of the doorway, knees tucked to chest.

"Greer?"

Greer's sandy head rose. She looked at him, then quickly looked away. In a flourish of limbs, she rose to her feet and hurried down the lawn, brushing past Jack.

"I shouldn't have come," she muttered as she made her way to the curb.

"Why did you?" Jack called after her.

Greer stopped by the driver's side door of her little blue car. "I just . . ." Finally, she turned to face Jack. "Is it done?"

Jack cocked his head. This was somehow more baffling than being cornered in a bathroom by The Eagle. "Is what done?"

"This . . . this thing. The job. The list. I'm assuming you're done with it now, right? It's not happening anymore?"

Jack tried to find pockets in which to bury his hands, but the pencil skirt swaddling his lower half offered no such comfort.

Instead, he folded his arms over his chest. If Greer had turned up that morning and asked him that question, the answer would have been an easy yes. He was done. With everything. But after The Eagle's mysterious message and the hint that his afterlife might be taken away, he suddenly wasn't sure about anything. It was a dizzying roller coaster to ride.

"I don't know," he said honestly.

Greer just nodded. Her movements were sharp, bordering on panicked. She was desperate. It was a side to her he had rarely seen, and it ripped an ache through his heart.

"You really love him," Jack said before he could stop himself.

"What?"

"Nothing, forget it."

"My husband?"

Jack said nothing, a second ache in his heart picking up the slack from the first.

"Of course I love him."

The pain was sharper now, a hammer replaced by a knife. Now it was Jack's turn to nod as words failed him.

"Jack." Greer took a step toward him, then seemed to think better of it and locked herself where she was. "You know me better than that, don't you?"

"Than what?"

"Than to think I'd get married for anything less than love."

"Yeah, but the way you ran off with him like that, in the middle of everything . . ."

"Eloping gave me an opportunity to get away and I took it, I won't deny that. But the love was already there. It's the reason I didn't tell you. Why I couldn't tell you."

"I don't understand," said Jack. "You always told me the

things that mattered most to you unless they were bad. I thought that meant he must be a bad thing too."

"Right," said Greer. "Because that's what you wanted to think. Because that was what was easier for you to think, and that's always what you choose."

"I don't understand," Jack said again. He could feel himself loosening from Margaret's body, floating just above it, an untethered balloon on the verge of being swallowed by the sky. This conversation had played out over and over again in his mind throughout the years in a million different permutations, and as each possible outcome was eliminated, it felt as though the weight of all that potential had been the only thing keeping him earthbound.

"We're actually going to do this?" Greer sighed.

Jack had to swallow down the urge to say he didn't understand for a third time. In truth he wasn't even sure he still had enough control over Margaret's tongue to form the words.

"Jack, I'm not a complete idiot, okay? I know you. Sometimes better than you do, I think. I know how you felt when we were growing up, and maybe even now."

This sent Jack plummeting back to earth. His stomach dropped, heart quick to follow, and he had never quite felt so decidedly in a body before, so raw and vulnerable and easily bruised.

"What?"

Greer turned away, whether out of embarrassment or frustration or something else, Jack couldn't be sure. "It was obvious. Not to the guys, I don't think, and not to Jules—she hated that kind of thing. But to me. That's why I couldn't tell you when I eloped. I didn't want to hurt you. And it's why I couldn't tell you who the money was actually for. Because I thought—because I feared—that you'd change your mind about the job if I did. I need that money, Jack. Curtis needs that money. I didn't know what else to do. He's the most amazing man I've ever known. I don't want the girls to live without him. I don't want to live without him. I don't think I can."

As she spoke, Jack had hit earth and kept going. Now he felt as though he was somewhere deep below the dirt, rotting with the worms and beetles. Greer knew. All this time, she knew. Of course she knew. She knew and she didn't feel the same. She knew and she hid it from him. She knew . . . and she still let him in. She still let him be her friend. She still let him be a part of her life. She let him love her even if she didn't want it, because at the end of the day, she still wanted him, in her own way.

Jack climbed out of his own grave and back into the body standing in front of Greer, and without a second of doubt or hesitation, he finally, finally said it. "I love you, Greer."

Greer looked back at him. She had tears in her eyes. So did he, he realized.

"Jack, please." That note of desperation again.

"No, Greer, listen. I love you. I do. I think you're clever and brave and stronger than I could ever be. I love having you in my life and I never want to lose that again. And I want you happy. That's all I've ever wanted. It doesn't have to be with me, but I'd like it to be *because* of me as much as I can swing it. Because I love you, as a person, as a friend, as a you. And I'd like to continue that, if you'll let me."

"Just like that?" Greer was all narrowed eyes and skepticism. "Even knowing I won't change my mind?"

"Yeah," said Jack. "Just like that. Just like it always used to be. It was enough for me then. It's more than enough for me now."

She raked a sleeve across her face. "I am sorry, you know. For leaving like that. After Jules, I just couldn't. You were a reminder. You were the reason we'd all been there, the reason it all . . . and I just couldn't. But I should've talked to you."

A familiar pain ripped at him. One he'd so often inflicted upon himself over the years, when he actually let his mind wander unrestricted to the past. He was the reason she was dead. But this moment was not for that thought. This moment was for Greer. And so, like he'd done every time this old wound opened, he slapped a Band-Aid on top and pretended he couldn't feel it at all.

"We were kids," Jack said, as if he'd grown since. As if he'd changed. As if the Jack McCoy of those long-ago days was in any way different than the one standing there on the lawn, beyond the differences in appearance.

"We were." She sniffed. "And I do too, for what it's worth. Love you, I mean. Not, you know, like that, but you were my childhood. When I left you all, I left that behind, and some days I really miss it. I miss you."

"I've missed you too."

Another sniff. Greer looked down at the elderly woman housing her oldest friend and extended a hand. "Friends?"

Jack wrapped a liver-spotted grip around it and held tight. "Always."

They shared a smile that felt like breathing.

Jack had been in love with Greer since the first day they'd met, and that love had become one of the things that made Jack,

Jack. But as they stood there in the golden light of sunset, tendrils of fading warmth wrapping around them in a soothing embrace, that part of him inhaled a final breath and moved on to wherever it was the rest of him had been meant to go the day he died, leaving him a little less Jack than he ever had been. And a little more of something new.

35

The rest of the You Agains turned up less than an hour later in response to Jack's SOS text. He'd need all hands on deck if The Eagle's information was to be believed.

Once his team had assembled, Jack relayed the so-called intel he'd received that afternoon.

"You sure we can trust this guy?" Carter asked.

"No idea," said Jack. "But if anyone knows what's going on in that office, it's him. He's always in everybody's business. It's really made possessing someone more difficult than it should be."

"What does he think the archivist has to do with anything?" Dale asked. "I dunno, Jackie, if he's that nosy, maybe he knows what's going on and wants to get to the list before you do."

Jack hadn't considered that possibility, and it took him a double take at his right-hand man to process the fact that Dale actually had. Still, it felt unlikely. The Eagle seemed to live for his job, if for no other reason than it provided an endless supply of strange deaths and stranger souls to keep his curious nature satisfied. Jack had trouble imagining the man risking all that for monetary gain.

"It's still an avenue worth investigating," Jack decided aloud. It wasn't like they had much else to go on at the moment anyway. He swiveled to Eli. "Anything on Greta Summers yet?"

A flicker of sheepishness passed over Eli's stoic face. He shook his head. "I just keep getting that older lady every time I try. You sure her last name is 'Summers'? Could she have gotten married recently or something?"

Jack tried to picture the kind of person who'd willingly walk down the aisle with the animate ice sculpture that was the new archivist. Stranger things had certainly happened; he was nonliving proof of that. "Good thought," he said. "All right, try searching Gretas with other surnames working in the transportation field and see what you find. In the meantime, I'll head back to the archives tomorrow and see if I can sniff out anything new."

"You sure that's a good idea, Jackie?" Dale asked. "I thought you were worried she'd start catching on."

"It's the best we have to go on right now."

Dale nodded at that. "Maybe I should come with you."

"Absolutely not," said Jack, more harshly than he'd meant to. "You know what happened last time I brought you to the office."

"Yeah, sorry, Jackie. I'm just getting a little bored here, I guess."

For the second time in one conversation, Dale's words gave Jack pause, a wave of guilt splashing him in the face. All this time he'd been so consumed with making his own afterlife as full and satisfying as it could be without giving any thought to Dale's. While Jack had the luxury of a body to move around in and two jobs—one paying and one scheming—to keep him occupied, Dale only had the couch and television for company. There were still two weeks before Dale would need to move on to processing in order to avoid being trapped on earth as a ghost forever. With any luck, this archivist lead would bring the You Agains to the Master List with enough time left over for Jack to make Dale's last days on this plane special. He owed him that at least. After all, Dale had been the one to come up with this plan in the first place.

JACK BIDED HIS TIME AT HIS DESK, SIFTING THROUGH FILES AND dodging weighty looks from The Eagle, whose face kept appearing over the cubicle wall like a Whac-A-Mole. He needed a buffer before venturing into the archives in order to avoid rousing suspicion from his colleagues, which meant giving himself enough time to have theoretically attempted to wrangle a difficult case on his own before requiring some of the knowledge housed within the office basement.

After what felt like enough time had passed, Jack abandoned his desk and made his way to the lobby, giving The Eagle what he hoped was a conspiratorial head tip as he went. It felt only right to throw his cubicle neighbor a bone, and given the way The Eagle's eyes lit up at the gesture, he appeared to catch that bone in hungry jowls.

As Jack padded down the stairs to the archives, the temperature seemed to chill, growing colder with each step. It was as though the icy archivist beyond had molded her new lair to reflect her demeanor. The door closed behind Jack with a metallic bang, forcing Greta to drag her focus up from her computer screen. She found Jack at the entrance of her domain and her face fell in what could only be the deepest form of annoyance.

"Oh," said Greta. "It's you."

"Just need to see some old case files." Jack approached the desk with a nonchalant swagger.

"Again." The word was as sharp as an icicle.

"What can I say?" Jack tried. "Us old-timers are big on research. It's a dying art, if you'll pardon the pun."

"I'm not sure I have a choice," said Greta. "What files are you looking for?"

The hip pocket of Jack's paisley-printed trousers buzzed against his side, but he ignored it. "I need everything you've got on death by plunger bludgeoning." He'd read an article about one such case back when he was still alive: an on-the-job dispute between plumbers, apparently. It had stuck with Jack ever since, in much the same way the toilet plunger had stuck to the cranium of the victim.

Greta gave him the kind of fixed stare that suggested it would be a particularly colorful cuss word under less professional circumstances. Jack, for his part, continued to smile politely up at her as his pants pocket buzzed again.

"This is for a case?" Greta asked on a barely perceptible sigh.

"Naturally," said Jack.

Another buzz.

Greta gave a reluctant swivel back toward her desktop and her fingers tip-tapped across the keyboard with the stiff precision of a military march.

"We sure are lucky to have you here," Jack said as she typed. This prompted a pause in her marching fingers. Her eyes flicked down at him barely long enough to land before returning to the computer screen.

"It was unfortunate to lose Gerard, of course," Jack carried on, pretending not to notice the way the iciness in the air grew sharper. "But you run a tight ship. We need that around here. It's almost as if you've been in charge of more than the archives before. What branch did you say you transferred in from?"

"I didn't," Greta said through teeth clamped so tightly Jack worried one might pop out.

His hip buzzed again.

"No," Jack said. "I guess you didn't. Nice of them to lend you out, though. I know how important the archivist role is at S.C.Y.T.H.E., so your old branch must be in a lurch without one. In fact, I'm surprised they let you go at all, since it means they're down a crucial team member. That means someone must have really pushed for the transfer on your behalf. A director, perhaps."

Greta's fair cheeks colored. She kept her eyes glued to the screen.

"I get it," Jack continued. "This is a great branch. Newly renovated facilities, nice managers, easily accessible information. And if there's one thing archivists love, it's information. Files, documents . . . lists."

Her head lifted sharply. "I have no idea what you're going on about."

Yet another buzz. No one was ever this insistent on getting hold of him, but he couldn't waver now. Not when he was beginning to see the cracks in Greta's facade.

"You sure about that?" said Jack. "Why are you really here?"

The tendons in Greta's neck twitched. She chewed her cheek, then said, "The information you're looking for is in Row 52, section E."

A sixth buzz. He could continue to push, but there wasn't much more he could say without tipping his hand. He needed a moment to regroup. To think. To figure out his next move. He gave a tight nod and headed in the direction she pointed.

Tucked into the aisle, sandwiched comfortably between shelves full of paper, Jack rested an arm against a metal rack and recalibrated. Greta's reaction told him he was on the right track, but the question now was where was she hiding the list? That wasn't something she was likely to answer no matter how hard he pushed. He'd need to start thinking like Greta. In her shoes, where would he hide something so important? It wasn't an easy answer to dream up with so little information about the woman. Anyone with common sense would take their stolen goods off the property, and Greta struck him as someone who had a respectable amount of common sense. But without knowing where she lived or spent her time outside of work, it was impossible to speculate where she might have stashed the list.

He could try Brenda again. She may have, rightfully, labelled Greta as terrifying, but that didn't mean she didn't know more information about her. After all, she'd have had more interaction with Greta than anyone on Jack's level.

For that matter, someone like Ian Grant would have even more knowledge about the woman, since they were direct colleagues. Greer wouldn't be thrilled by the prospect of another visit, but she was the one who most wanted to find the list, so in the end she was sure to come around.

He continued to puzzle over options when his pocket buzzed again. In his whirlwind of thoughts following his interaction with Greta, he'd all but forgotten about his phone. As it vibrated against him like a purring cat, he found himself annoyed by the interruption. He'd nearly done it. Greta's behavior basically confirmed she was the one behind the theft. He needed time without distractions to plot his next steps. Now it was his turn to reclaim his rightful role as thief.

More from annoyance than interest, Jack finally released his phone from its fabric prison. The screen lit up with five missed calls and two texts from Eli.

ELI: found her

ELI: call me

Jack's thumb immediately sought Eli's number, but he stopped himself from pressing it. He couldn't make that phone call here, but he'd risk rousing suspicion if he left the archives now and then had to return. Instead he directed his thumb to the little box at the bottom of the text conversation.

JACK: u found Greta?

Less than a minute later:

ELI: better, I found Gretas

JACK: ???

ELI: your new archivist is Greta Nelson, not Greta Summers

JACK: ???

ELI: there's 2 of them, dumbass

JACK: 2 Gretas?

ELI: yup

JACK: so this Greta isn't 1 of the directors?

ELI: no

Jack stared at the screen. How could that be? He'd just figured it out. He'd just confirmed it. Greta Summers was there in the archives after weaseling her way into this branch to steal the Master List. There was no other reason for her to be so shifty. There was no other reason for her to be *there*. Except, if Eli was right, that wasn't Greta Summers at all, which meant she might very well be an actual archivist with every reason to be exactly where she was, which, in turn, would mean Jack was wrong about everything and back at square one again.

Another text appeared in a glowing little box on Jack's home screen.

ELI: but that's not the best part

Jack stared at the message as though it was written not only in a language he didn't speak, but one he'd never even seen written down before.

JACK: ???

ELI: FFS stop doing that

ELI: guess who Greta Nelson's stepdad is

Jack went to type more question marks but quickly stopped himself. His mind became a question mark instead. What the hell was Eli talking about? And more importantly, why was he talking about it? Not three minutes ago, Jack could feel the Master List in his grasp. He had been so close. Now, just like that, he was as far from completing this job as he ever had been, and Eli was texting him about his colleagues' family trees.

JACK: no idea

ELI: Omesh Bajwa

Bajwa. The name echoed like a memory through Jack's mind. He knew that name. Why did he know that name? And then it hit him.

Bajwa. Summers. Cook. F. Ian Grant.

The directors of this branch of S.C.Y.T.H.E. The names scribbled in initial form on the whiteboard in the Room of Records.

Ms. G. Summers. Mr. O. Bajwa. Mr. J.F. Mr. Ian Grant. Ms. P. Cook.

So there *were* two terrifying Gretas working at this branch of the company, and one of them was the stepdaughter of the only director Jack had yet to investigate. One of them appeared just before the list was stolen. One of them could have been placed in a position of power by a relative with even more power. Had it been Jack plotting the theft with the same resources available, it was exactly what he would have done. Jack had been so distracted, first by Greta Summers and then by Ian Grant, and then by Greta again, that he'd yet to even begin tracking down Mr. O. Bajwa, and yet an extension of him had been right under Jack's nose all along, with unfettered access to classified information about the inner workings of the organization. So it *was* Greta, but not as a director who'd taken a secondary job at this branch for closer access to the Master List. Instead, she was working as an undercover agent for a director Jack had all but forgotten about, here to do his bidding by proxy.

Jack tapped his thumbs across his phone a final time.

JACK: well shit

Then he abandoned the aisles and doubled back to confront his rival thief.

36

"Find what you were looking for?" Greta asked robotically as Jack approached her desk again.

"I think I did," he said, trying not to let too much glee seep into his tone.

She kept herself fully immersed in whatever it was she was reading on her computer screen. "Good. Is there something else you need?"

"The truth," Jack said. He hadn't meant to bring quite so much drama into the equation, but it felt right for the moment.

Greta's breath shallowed, but still she carried on staring at her computer.

"I know why you're really here," Jack continued.

Whatever weak color Greta had in her alabaster complexion all but abandoned her in that moment, giving her the appearance of a translucent anglerfish trying to maintain its composure despite the underbite.

"I don't know what you think you know, but—"

"It's Greta Bajwa, isn't it?" This time a little bit of glee did sneak in.

Greta finally abandoned her pretense of working, her focus landing sharp on Jack. "Will you keep your voice down?" she hissed.

"I could," Jack mused. "Or I could take this directly to the higher-ups."

"There's no need for that."

"I disagree," Jack boomed, enjoying himself now.

"Why are you doing this?"

"Because," said Jack, "you have something I want."

Greta gave a frantic look around her, at the computer, the shelves, the desk. "My job?"

Jack blinked at that. "What? No. The list. But if you tell me where it is, I won't tell anyone you took it. You and your stepdad won't face any issues from me."

Now it was Greta's turn to blink. "List? What list? What are you talking about?"

"Don't play dumb with me, Greta. I know you have it." It took only a prolonged look at her expression, though, to tell Jack she wasn't necessarily playing at all. "You do have it, right?"

"I don't have anything," Greta said, and her tone shifted into something Jack didn't recognize. Gone was the human exclamation mark with all its intensity; melted was the ice surrounding her. "Except this." She gestured at the archives around them.

"Wait, what?"

"That's what this is all about, isn't it?" Greta said weakly. "My job here. You know."

"Yeah," Jack lied, because he once again wasn't sure he knew anything at all. "Your job here. That's what this is about."

Greta's sharp shoulders sagged. "Please, please keep this between us."

"I'll consider it," said Jack. "But, uh, in your own words, can you tell me what 'this' is? Just so I'm sure we're on the same page."

Greta abandoned her post, crossing briskly to the door and clicking the lock before returning to the safety of her desk. Even with the door locked and only the two of them in the basement chamber, she still threw a look over her shoulder, as if someone might be lurking in the shelves behind her.

"How did you find out?" She shook her head. "It doesn't matter. It's all so humiliating."

"What is?"

"Being fired. Twice. Something about my temperament. Utter nonsense, of course."

"Of course," said Jack.

"I couldn't find another job for the life of me. No other libraries would hire me. My reputation was ruined."

"So you needed the money," said Jack. "And that's why you stole the list."

Greta just gave him a blank stare.

"Or maybe not. Go on."

"Well, when the last archivist died, Omesh thought I'd be a good fit. I could finally get back on my feet. But, of course, I was never supposed to know this place existed. Plus archivists spend years training to handle all the sensitive material that comes their way. My time studying library science doesn't mean much around here. Some nonsense about how traditional college learning is more focused on the Dewey decimal system than the rules of life and death. People die in libraries sometimes, Ms. Chen! It's really not that different."

Jack took a full breath cycle to catch up to what Greta was

saying. All her secrecy, all her tenseness and recent attempts at subterfuge, it wasn't because she was here to steal a priceless artifact. It was because she was a nepo baby.

"So what you're saying is you're worried that if anyone finds out that you're not qualified and the only reason you're here is because you're related to one of the bosses, you'll lose your job?"

"Of course," Greta said, as if that should be obvious. "I cannot be fired for a third time, Ms. Chen. I simply cannot. Plus this job has dental."

Jack made a mental note of that. One of Margaret's remaining teeth had been acting up recently.

"Right," he said, still recovering from the whiplash of his back-and-forth suspicions that afternoon. "Okay."

"Will you tell?" The sudden fragility of such a prickly figure unnerved him, but he couldn't help empathizing with her plight. Everyone had a secret that could destroy them. He kept his own close to the chest that wasn't his.

"Nah," he said.

"Wait, really?"

"I mean you're clearly a solid archivist," said Jack. "And you're not hurting anybody by being here. No reason to get you fired for a little bit of secret nepotism."

"Oh," said Greta. "Thank you."

"It's cool," said Jack. Then, re-Margaret-ing, he added, "I mean, it's my pleasure, dear. No one else could find the section on plunger-related deaths as quickly as you."

If Jack squinted hard, it would almost have looked as though this drew a tiny smile from the woman in front of him.

"Well, if there's anything else you require assistance in researching, I would be happy to help."

Jack wasn't fully convinced that "happy" was the word she actually wanted to use, but it sounded nicer than "duty bound" or "guilted into," so he let it slide.

"Actually," he said, in a last-ditch effort to take something productive away from this whole endeavor, "when Gerard was still alive, he mentioned in passing that some people had access to a special skeleton key that could open up a glass dome hidden somewhere in the building."

Jack studied Greta's face as he spoke his lie; her expression soured slightly.

"He really wasn't supposed to talk about that," she said.

Jack powered on. "Well, what can I say? Old Gerry and I had a special connection. Anyway, it got me thinking. Who actually has access to that key?"

Jack watched a debate play out across Greta's stern features. He wasn't supposed to know that the key, or the dome it unlocked, even existed, and talking about it likely went against the protocols of Greta's job. But at the same time, Jack had just spared her that very job, and she clearly felt indebted for that.

Finally she sighed. "There are six copies of the skeleton key. Only branch directors and archivists have a copy. Does that satisfy your curiosity?"

Jack had hoped there'd be new names on the list of people who knew the whereabouts of the key, but he hadn't expected Greta's to be one of them. "You've never been tempted to use it?"

"Ms. Chen," Greta said, "I'm holding on to this job by the skin of my teeth. It best behooves me to keep my head down. Besides, archivists are only given a copy of the key in case a director misplaces theirs, not so that we can go rooting around where we don't belong. I'm certainly not about to risk anything for the sake of satisfying my own curiosity. In truth, I don't even know where the dome is located or what might be inside it, and I prefer to keep it that way."

As much as Jack wanted Greta to be the Master List thief, as much as she absolutely had been the thief only a short while ago, at least in his mind, he had to loosen his grip on that theory. He had to accept the fact that he was, once again, outfoxed by someone he'd yet to discover. And with the next Bleak Market auction around the corner and Dale's days numbered, he was running out of time to expose that someone before the list was permanently beyond his grasp.

37

The You Agains were a wreath around Margaret's kitchen island once again, wedged shoulder to shoulder and, in a few cases, butt cheek to butt cheek on the handful of bar stools around the marble surface.

"So it's not this Greta person, then?" Greer's voice was tight, disappointment wafting off her like cheap perfume.

"Doesn't seem like it," Jack said on a headshake. "Her only crimes seem to be a powerful stepdad and a fireable personality."

"What about this Bajwa guy, then?" said Carter. "He's the only one we haven't looked into, and we know he's not opposed to breaking rules when it serves him."

Jack had already thought of that, which was why he'd called Eli on the way home from work with a new target to look into. He turned the floor over to Eli with a tip of the head.

"It couldn't be him," Eli said. He flipped his laptop to face the others. "Bajwa was in Boston running the marathon that week. There are location tagged pictures all over his social media and an article about the growing popularity of marathoning among the over-fifty crowd that he's quoted in. Unless you think his stepdaughter would have done the actual thieving for him?"

Jack thought back to his conversation with Greta. He'd hoped that might have been the case, and even questioned her to test if it was, but in light of all he'd learned, he just didn't think it could be her.

"I doubt it."

"So that leaves us with nothing," said Greer. "No leads, no list, no money. Nothing."

"We'll figure this out," Jack said, as much to convince himself as to comfort Greer. The truth was, they'd eliminated all their suspects and were somehow even more in the dark than they'd been when they first found out the list had been stolen.

"Will we?" Greer seemed to shrink into herself, her desperation whittling her down to a soft voice and a diminished presence. "Jack, I'm not so sure. If that list ends up at the market, we'll have no chance of getting the money from it. We only have like a week; what's to say it's not already there now?"

"There's always next month's list," Jack said. "We can try again."

"There's no reason the other thief won't get there before us again. And besides, I'm not sure Curtis has that long." Her eyes glistened even as she tried to blink the sheen away. With a headshake, she slid from the stool. "Sorry, I just need a minute."

Greer hurried upstairs before Jack or anyone else could stop her.

"Jeez," Dale said on a whistle. "I don't think I've ever seen her like this."

Eli closed his laptop, teeth working at his bottom lip so hard he drew blood. "We have to do something."

There were two important things about Eli Jack knew for certain. The first was that nothing good ever came from him saying that sentence. The second was that he could never bear to see Greer upset. The combination of the two, Jack decided, could only be cataclysmic. The fact was, at this moment, there was nothing they really could do. The list was gone, and whoever took it remained a mystery Jack wasn't so sure he had the capacity to solve. He was used to being the one committing the crimes, after all, not preventing them. Short of finding another afterlife retail establishment and somehow passing off their knockoff list as the real deal, they were shit out of luck.

Jack put a hand on Eli's shoulder, gently pushing him back onto his seat. The man was primed and ready to do something reckless, which meant it was up to Jack to do something sensible instead.

"I'll talk to her," he said, and he gave Carter the kind of hard eye contact he'd used many times to alert one of his cooler-headed friends that they were in charge of babysitting Eli's emotions for the time being. Carter gave a nod and Jack slipped upstairs.

His bedroom door was shut despite him leaving it open that morning, which meant either the house was haunted by a more agile entity than Dale or that Greer was inside. Jack gave a soft rap on the door, which was met with a series of sniffs and a weak "Come in."

Jack pried the door back and found Greer slumped on the side of the bed, face red and wet and blotchy. In all their years of friendship, he'd only seen her cry on two occasions, and one of them was her fake tears on Mrs. Sullivan's doorstep the first day they'd met. The other, he was crying too, so it barely felt like it counted. He pushed the thought away and ambled over to her and lowered himself to the bedspread.

"It doesn't have to be this, you know," he said. "Selling the list, I mean. There are lots of ways to make a fast buck. Home robbery, bank robbery—mostly robberies, when you think about it. No one would see an octogenarian bank robber coming."

Greer sniffed again at that, though Jack couldn't tell if it was a small chuckle or just snot.

"No," said Greer. "I can't risk anyone getting caught and going to jail or . . . or worse. The list made sense. Your job, that world, it operates under different laws. It felt safer somehow. But knocking over a bank or breaking into someone's house . . . no. Not after last time."

Of course she'd say no. None of the You Agains would ever travel back down that road. He should have known as much. But in truth, he didn't know, or at least he didn't remember. It was what he'd become most adept at over the years: forgetting some things and remembering others. Sometimes the best way to survive was to swallow down the painful things so they burned a hole through your stomach. You never had to look at them there. It was what kept him alive, even past his death. So to Jack, even after everything, the idea of robbing a home or business sounded like a good time. And on many occasions it had been. The You Agains were no strangers to that particular category of crime. But things were different now, even if Jack struggled to let them be.

That meant they had to find the list; there was no other choice now. And so he decided they would. The question that hung over him like an angry rain cloud was how, but he didn't have to answer that in this moment. Right now the only thing that truly mattered was that Greer was crying on his rose-patterned bedspread. He let a hand fall tentatively onto her back, still wary about giving the wrong impression after their discussion in the front yard.

"There, there," he tried. Jack had always been better at plotting and scheming than handling emotions, regardless of who they were coming from.

"You're really bad at this," Greer said through sniffles, as if reading his thoughts.

"How can I be better?" Jack asked, the earnestness nauseating to his own ears. "How can I help you stop crying?"

"I think I just need to cry," said Greer. "Sometimes that's important. With grief, that's really all you can do at times."

"Really?" Jack tried to think back to his own grief, but it was another one of those things he never let himself properly feel, much less remember. After all was said and done back then, he was right back to his old ways again in less than half a year. Greer was off starting her new married life, and it wasn't long before the other You Agains graduated high school and started down the paths they'd travel for years to come: Dale picked up odd jobs in town and met Savannah, Carter went off to college for graphic design and illustration, and Eli continued his merry-go-round with the law. But as high school faded from being the core distraction of his life into a memory, Jack simply carried on as he always had. He'd shed some tears in that hard wooden pew next to the others, but otherwise his grief hadn't seemed to require much taking care of. He'd felt bad about that from time to time, as though he should have suffered more, as though it should have taken him longer to start living again in the face of death, but he couldn't help it. At the end of the day, Jack McCoy would always be Jack McCoy. It was the only thing he knew how to be. It was the only thing that made sense to him. And when everything he thought he knew about the world was upended one summer night, it was the one thing he'd needed most. The rest was for another time. Another place. Another life.

"You don't have to stay," said Greer, dragging Jack back into the present. "If it makes you uncomfortable."

"I can handle it."

Greer leaned her head on his shoulder, tears still dancing freely down her cheeks. "Is this okay?" she asked.

As the warmth of the tears seeped into the satin fabric of his tasteful cream blouse, he realized that, for the first time in their friendship, Greer was letting him see her shadows. Something between them had shifted since they'd spoken the previous day, something important enough for her to trust him with her tears when she never had before. It was like by clearing the air, they had also cleared enough space to pack in all the parts of life that didn't quite fit between them before, as if defining their friendship as just that and removing the hopes or fears about anything more meant they could properly, truly, deeply be friends.

"Yeah," said Jack. "This is okay."

38

Jack and Greer reemerged a short while later, having spent the better part of half an hour in a comfortable silence as Greer let her tears run their course. When they returned to the kitchen, one of the stools around the island stood empty.

"Where's Eli?" Greer asked before Jack had the chance.

Carter gave an apologetic shrug. "I tried to keep him here, but he wouldn't stay."

"Dude," said Jack. "Come on, you were in charge."

"I know," said Carter. "But you know how Eli can be. Besides, you said yourself we have no leads right now. What trouble can he possibly get into over this?"

"Have you met Eli?" Greer cried. "Fuck. I'm calling him."

"Good idea," said Jack. Then to Dale and Carter, "Did he give any indication about where he might've gone?"

"Sorry, Jackie," Dale said. "He just said he needed to go and then dipped."

"I don't think so," Carter said. "I really did try to talk him down, man, I promise."

"He did," Dale testified. "Got in Eli's face and everything."

"I reminded him about how much he wants to stay out of jail," said Carter. "Told him if he does anything stupid, he'll end up right back there, but I don't know how much he was listening. He was like a man possessed. But like, not in the way you are. In a feral way."

"Shit," Greer said, phone to her ear. "I should've known to watch my tongue around him. He didn't need to hear me so upset."

"No answer?" Jack asked with a tip of the chin at her phone.

Greer shook her head. "This is my third time trying. It keeps going straight to voicemail."

Jack felt a rush of adrenaline surge through him. If Eli's history with decision-making was anything to go by, this would not have a happy ending.

"Okay," he said, slipping reflexively back into his usual role. "Greer, take Carter. Go check his house, his usual haunts, anywhere you think he might go under the circumstances. I'll keep calling him, and Dale and I will stay here in case he comes back."

The words came easily to him, the plan fully formed before he'd even been aware of it. And just as Jack McCoy returned to the helm, the others moved to carry out their instructions without a second thought.

"You always know what to do, Jackie," said Dale as he made his way back to the couch.

Jack walked Greer and Carter to the door, offering a quick hug to Greer as she stepped onto the front stoop. "We'll find him," he said into her hair.

"I just hope it's not at the police station this time." Greer squeezed him back and followed Carter over to her car. Jack waited until they'd pulled away before slouching to the living room. He threw himself down on the sofa beside Dale, the leather cool on his skin. As much as he feared for the outcome of whatever mayhem Eli was currently causing, he couldn't help but worry for Greer. She was already so consumed by caring for her ailing husband; the last thing she needed was another loved one in jeopardy.

He took a breath to examine his heart. As much as it broke for Greer in that moment, and as heavy as it was with love for her, it felt different somehow. A new sort of love. And as he allowed that love to settle across him, it was met with a breath of relief, as though he could finally put down the torch he'd carried all these years and stretch. What they had now was something they could carry together, and at this new stage of afterlife, he decided he preferred that.

Time crawled slowly through the late spring air that evening. It barely seemed to acknowledge the natural speed of its passing, determined instead to drag out every second, every minute, like an analog clock dipped in molasses. Jack kept trying Eli's phone but was only ever met with his tinny voice on the other end telling him to leave a message after the beep.

Greer called around midnight. They'd searched everywhere she could think of and come up empty. She needed to get home. Curtis had an appointment early the next morning. Jack knew she wouldn't sleep that night.

Between attempted phone calls, Jack scrolled through his phone and bounced around news channels on the TV in case Eli's fate ended up covered there, the prospect grim but too plausible not to follow up.

By two a.m., Jack's stolen age crept over him in a wave of exhaustion. His new circadian rhythm had him in bed before ten p.m. most nights and up at roughly the crack of dawn. He shuffled to the kitchen and retrieved a tray of ice cubes from the freezer, dropping one down his shirt every time he felt himself drifting.

For his part, Dale tried to keep Jack occupied with conversation that was at once dry and inane, which only made the drowsiness worse despite the thoughtful gesture. He couldn't be sure quite when it happened, but at some point Jack must have drifted off in spite of himself, leaving him lost to slumber until a sharp knock on the door pulled him back into consciousness. Jack ran a hand over his wrinkled face, disoriented. He took in his surroundings: not Margaret's bedroom but the living room below, TV on, phone in his hand, Dale on the arm of the sofa. He was down here for a reason, he remembered. Eli.

Another bang at the door. His glowing phone screen told him it was after four in the morning. Eli had been picking the lock to Margaret's house for weeks now; he had no reason to knock. Jack's stomach plummeted. Was this a police officer at his door? Someone with news about Eli? News too heavy to send through a text?

Jack peeled himself from the couch and hurried his aching body into the foyer, flipping the lock and opening the door with as much force as his old muscles carried. There, on the doorstep. Not a cop. Not a grief-stricken Greer. Not a Carter with head bowed and hands in his pockets. Eli.

The hollows under his eyes were purple, the eyes themselves wide, his face drawn and sunken in, in a way it hadn't been only hours ago. Jack had seen him like this once before, and suddenly he knew exactly where Eli had been, what reckless thing he'd been up to. And it was so much worse than anything Jack could have dreamed up.

39

Wrong

July 2009

There were still three packed cardboard boxes stacked in the corner of Jack's room. One had the word "kitchen" scribbled across it in black Sharpie; the other two were unmarked. He'd get to them eventually, he told himself. Even if unpacking them would mean there was really no turning back. A frenetic bass rattled the wall he shared with one of his three new roommates, vibrating in his skull as he lay in bed. This wasn't exactly how he'd pictured his last months as a teenager, but it would have to do.

Someone knocked on his door. "Bro, somebody's here to see you," came the voice of one of the other guys sharing the apartment. Mike, maybe? Or Tom? Or the one with the dirty sock collection? They all kind of blurred together in a swirl of graphic T-shirts and questionable hygiene.

Jack hauled himself out of bed and opened the door to see

the sock guy retreating down the hall toward his own room. On a sigh, Jack made his way to the apartment door. Sock guy had left it open, and in its arch stood Eli. Or at least Jack was pretty sure it was Eli. The young man in front of him was devoid of color, crescent moons of indigo beneath bloodshot eyes, cheeks sunken into hollows.

"Jesus Christ," Jack said on a gasp. Then he noticed the trickle of blood dripping in steady droplets onto Eli's sneaker. Jack followed the flow with his eyes, finding a stream pooling on Eli's left index finger from an angry gash on his palm. "What the hell did you do?"

Eli continued to stare at Jack with an empty gaze, as though he wasn't fully in his body. Jack wrapped gentle fingers around Eli's scrawny wrist and guided him carefully into a living room furnished by a forest green futon in front of a television propped on empty milk crates. Jack eased Eli onto the futon and disappeared into the bathroom, returning a moment later with a full roll of toilet paper. He grabbed Eli's bloody hand and pressed a wad of toilet paper against it, adding more and more layers until the makeshift bandage was too thick for the blood to seep through. He'd dealt with You Again injuries before: scraped knees from jumping out of low windows, black eyes from scrapping, even a broken bone or two. But this injury was different. The cut was too clean, too deliberate. This had been a choice.

"Eli, what happened?" Jack slid onto the futon beside his friend, but Eli's gaze was still so far away Jack felt as though he'd need a plane ticket to find him.

He gave Eli a nudge with his shoulder. Nothing.

"Dude," he tried, a wave of panic rising from the acid in his stomach. He should call somebody. He should call Greer. But

Greer had barely spoken to him since she got married. Did he still have their mom's number? He could check his phone, but it was nearly midnight and the odds of getting ahold of her seemed slim. No, Jack had to bring Eli back to earth himself.

He gave Eli's thigh a hard pinch, but while it elicited a wince, Eli's gaze remained locked on the middle distance. This called for desperate measures. Jack left Eli on the futon and knocked on sock guy's bedroom door. It took two tries to get an answer and four to get his cooperation, but eventually Jack returned to the living room with his mission accomplished. He plopped back onto the futon, the movement bouncing Eli but still failing to rouse him. That was fine. Jack had a bigger weapon now. He unzipped the lid of a hefty reusable bag stuffed with old gym socks and waved it under Eli's nose like smelling salts. Eli's eyes began to water, and after only a few wafts, he sputtered and pushed the bag away.

"Fuck," he wheezed.

Jack lowered the bag, exhaling a breath of relief. Whatever happened, whatever awful, horrible thing Eli had done to put himself in that catatonic state, he was back now, and that was all that mattered. At least until the relief eased, and then Jack needed answers.

"Okay, what the hell?" he demanded as Eli's cheeks regained a small wash of color.

Eli just shook his head.

"Dude, come on. You can't show up on my doorstep in the middle of the night acting like a zombie and bleeding all over my futon and not tell me why."

"You wouldn't believe me if I tried."

There was very little Eli could get up to that he wouldn't

believe, but saying as much would only hurt Eli's feelings, and Jack wasn't about to be the reason he went catatonic again.

"When have I ever not believed you before?" he said instead.

Eli shifted on the futon and scratched the brown patch on his chin that feebly passed for facial hair. "Remember that guy I used to buy weed from in high school?"

"The guy with the skunk hair and all the chains?"

Eli wiped his nose with the heel of his right hand, the left still doing its best to bleed through the toilet paper wad. "He always talked about weird shit. Like, he could do stuff. I don't know. Like he knew how to see the dead and stuff. Which was bullshit, obviously. I knew it was bullshit. How could it not be?"

"Right," said Jack. His mom had taken him to church until he was about eight or nine, when they both gave up; her because there just wasn't enough time in her schedule as a working single mother for the commitment of faith, and him because, well, he just didn't really believe in what he was hearing. When he first heard some of the other kids at school talking about how dying just meant you became worm food, it made sense to him. As far as Jack was concerned, the idea of an afterlife was utterly absurd.

"Except that it wasn't."

Jack blinked at Eli. Had the blood loss made him a little loopy, maybe? Or was he just high? Both seemed equally plausible at this point.

"What are you talking about?"

"I tracked him down. I needed to . . . I wanted . . . I just needed some answers, I guess. After Jules. I didn't really think anything would happen, you know? But I wanted to try, just in case. I wanted to see, because . . . Whatever, it doesn't matter. The point is, I was wrong."

"Wrong how?"

Eli pulled his wounded hand onto his lap, flexing the fingers, staring at the bloodied toilet paper.

"He was telling the truth, Jack. He showed me. We had to do some fucked-up shit to make it happen—I mean, I don't think anyone's supposed to be able to see that shit, you know? But it worked. I saw . . . I saw death, I guess."

Eli was right, Jack did struggle to believe him in the end. Eli had spent the past few years getting high off anything with the slightest possibility of doing the job, which made his grasp on reality more than a little bit sketchy at times. And yet, there was something in his voice that weakened Jack's skepticism ever so slightly. A note of unwavering conviction mingled with terror. And Jack found himself asking in spite of himself, "Did you see . . . ?"

"No," said Eli. "She wasn't there."

Jack quickly pushed down the parade of emotions marching up his throat. This was all too much to believe. This was all too much.

"But Jack," Eli continued, "it wasn't . . . I don't know how to explain it. Like, obviously no one living is supposed to see the other side. I get that. But there was something about it, something *off*, something *wrong*. He said it didn't used to be this way. It's getting worse. Death, I mean. It used to be different, but now it's all . . . screwed up."

"Dude," Jack said. "I'm sorry. You're freaked. Whatever happened, it sounds fucked. You need to stay away from that guy, all right? Promise me, man. Whatever he's been giving you, it might be laced with something, or I don't know, it's not good."

"You don't believe me."

"We should get you to the emergency room. You'll probably need stitches."

"McCoy."

"It's just hard to wrap my head around, okay? Like, if it was real, she would've been there."

Eli rose on unsteady legs, swaying slightly as he reached his full height. "Whatever. I'm going home."

"Eli, no. Look, I'm sorry. I'm trying to believe you, I promise. But dude, you've gotta get that hand checked out."

"Later, man."

Eli wobbled cautiously to the living room doorway and slipped out of view. Jack couldn't bring himself to follow; he was too confused, too shocked, too overwhelmed by the prospect of all Eli had said. But of course it wasn't true. It couldn't be. Jack was certain of it.

JACK GUIDED ELI TO THE LIVING ROOM SOFA BY THE WRIST, EASING him onto a cushion and dropping down beside him.

"Yo, what the hell's wrong with him?" Dale asked from the other end of the couch, face screwed up in alarm.

"You went to see Cyrus," Jack said to Eli. There was no need to ask. As Jack spoke, he ran his eyes over Eli's hands, searching for blood, but all that decorated his palm was the raised scar from years ago.

Eli slowly turned his head to face Jack. Good, he was alert enough to hear Jack's words. Whatever had pulled his features into this twisted mask wasn't enough to steal his senses from him at least, and Jack took some small bit of solace from that.

"Yeah," Eli confirmed. His voice was raw and gravelly, as if his throat had never known water.

"Dude. Eli. Why?"

"We're running out of time. Greer's running out of time. We can't keep pissing around playing games. I thought maybe Cyrus might know more than we do."

He was shaking, limbs vibrating like a chihuahua in the cold.

"And did he?"

"Yeah," Eli said again.

As much as Jack wanted to know more, there was a more pressing question on his lips. "What did he ask for in return?"

"Not important," said Eli.

Jack gave him a hard look, but Eli didn't waver. Instead, he dropped his head into his hands. "Someone contacted him about the list. Saying they had it and wanted to sell."

"Who?" Jack almost leapt to his feet.

"He didn't say. But the handoff is happening tomorrow night. Midnight. Cyrus wants the list before the auction next week so he has enough time to authenticate it. It took some work, but I got the coordinates. He doesn't care who he buys the list off of as long as he gets it, so I guess he doesn't mind if we show up and confront the guy. Hell, if things get real hairy, it would mean Cyrus wouldn't have to pay anyone at all."

"Eli, what did you have to do for this?"

Eli shook his head. "Greer's getting her money."

This was a losing battle, Jack was sure of that. Eli was a reckless man, and the depth to which he cared about others only made that recklessness worse. Jack had always known Eli loved his sister fiercely and would move heaven and earth for her, and tonight he might have literally done just that. There would be no arguing the point or trying to right whatever wrongs he'd endured. It was all a worthwhile means to an end for Eli, and if his information was accurate, that end was only twenty-four hours away.

"Okay," said Jack. And then, in a sentence that had left his lips more times than he could count: "Give me the details and I'll come up with a plan."

40

As far as clandestine meeting locations went, Jack had made use of everything from playgrounds to cemeteries to the occasional back alley when he was feeling less creative. What he had never thought to use, for what he figured were pretty obvious reasons, was the sewer. But the original sewer system that ran in archways of abandoned brick beneath the town corresponded with the coordinates from Cyrus that Eli had scribbled on the back of his hand the night before. In fact, until Eli relayed the information, Jack hadn't even been aware that there was an old, disused sewer system down there. He'd always kind of figured there was just the one with all the poop.

Sure enough, when Carter matched up old Victorian city blueprints to the current layout of the town, he found that while the coordinates didn't lead to anything notable aboveground, they happened to land directly over a passage of the old sewers. It was only the first job Jack had assigned Carter that day. Everyone had their roles. Except, of course, for Dale, who seemed perfectly content to stay home and watch the game while the others were busy crawling around underground.

When plotting something, Jack typically liked to identify as many variables as possible in advance, but because Cyrus had withheld any information about the seller of the list, Jack had to plan something a bit more general than he'd have preferred. He called off work that day, ostensibly so he'd have more time to ready himself and the You Agains for what was to come, but also in large part so he could spend the afternoon napping in preparation for a late night.

Eli had stayed over the night before, too shaken to go home alone after his encounter with Cyrus even if he wouldn't admit as much. Instead he said he was too tired to drive, and Jack pretended he believed him. The three of them, Jack, Dale, and Eli, didn't leave the couch until just before the first shreds of light streaked the sky beyond the living room window. Their conversation rattled the still night air, ranging in topic from mindless small talk to the memories that stitched them together like the yarn of a sweater. Despite the bleakness of the circumstances, Jack couldn't help but be warmed by the familiarity of the scene. How many nights had he spent just like this? Too many to count. The way Eli's knee bounced restlessly as he listened, jokes falling flat and eliciting a bigger laugh than if they'd actually landed, the dizziness of exhaustion giving way to disjointed sentences and bubbling giggles. Every hard time that befell a You Again was solved this way. And despite the years between those nights and this one, despite the evolution from teenaged heartbreak to mortal fear, Jack couldn't help but believe this would be enough to solve everything again.

Greer arrived at Margaret's around three, and Carter joined them after his workday was done. The air around the kitchen island was abuzz with anticipation and anxiety, as though a million hornets hid in the walls, keeping everyone just a little on edge. Midnight still dangled just out of reach above them. Dinnertime rolled around and Jack ordered pizza for the group, laying boxes out across the island. He felt like a medieval king providing a banquet for his knights before they all rode into battle. Like the night before, this was another ritual for Jack and the You Agains, the pizza order delivered from the same place between the 7-Eleven and the old barber shop. But unlike last night, the conversations felt too slippery for Jack to grasp, and the memories he held out to the others went unnoticed. Instead everyone seemed only too eager to focus on aspects of their lives Jack hadn't been part of.

"Did I tell you we're designing the branding for a new brewery?" Carter said through a slice. "They're going for a family-friendly vibe, apparently. I've got a gift card. Greer, you should take the kids."

"How the hell do they make a brewery family friendly?" Eli jumped in. "Put the beer in a sippy cup?"

"They have a children's area with a ball pit," said Carter.

"Great, so the kids can play while mom and dad get hammered." Greer shook her head. "We're more of a museum family, but thanks anyway, Carter."

"Since when?" Jack said.

"Since my oldest went through her dinosaur phase," said Greer.

"God, I forgot about that," Eli said on a laugh. "She used to ask if I found any bones every time I was out digging the foundations for a new build site."

"Well, you did, that one time."

"Oh yeah," said Carter. "They had to get forensics out there for that, didn't they?"

"Held up construction for weeks," said Eli. "Turned out to be the family dog of whoever lived in that old farmhouse before we tore it down for the condos."

"Ugh, speaking of, Mia keeps begging for a dog. I told her to convince Uncle Eli to get one so she could visit."

"Not a chance," said Eli. "There's barely enough room in my apartment for me."

"I've actually been thinking about getting one," said Carter. "Now that I own my own place and don't have to worry about pissing off landlords."

"Great, then I'll send her your way," Greer said.

Jack looked between them, watching this exchange like a spectator at a sporting event. He wasn't even on the sidelines, he realized. That would imply he had the skill set to jump into the game. As the others spoke about their new lives, he knew he was on the outside looking in, and he couldn't quite figure out how to join them. Their worlds had kept turning, their lives had kept evolving, and they had just let it happen. It was a strange and uncomfortable thing to be made so acutely aware of, that despite Jack being the one in a new body, they'd all changed in more significant ways while he'd remained in the past. It was an easier place to be. A time before responsibilities. Before expectations. Before Jules . . .

It was okay, he told himself. He just had to bide his time. In a few short hours they'd be on the road to complete the most important job of their lives, and that would bring them all right back to where they used to be. How could it not? That night's Master List heist would be everything the You Agains had ever been and then some. All that had happened in the intervening years paled in comparison, and soon they'd see that. He just had to wait.

JACK FLICKED TO THE GAME FOR DALE AND HE AND THE REST OF THE You Agains piled into Margaret's Mercedes. It was forty minutes until midnight, and they needed enough time to set up before the Master List thief arrived at the meeting spot. A plan was only as good as its execution, after all.

Eli mic'd Greer up from the back seat with equipment he'd rented for the occasion and handed out earpieces and little round disks.

"Your phones might not get a signal down there," he explained, indicating the disks. "These will help me track your locations so I can guide you through the tunnels. Keep them in your pockets, and make sure this button is turned on." He flicked a little switch on the underside, summoning a glowing green light. "Greer, mic test?"

Greer counted to five and her voice came clear through the earpieces.

"Good," said Eli. "The mic seems to be working well, so we should be able to stay in touch."

"Great," said Jack. "Carter?"

From his back jeans pocket, Carter pulled the sewer map and flattened it on the car's center console. He traced a finger along the labyrinthine paths.

"The only accessible entrance left is here." He pointed at a spot that corresponded to a location a few blocks away. "The handoff will be here in this area, so Greer and I will go down this tunnel and turn down that way. Jack, you're going off into this little alcove here at the fork."

Jack nodded. "This should be pretty straightforward," he said. "Whoever the thief is, they have no idea we're going to be there. Greer, you'll turn on the waterworks, and with any luck they'll turn over the list without issue, but if they do give you any trouble, you've got Carter there for muscle. I'm hoping to stay in the shadows. Whoever the thief is, they're someone I work with, and seeing me there might scare them off before you get the chance to convince them to give up the list. But if you need me, Greer, just say so. I'll hear you through the earpiece. You good?"

Greer gave a stiff thumbs-up. She always got nervous before a job. Out of all the You Agains, she had the worst prejob stage fright, but it never impeded her performance in the end.

Jack stepped out of the driver's seat and Eli took his place, slipping his laptop out of its case and setting it up on his lap. Three little dots in different colors blinked from a map on the screen: one green, one blue, one yellow. They were clustered together, one a fraction removed from the others, corresponding to where Jack stood by the car.

"That's you guys," Eli said, pointing to the dots. "I'll have an eye on your movements here. I can also communicate through the mic on the computer. Can you all hear me okay?" He pressed a button on his keyboard, his voice filtering steadily through Jack's earpiece.

"Got you," said Jack. "All right, let's get in position before the seller gets here."

The trio strode through the neighborhood toward a rolling field crisscrossed with power lines.

"You're gonna veer to your left," Eli said in their ears.

They adjusted course accordingly, coming to a stop at the base of a grassy hill. Carved into the hill was a wall of white stone, a gaping circle in the middle baring metal teeth. In the center of the rusted bars stood a door, the handle chained with a padlock.

"Door reached," Greer said into the mic under her T-shirt.

"Copy," Eli replied in their ears.

Jack crouched by the padlock, examining the keyhole. A tiny smile tickled his lips when he realized it was built for a skeleton key. He dug through the purse on his shoulder for his lock picking kit and pulled out the same tool he'd used in the Room of Records. He slipped the tool into the lock and gave a few twists and jiggles before hearing the satisfying click of success, the lock and chains falling away.

"Door breached," Greer reported to Eli.

"Copy," came Eli's voice again.

Jack hauled the door open, its rusted hinges resisting with a disgruntled creak. He hopped over the raised stones surrounding the metal bars and stepped inside. The cavernous sewer beyond exhaled a breath of cool, musty air, the ghost of human refuse past still haunting the space with a sour pungency. The others filed in behind him and Jack turned on his phone flashlight, leading the way down the decrepit, brick-lined tunnel. Dust motes danced in the phone's yellow beam, celebrating their first encounter with light in what must have been decades. The air continued to chill with each step, the stillness around them so absolute that every footfall echoed back to them like a gunshot.

Eventually they reached the fork Carter had circled on his blueprints, the tunnel splitting into three like the heads of a man-made hydra.

"All right." Eli's voice returned to their ears. "Jack, you're going right. Greer and Carter, keep going straight."

For a moment, they all lingered at that break in the path.

"Okay," Jack said, adrenaline rushing through his veins like rapids on a river. He had nothing to be nervous about, of course. Despite the importance of the outcome here, he'd taken on infinitely more difficult jobs before he was in high school. This should be a breeze. He'd thought of every possible outcome, put in every possible fail-safe. And yet, something in Margaret's body told him to panic. Call it woman's intuition.

Jack checked his watch. It was now quarter to midnight. Cyrus would be arriving any minute, and the seller only a short while after that.

"Okay," he said again. "You know where I'll be if anything goes sideways."

"We'll be fine," Greer said tightly, her eagerness to get that list and, subsequently, the money from Cyrus hurrying her away from Jack. "We've done this shit a million times."

"Yeah," said Jack, but something still tugged at him from somewhere that wasn't entirely his. For all their months together, Margaret's presence had never felt stronger, and that terrified him. "Be safe."

Greer was already on the move again before Jack could finish his plea, but Carter gave him a clap on the shoulder. "We'll be good."

Then he, too, was gone and Jack stood in the echoing darkness alone.

After a breath, he tucked himself down the narrow tunnel to the right, the chipped brick walls tapering slightly as he made his way to his designated hiding place. The walls drew together in a small, round chamber, a concrete-filled hole carved into the ceiling where a manhole cover had once been, the staple-shaped steps of a metal ladder still sprouting from the bricks at the back of the space.

Jack hunkered down, leaning his weight against the wall as he waited. His lower back already ached, and his compression socks weren't doing much for his varicose veins. The late hour weighed heavily on his eyelids.

"Hey, team." Eli's voice in Jack's ear. "I'm opening the channels now so Jack can hear what's happening with Carter and Greer."

"Cyrus is here," Greer said through the earpiece. "Still no sign of the seller."

It was five minutes past midnight. The thought occurred to Jack that this might not actually happen: that the seller might have gotten cold feet or found a better offer or simply had a change of heart, and this would all be for nothing. Then a few muffled words came crackling through Greer's mic, a collection of voices all layered over one another. The words themselves were impossible to make out. All Jack knew was that something was off. The voices rose in volume. Someone was yelling. And then, before Jack could move or breathe or think, he heard it. A familiar metallic click.

41

Click

August 2007

The heat wave was verging on unbearable. Two straight weeks of sticky skin and ice cream that melted before you'd even paid for it. But Jack McCoy had a plan. Jack McCoy always had a plan. And this was a brilliant one.

"This is moronic," Greer declared from her seat across the booth at Billy's. The diner's air-conditioning was on the fritz and the single ceiling fan rotated at a pace suggesting it knew it was the only thing standing between the patrons beneath and heat-stroke, and it relished the power. "The risk isn't worth it."

"Greer's right," said Eli. "I'm one strike away from juvie. I'm not risking it for this."

Jack had known there would be pushback. After almost a decade as the democratically elected leader of the You Agains, Jack knew every thought bound to enter his friends' minds, often before they'd thought them. It was a necessary skill, one that enabled him to strategize for an inconveniently timed conscience or concern. He also knew that, for a plan like this, all it would take was one You Again to fall and the rest would topple after them like dominoes. He shifted his focus to Jules.

"Don't tell me you're chickening out too," he poked.

"Jack, come on." Greer gave a warning hiss.

"What? I'm just saying. I get it, the rest of you are down to spend the summer with swampy butt cracks, fine, but Jules isn't afraid of a bit of fun."

"Jack, I'm serious," Greer said. "Stop dragging her into your bullshit. She's just a kid."

Jack caught Jules stiffen beside Greer from the corner of his eye. His domino was wobbling. She just needed a little tap now.

"You're right," Jack said. "Sorry, Jules. I know you got grounded last time. I'd hate for you to get in trouble again because of me. Not when you have your whole future ahead of you, kiddo."

Jules's nostrils flared at this, and just like that, the first domino fell.

"I am not a kid," Jules spat. "And I'm sick of you buttmunches acting like I am. I don't need your pity and I don't need you to babysit me." She raised her chin at Jack. "Besides, I'm over my armpits smelling like pepperoni. I need a break from this heat."

Jack bit back his smile as he turned from her to the rest of the You Agains. Carter toppled next on a heavy sigh.

"Yeah, fine, I'm in."

"I think it's a brilliant idea, Jackie," said Dale, confirming what Jack already knew. Three down, two to go.

"Eli?" Jack prompted.

Eli glared morosely up at the passive-aggressive ceiling fan. "If I get in shit for this, you're a dead man, McCoy."

Jack cheesed a grin at Greer. "Majority rules," he said. "You don't have to come, you know. I'm sure you have some college friends around you could talk about Descartes with or whatever."

Greer held his stare for a long moment. "Ugh, whatever, I'll come, but I want it on the record that I'm technically against this and think it's a very dumb idea."

"Consider it formally noted."

And so the plan was set. That night, as the neighborhood lay sleeping, the You Agains crept from the seedy streets they called home to the blocks of three-story houses with perfectly manicured lawns stretched out before them on the other side of town. Jack had walked by these houses every day on his trek to and from his summer job slinging hot dogs at the movie theater, had even said hello to a few of the moms in capris with chunky highlights in their hair and the dads on riding lawnmowers. One family even offered him lemonade on a particularly hot day. It was why he knew that very family would be out of town for the week. A family that, most crucially, had a pool.

Jack had never been inside a house with so much unused space. There was a whole dining room all to itself, a kitchen with sprawling marble counters, and a living room vast enough for multiple couches.

"Don't touch anything," he hissed at the others behind him as he slipped his lock pick back into his pocket. They slunk through the kitchen, toward the door to the backyard.

"Can I touch one thing?" Eli asked as they made their way outside.

Jack cocked his head in a question mark.

With a cheeky grin, Eli opened the fridge by the back door.

The shelves contained an array of cheeses and meats and a twelve-pack of beer. Eli grabbed a can and tossed it at Jack. Jack should've protested. They weren't actually here to take anything, they'd just come to cool down. But the icy can curved so effortlessly against his palm, it seemed almost rude to say no.

Jack pulled the tab as Eli passed the other cans around, and soon the You Agains were in the pool with a buzz gently fogging their minds. The sky above them was clear, a spattering of stars winking down at them. The pool lights gave the water an aqua tint, as though they were swimming through a cartoon. The whole night had a not-quite-real quality to it that was only enhanced by the alcohol and the unrelenting heat. Jack leaned back on the inflatable pink flamingo chair gliding him over the water and breathed in his success. Now *this* was how you spent your last few days of summer.

Greer swam over just as Eli blasted the water with a cannonball. She was a mermaid glistening in the moonlight, wet hair slick to her scalp, eyeliner running. Jack could feel his face stretch into a dopey smile even as he told it not to.

"Jack," Greer said, and Jack nearly fell upward into the stars. "I'm worried about Jules."

This snapped Jack back to earth. "What? Why?"

"She's on her second beer, and I don't think she's doing great with it. She's never had alcohol before, has she? I mean, she is still just a kid, whether she wants to be or not."

Jack scanned the pool surface and the artfully placed stone slabs surrounding it, searching for Jules. Shit. Where was she? She wasn't the best swimmer in the group. Gym class was an unrelenting nightmare for her for a multitude of reasons, her lack of proficiency in anything beyond the doggy paddle being one. But swimming when buzzed? He should have known better than to let her drink tonight.

Finally he spotted Jules sitting on the pool's top step, lying back on the ground, face angled up toward the sky. Was she breathing? From the other end of the pool, he couldn't be sure. Heart rate climbing, Jack scrambled off the floaty and swam over to her as fast as his arms could drag him through the water. He emerged beside her and she gently lolled her head toward him. Jack allowed himself to breathe. She was fine. Thank god she was fine. He'd made a promise to protect her, and tonight he'd done a pretty shit job of it. Well, that all changed now. He wouldn't leave her side until they were back on dry land and out of harm's way.

He sat himself on the step beside her and laid his head next to hers.

"You good?"

Jules went back to looking at the night sky. "You ever wonder what we look like from up there?"

"Small," Jack said. "I bet we look small."

"Like the way stars look from down here?"

"Even smaller."

"Yeah, that makes sense," said Jules. "You think we glow?"

Jack found Jules's freckle-spattered face from the corner of his eye. "Some of us, maybe."

"Hmm." Then she took a deep breath. "It's gonna suck with you gone."

Jack couldn't argue with that. He was at once thrilled by the prospect of freedom after graduation next June and concerned about what would happen to Jules without her friends at school to protect her.

"We'll still be around," he promised.

Jules opened her mouth to say something, but Jack held up a hand. Was that a car door slamming? He listened, straining to hear anything beyond the crickets and rustling leaves and laughter in the backyard.

A light flicked on in the house. Then a light in the kitchen, where the counters now lay beneath piles of empty beer cans. The lemonade family must have come home early.

Jack cupped his hands around his mouth and shouted, "Abort mission!"

The splashing and giggles stopped. Every head swiveled first in Jack's direction and then to the illuminated kitchen windows. Without another word spoken, the You Agains flung themselves out of the pool, gathering their clothing in their arms and taking off at a run as the back door opened, the silhouette of a large man nearly blocking the doorway.

Greer was the first over the back fence, tossing her sundress over the tall slats of wood and scrambling agilely after it. Carter was next, then Eli, with Jack and Jules bringing up the rear. Jules was still too buzzed for quick movements, and Jack had a personal policy to never leave one of his own behind. The man was gaining on them, still just a silhouette against the night. Jules was nearly at the fence now, Jack urging her on with waves and gestures like an air traffic controller. Just a few more feet and he'd help hoist her up and over the fence to safety. Just a few more feet. Come on.

She was nearly within arm's reach now, dizzy smiles of relief growing across both of their faces as they reached for each other. But before he could take her hand and drag her with him, something rattled the silence. Something Jack wouldn't let himself comprehend. Something sharp and piercing. A metallic click.

42

A gun.

"Jack?" Eli was back in his ear. "Greer? Is everyone okay? What's going on? Was that . . . ?"

Jack staggered out of the sewer alcove as fast as his elderly legs would carry him, racing heedlessly in the direction of Carter and Greer. He wheeled into a high-ceilinged space encased in brick and grime. By the far wall, Cyrus stood with hands raised, as though he'd been ambushed by the police. Jack ran frantic eyes around the room until they landed on Carter and Greer, backs to him, facing a wall around a sharp corner. A gun pressed into the flesh just behind Greer's ear.

The person holding the gun turned slowly, attention drawn by the sound of Jack's sensible heels skittering on the concrete floor. Jack's blood chilled, skin prickling with goose bumps.

"No." Disbelief wrapped strangling hands around his throat, his strained voice bouncing off the high ceilings and back at him with almost enough force to knock him off his increasingly unsteady feet. "You're . . . You're dead."

"Technically, so are you." Gerard's eyes twinkled with the same delight they'd held when he'd talked about pigeons all those weeks ago. "Faking your own death is delightfully simple when you're the one with access to all the company paperwork." He lowered the gun from Greer's head and aimed it at Jack. "It's lovely to see you again, Margaret. Or should I say Jack?"

Jack's mouth was a desert, his tongue too busy searching for moisture to form coherent words. "Huh?" was the best he could come up with.

Gerard's wrinkled features lifted in a soft smile as he returned the gun's nose to Greer's temple. "I owe you and your little pal a debt of gratitude. If it weren't for your mischief, I would never have known to play dead in order to save my afterlife."

The words came muffled through the whoosh of Jack's thudding heart. All he could focus on, all that mattered, was the gun against Greer's head. Eventually Gerard's voice pierced through the fog in Jack's mind with the force of a bullet, scattering his thoughts in too many directions. He scrambled for one and let it pass through his lips.

"What pal?"

"Not bad, huh, Jackie?" said a new voice echoing through the cavernous space. New and yet as familiar to Jack as scraped knees on a summer night, as stale coffee at Billy's Diner, as the life Jack had lived once and now lived again.

Jack whipped around. Hovering at the entrance of the chamber, face pulled in a smug grin, stood Dale. He looked different, somehow. Chest puffed, chin lifted, back straightened to full height. He looked like . . . Jack.

"All these years I never thought I could come up with plans as good as yours." Dale took a weightless step forward, staring down at Jack. "Turns out mine was even better."

"What are you talking about?" Jack could feel himself slipping from his earthly tethers again, the utter bafflement loosening his grip on this plane. Margaret crept up from somewhere beside him, steadying the legs they shared just enough to keep him upright.

"No offense, Jackie, but you don't have the same skills you used to," said Dale. "You were taking forever to get things moving, and I don't have forever, you know?"

"What the hell is going on?" Cyrus barked from where he still stood by the far wall, his back to the center of the room.

"Dale," was all Jack could say.

"Who?" came Cyrus's strangled reply.

A muscle in Dale's jaw twitched. "Tell your goth friend it's okay, I'm used to it. No one remembers the lackey. Not unless he does something worth being remembered for."

"So that's why you're doing this?" Jack sputtered. "Because you're having some afterlife crisis?"

That got a scoff from Dale. "Real rich coming from you, Jackie. Look at you, wearing an old lady just to stay alive. And for what? Face it, you're slipping. There was a time when you'd have snatched that list and been rich before anyone could think to beat you to it. I remember that Jack McCoy. I learned from him. But he's dead now. This was the way it always should've been—you get locked up or struck down and your right-hand man takes your place. That's the natural order of things. But not for Jack McCoy. Nothing ever touched you, and then when it finally did, it got me too. I never got the chance to be that guy, so I had to take it. You get that, Jackie, I know you do. And now you get to see how all my hard work paid off. A little bit of that pizzazz you always loved. What do you think, Jackie? Not too bad for the invisible friend, huh?"

Jack's glance darted back to Gerard and the gun pressed to Greer's head, but Dale just tutted.

"Don't get cute, Jack. We didn't come to hurt anyone, but that doesn't mean we won't."

"Just let her go," Jack pleaded. "She's your friend, she doesn't need to be caught in the middle of this."

"Yeah, I think you're wrong there," said Dale. "Because I think she makes a pretty compelling bargaining chip, don't you? Like I said, Jackie, I learned from the best."

"I'd never do this."

"No, you wouldn't have. Things would have been different with me in charge. So here's how this is going to work. You're going to give up on the list, all of you. You'll walk back out of here knowing I won, unless you're ready to join me. Because I've got big things planned, Jackie, for all of us. Turns out once you start, it's addictive. A guy could get used to it, you know? Being you."

This was useless. Dale was so hopped up on his own ego he couldn't see beyond it, but Jack could, and what Jack could see horrified him. Greer's cheeks were lined with a steady flow of silent tears. Every time Gerard shifted even slightly, a bright red indent revealed itself on Greer's temple from beneath the gun's barrel. Bile and anxiety rose up Jack's esophagus. He needed to do something quickly, before Dale's power trip completely overtook him, but any wrong moves would put a bullet in Greer's head. He was running out of options. Dale was a lost cause. The only choice now was to appeal to the man holding the gun.

"Gerard," Jack said carefully, "you don't have to do this. Dale promised you a cut of the take, right? Whatever it is, we'll double it. Just put the gun down. Please."

Gerard studied Jack, seeming to contemplate this proposal on a long inhale.

"He's here because of you," Dale said before Gerard could reply. "This is what I mean when I say you've lost your touch, Jackie. See, Gerry saw us on the archives' security footage that night we broke in. The old Jack McCoy would never have let that happen. The next day, he dropped by for a visit. I guess he was too sweet on Margaret to turn her in without talking to her first. But you were out, and I decided to see who it was. Never expected it to be someone who could see me too. That's when it hit me. The reason all your plans worked. It wasn't because you were some genius, it was because you had a brilliant right-hand man doing all the dirty work for you. And suddenly I had mine. Good thing you kept that spare key under the flowerpot. Made it much easier to meet with ol' Gerry here."

Jack's mind whipped back to all the times he'd come home to find Margaret's front door unlocked. He'd always assumed it was Eli letting himself in with his lock picking skills, but that, along with everything else he thought he knew, was clearly not the case.

"We just needed to stay one step ahead of you, and no offense again, Jackie, but you made that pretty easy. Especially because I got to hear all your plans before you ever followed through on them."

Jack's head was spinning. He had known Dale almost all his life, and yet the spirit in front of him was little more than a stranger.

The sound of loose pebbles skittering across the ground pulled his attention back across the chamber just in time to catch Carter dissolving into a blur as he bolted headlong toward Gerard, who whipped around, gun raised. The shot rang out like a scream, its piercing echo bouncing off every surface. Jack held his breath as a plume of dust erupted from above. As it settled, Carter's silhouette emerged upright and unharmed in its wake, a bullet lodged in the stone just above him.

"Consider that a warning shot," Gerard snarled with a feral quality Jack had never heard from him before. "I was a military man most of my life. I won't miss again." Then he shifted the still-steaming gun back to Greer.

Carter took a wobbly step back. Cyrus was on his knees now, muttering unintelligibly. Jack still hadn't exhaled.

"Okay, whoa," said Dale, making his way over to his gunman. "Easy. Let's not get too trigger-happy here, Gerry. We've been over this."

"We have," Gerard sneered back. "We've been over a lot. Charming you think I'm actually listening to any of it."

That seemed to hit Dale like a blow to the gut. His brows tightened toward each other. "What are you talking about?"

"You're morons, the lot of you. Have none of you taken a single moment to read this list you all so covet?"

To the silence, Gerard continued. "Of course not. It's just a way to make a fast dollar for you. But if you glanced at it, even once, you'd see my name right up at the top. Of course, I'd never have known it was there if you lot hadn't brought the Scroll of Souls to my attention in the first place, which I suppose I must be grateful for. But you'd sell my soul, and the souls of everyone else on that list, to some twisted associate of that morally bankrupt individual"—he waved the gun in Cyrus's direction—"to do god knows what with, and I won't stand for it. Margaret—Jack, I used to see you in the archives, poring over all sorts of S.C.Y.T.H.E. literature. You must've read about afterlife experimentation, so you know souls are vulnerable to those with ill intent. I thought it would be enough to take the list before you had the chance so that its contents couldn't be sold off, but you've proved too stubborn to see reason. If I must harm the few to spare the many, then so be it. It wouldn't be the first time."

Gerard's finger danced on the trigger again, the barrel still aimed toward Greer. Before Jack could find Margaret's feet to move or her tongue to speak, Eli tumbled into the room, eyes wild as they landed on the scene before him.

"Greer!"

Another blast barely missed its target as more rock loosened from the wall just behind Eli and showered onto him, a heavy shard of stone shrapnel cracking him across the forehead. The curls above his left eyebrow grew slick, a thick ooze of red cascading down his cheek. The blue at the shoulder of his T-shirt quickly purpled as a thick, dark liquid dripped down in fat splashes. Eli staggered back, grasping the wall behind him for support.

"Dude, stop!" Dale shouted over the reverberation. "Enough. We're not doing it like this."

Gerard didn't even look in Dale's direction as everyone froze breathlessly in place, the gun tipping back toward Greer.

"Hey," Dale tried again, desperation fraying his tone. "Gerry. Dumbass. I'm in charge here, remember?"

A snort from Gerard. "Of course you aren't, boy. You never have been."

Jack braved a glance over his shoulder to where Eli stood several feet behind. Through the pain, a glimmer of recklessness shone in Eli's eyes like sunlight on a tumultuous sea. Jack knew that glimmer, and it terrified him nearly as much as the weapon in Gerard's hands. Eli moved like a flash, but Jack was ready. As Eli barreled headfirst toward his sister's captor and Gerard raised the gun to face Eli, Jack was already on the move, screaming a heedless war cry that echoed with a voice not quite his and not quite Margaret's, one that had been gone for too long.

In a heartbeat, Jack flung his full body weight onto Eli, dragging both of them to the ground in a tangle of limbs as another bullet hissed past. Margaret's entire mass pressed across Eli's torso, knocking the wind out of him long enough for Jack to scramble to his feet without risk of Eli following. The gun's barrel followed him as he rose, its metal gaze locked on his, and for the second time in his existence, Jack found himself staring directly into the eyes of Death. When they'd met before, he'd been a different man in so many ways, and Jack McCoy had done what he always had when trouble caught up with him: he'd come up with a plan and evaded the consequences of his actions. This time he greeted Death with a very different goal. No one else would die because of him. Not again. He'd spent his whole afterlife running from Death and only now he realized it had never been his own he couldn't handle. If the next bullet came for him, he was ready for it.

Not yet.

The voice inside his head was so jarringly not his own, it knocked Jack off-kilter, sending him stumbling just enough that the bullet he'd begun to accept as his fate ripped through the curls on one side of his meticulously coiffed hair, narrowly missing anything more substantial. Eli staggered to his feet just behind Jack, who was already preparing for another round of playing human shield when a wet crack tore through the tumult of the scene. Jack swiveled toward the center of the room to find Greer in the final throes of a headbutt, Gerard's free hand flying to his nose as a geyser of blood erupted from it. Without missing a beat, Carter charged the hand with the gun, but Eli beat him to it. He'd moved so fast, Jack hadn't even realized he'd slipped out from behind him.

Eli wrestled the gun away with ease, Gerard still distracted by the pain of his freshly broken nose. Greer turned her gaze to Jack as something raw and primal settled over Eli's expression.

"Eli," Jack said quietly, "you did it. You got the gun. Everyone's safe now. Let's just put it down, all right?"

But Eli wasn't listening. He wasn't there. He was back at the pool they never should have been at on that summer night all those years ago. Jack could see it in his eyes. In many ways, none of them had left. Jack had always been too afraid to, he realized. Because if he left, it meant admitting what happened after. It meant acknowledging it was all real. But if he continued to live his life in the past the way he always had, it would all happen again right here in the present. Jack would lose Eli. He had already lost too much.

Jules. He let her name into his mind in a way he rarely had the courage to before, let every memory surge through him until it possessed him like a wayward spirit. And for a moment, he nearly let it fully take the wheel.

No. It was time to leave that pool.

Eli's arm rose, steady in its conviction and yet trembling

under the weight of its mission. The gun glimmered in his grasp, Gerard's chest positioned squarely at the end of it.

Gerard himself had only just lowered his head after tilting it back to ease his bloody nose. "Go ahead," he said as he caught sight of the weapon. "I'm slated to die anyway. You'll only be expediting my fate and ruining the Scroll of Souls in the process." He gave a chest pocket in his cardigan a pat.

But that was the least of it, Jack knew. Eli would ruin himself and his chance at a future in the process.

Eli's finger hugged the trigger.

"Eli, no, please." Greer took a step toward her brother but quickly thought better of it, his body tensing at the sound of her movement. His eyes were rimmed red, a layer of tears dancing over them, their focus deep in the broken past. He was lost, too far gone for anyone's words to reach him. One wrong move and that gun would fire, if not at Gerard, then at someone he'd truly never recover from harming.

If Jack closed his eyes and listened past the chaos of that little sewer chamber, he could still hear it all. The click of the gun, the screams, the sirens. Eli wailing in the hospital hallway, Greer and the others too consumed by their own grief to hold his pain. That was the day it all fell apart, the day *they* all fell apart. And that was how it had been ever since. Jack never had the chance to put them all back together again. Had never let himself even realize he was broken.

He took a step. Eli's bleary eyes shifted his way, the gun following suit. Jack took another step. That finger hovered over the trigger.

Not yet.

The voice came again, but Jack decided to ignore it. He was inches from the gun now, Eli's arm still stretched out to its full length in front of him. An exhale sent Jack close enough to feel the weapon's cool metal against his forehead before he ducked beneath the outstretched arm and wrapped his own arms around Eli's torso in a tight, unrelenting hug. Jack could feel Eli tense beneath his hold. Every one of Eli's lithe muscles seemed to twitch, as though they'd been carrying something very heavy for a very long time and had only now realized its toll. Then he began to tremble, then heave. He was sobbing, Jack realized, tears pelting down on Jack's head like the bullets of a gun that had long been loaded with no release.

The real gun, the one in Eli's grasp, dropped gently to the floor as Eli crumpled, dragging Jack down to the concrete with him.

"It's okay," Jack said softly, giving Eli's back a pat as a tear wrestled loose from his own eye. They were both here now, for the first time in far too long. "It's okay, buddy. I'm so sorry. For everything."

Greer stumbled over and slumped down beside them, wrapping her arms around them both. Her cheek was wet where it pressed against Jack's forearm. Then came Carter, enveloping the lot in his muscles. No one spoke. There was nothing to say.

From the corner of Jack's eye, he caught Dale watching them from where he hovered by the chamber entrance. His bravado had slipped like a Halloween mask, revealing the lost little boy underneath, and Jack knew he'd never forgive himself for not seeing that boy there before. Then, in a blink, Dale was gone—a fugitive from death, skulking away into the night. But Dale was right about one thing: Jack had a way of escaping consequences that most didn't, and Dale's consequence would be an afterlife trapped on this earth as a ghost if Jack couldn't get to him first. But he didn't have time to worry about that now.

"Well, this is all very touching," came Cyrus's forgotten voice, "but what the hell are we going to do about him?" Cyrus had crept from his hiding spot and nabbed Gerard by the scruff of his cardigan as the older man attempted to escape. "I need that list."

Jack untangled himself from the You Agains, their warmth receding as he pulled himself to his feet. The voice in his head was louder now, and it hummed with information Jack never thought he'd receive, information Margaret had shut away somewhere he'd never previously been able to access. Information that meant there was another way. It was as though the brush with her own death had brought Margaret back to life, and suddenly she was feeling generous.

"Gerard's right," Jack said, and those two words were enough to force everyone else in that chamber into silence. "His methods are questionable," he clarified quickly, "but he's right. We can't just sell that list and risk who-knows-what happening to all those people's souls."

Greer peeled herself away from the others. Jack could feel her behind him, those hazel eyes boring into his back.

"Jack." That desperation in her voice again. "Please. I need this."

"No," Jack said gently. "You need money. But it doesn't have to be this. Menace without harm, remember? That was because of you."

The expression on her face held the same sting of betrayal Jack had felt when he'd seen Dale down there in that chamber with them. The fact that he was the cause of it was almost enough to make him take back everything he'd just said. But he had a plan. He always had a plan. "There's another way," he said. "I just need you to trust me."

Greer studied him a long moment, her gaze piercing deep into Jack's own, so deep he could feel its weight on his soul. Greer jerked back, blinking hard, as though for a moment she had seen him as he was. Not the scheming boy, but the man he'd become beneath the woman he wore. Who he truly was.

"Okay," she said in a weak voice. "If it means we can get out of this stinking sewer, then okay."

"And what the hell am I supposed to tell my buyers?" Cyrus spat.

Jack let his glance dart to Eli, still clinging to Carter as his wound painted his face. "Tell them what you saw the day you and Eli looked into the other side. See how bad they still want to play with death after that."

Cyrus said nothing to that. Instead he turned his hand over and examined the scar on his palm, and even from where Jack stood, he could see the hairs lift on Cyrus's pale forearms.

"Jack," Carter called. "Eli's bleeding out. We've got to go."

Jack nodded to Carter, who wrapped an arm around Eli's back, helping him up to his feet. Greer rushed over to help as Cyrus slunk from the chamber, leaving Jack face-to-face with Gerard. He looked into the old man's face, ready for hate and anger to consume him, but something unexpected emerged in their place: pity. When Jack had been faced with his own death, he'd stolen someone else's life without a second thought. In a way, Gerard's willingness to kill for the sake of his soul meant he had been prepared to do the same. They were two sides to the same desperate coin.

"I'll return the list," Jack said.

"You expect me to trust you?" Gerard hissed through his teeth.

"Not really," said Jack. "I catfished you with someone else's body, so trust might be a bit too much to ask here. But S.C.Y.T.H.E. thinks you're dead, so it's not like you can return it yourself. Plus, I get it. Death can change you. I don't like who it's made me. I mean, Margaret seems fun, but the rest of it? The desperation? It's not who I want to be. We're both on a clock here, and I don't want mine to run out like this. Do you?"

Gerard held Jack's gaze for a long moment. "All I want," he said, "is to rest in peace and to know that everyone else dying with me will get to do the same."

With tentative hands, he pried the scroll from his breast pocket, studying it with a labored breath. "Is she still in there?"

"Margaret? Yeah. Big-time. Getting louder by the minute, actually."

Gerard nodded and surrendered the list to Jack's careful fingers. "Then this is for her. I want her to be the one to return it."

There was a warmth to the paper that such an object shouldn't have, as though it were a living thing. Jack could almost feel a pulse. Somewhere inside him, he could feel Margaret smile.

"She will," Jack promised. He turned to hurry after his friends, but Gerard grabbed his arm.

"There's more," he said, voice strained.

"More what?"

"I can't rest until I know someone is doing something about the glitch."

"The . . . ?"

"Death is changing," Gerard said, that wild urgency back in

his eyes. "Something is wrong with it; a glitch, they're calling it. An imbalance between the natural order of life and death, allowing for things that shouldn't be possible: uncooperative essences, souls becoming ghosts before the end of their forty-five-day grace period"—he gave Jack a hard look—"possession. Of course, I really shouldn't know this, but as archivist I see all the paperwork related to the company, and there's been quite a lot about this glitch these past few months, though some literature dates back years. It seems to be getting worse at an accelerated rate. It's only a matter of time now before that glitch not only takes down the company, but the very balance of life and death, and no one is doing enough to stop it. I've spent months buried in research, combing through the depths of Section 301 D, to no avail. After I'm gone, there'll be no one left to fix it except the morons running the place, and most of them have never picked up a book in their lives."

"Jack!" Greer's voice barreled down the corridor beyond the chamber. Eli was still bleeding. The You Agains needed him.

"I have to go," he said.

Not yet.

Margaret held him there, rooted to the cement as Gerard's gaze continued its plea. "I promise I'll look into it," Jack said. And with that, his borrowed body returned to him, allowing a stumble out into the cavernous corridor as he raced after his friends.

43

It wasn't the first time Jack had to wash Eli's blood off his hands, but with any luck, it would be the last. The drive to the hospital was nearly silent aside from Eli's heavy breathing. As they crowded the waiting room, the events of the night bubbled in everyone's throats, and soon uneasy conversation settled over the stark, sterile space. Not long before dawn rolled around, Eli was finally deemed fully stable despite the concussion and blood loss, and as soon as the You Agains were given the go-ahead, they gathered around his bed.

Eli would have a new scar to show for it all, but he would heal. Maybe they all would.

For his part, Jack's grip on his borrowed body had weakened, its rightful owner making herself known in moments that kept catching him off guard. Just now Margaret heaved her wrist into view, displaying the time on the delicate gold watch wrapped around it, and Jack knew what he needed to do.

THE DOORS TO THE BANK HAD OPENED MOMENTS BEFORE HIS ARrival, and aside from the employees, he was the first through them that morning. A teller ushered him over to her desk and Jack told her he wanted to transfer some funds. Margaret had been generous enough to offer up the information he needed to access her accounts, and that meant he could remove just enough money for Greer's husband to receive the treatment he needed and not a penny more, which Margaret's newfound presence was keen to make sure of.

Jack was back at the hospital half an hour later with a tray of coffees and a box of assorted doughnuts. Eli was still pale from the whole ordeal, but the darkness that always seemed to haunt him had lifted somehow. He was propped upright on the bed, laughing at something someone had said before Jack entered the room. Jack put the doughnuts on the bedside table and pulled Greer into the hall.

"It's done," he said.

"What's done?"

He couldn't help it; a smile tickled his lips. "Check your bank account."

Greer furrowed her brow but pulled her phone from her jeans pocket all the same and opened her banking app. Her eyes flew wildly between Jack and the screen and back again.

"How?"

"I had a little help from a friend," said Jack, gesturing at Margaret's form in what he hoped was enough of an explanation.

"Oh," Greer said. "She . . . ?"

Jack began a nod, but before he could complete the motion, she'd thrown her arms around Jack's shoulders, effectively hugging both him and Margaret. "Thank you."

Jack hugged her back, squeezing tight enough to feel the joy radiating from her. Despite all the schemes he'd schemed growing up, all the loot he'd looted, this was the feeling he'd been hunting for but never found. This was something that actually mattered.

To both of their surprise, Jack pulled away first. He looked at Margaret's watch again. "Ah shit, I've got to go."

Greer mopped up her tear-streaked face with the bottom of her tank top. "What are you talking about? Go where?"

"Work," said Jack. "I'm already late."

Greer's face dropped in disbelief. "You're not actually going to work now? You haven't slept all night, you're probably still shaken from everything, plus you said out there in the waiting room that you were finally ready to move on."

"Oh, that. I didn't mean from life," Jack clarified to an eye roll from Greer. "I meant from the past. From how things were before. But I'm not done here yet. Not according to Margaret, anyway."

Greer sniffed. "Look, Jack, I don't want you to go. I really don't. But I'm worried about you. It can't be healthy, sticking around like this."

"I know," said Jack. "And I'm not gonna stick around forever. Honestly. But I told you what Gerard said: there's a glitch in the balance of life and death, one so bad it's destroying the natural life cycle. That's bad, Greer."

"And you're going to fix it?"

"I'm going to try," said Jack. "Since it doesn't sound like anyone else is. I just need to learn more about what's going on so I can figure out a plan."

One side of Greer's mouth quirked up in a smile.

"What?"

"Nothing," said Greer. "I just like it when you use your

powers for good." She shifted her weight. "I should get home to Curtis. He was so worried when I told him we were at the hospital. Obviously he doesn't know the full reason, but I should show him I'm okay. And the girls, they've been texting."

"You need to use your powers for good too," said Jack.

"I know you think I gave up on my dreams for Curtis," she said. "But I didn't. I just found a new dream, and until he got sick, I was living it."

"I know," said Jack. "I may be nearsighted now, but I can still see that. Go be with your family. Carter's here with Eli, and I'll pop back in at lunch."

Greer nodded. "It's funny, sometimes you say something so wholly unlike the Jack I knew that I think it must be Margaret's influence, but really, I think this might just be the Jack McCoy who's been in there all along. It's nice to see him, even if he does look remarkably like an eighty-year-old woman."

44

The chill in the archives had eased somewhat since Jack's last visit, Greta's exclamation mark–like demeanor softening to a semicolon, or perhaps an em dash. She greeted Jack with a curt nod as he approached the desk.

"How can I help you this morning, Ms. Chen?"

"Have you been filing any information about a glitch in death?"

Greta stiffened.

Jack didn't wait for a reply. "I need everything you have about it."

"I'm afraid that information is highly classified. Even I'm not supposed to read it beyond the details required for classification."

"But you *have* read it," said Jack. "Haven't you?"

Greta's pale eyes shifted away. "Some of it."

"Then you know that if nothing changes, S.C.Y.T.H.E. will end up defunct and you'll be out of a job again."

A sharp exhale. "What do you want with that information?"

"We're dealing with a glitch here, right?" said Jack. "Glitches can be repaired."

"And you know how to do that?"

"Not even a little," Jack admitted. "But I promised someone I'd try."

"I'm sure there are others trying. Why would you be any different?"

"Let's just say I know enough about death at this point to know that when it functions well, it can be pretty scary. But if it stops functioning? If something goes wrong?" Margaret sent a small shudder through their shared body. "That's terrifying. I don't want anyone facing that. I don't think you do either."

Greta's gaze kept evading his.

"Plus going back on the job hunt without your stepdad's pull would really suck," Jack said. He could feel the hit landing. Greta flinched.

"Low blow, Ms. Chen."

"Yeah, sorry," said Jack. "Worrying about the balance of life and death makes me a little irritable."

A heavy sigh. Greta slipped her lanyard over her head, offering up her key card.

"Section 301 D should have what you're looking for," she said. "Ignore the boxes in the corner; the previous archivist clearly never got around to filing them and I haven't had a chance myself just yet."

"Thanks," said Jack, looking down at the key card. It still had Gerard's name on it.

45

Section 301 D was as musty and uninspiring as Jack remembered it. He grabbed a few books from the shelves and lowered himself to the floor to read through them. This position wouldn't be sustainable for long; elderly bodies were not made for floor sitting, but nothing could be removed from the small room at the back of the archives, and Jack was already breaking enough rules—and forcing Greta to break them with him—to risk adding another to the list.

Before long, his lower back was aflame and there were more open books and files around him than he could possibly read in a day. Greta was going to have to get used to his company down there. The information he'd already uncovered sent his head spinning, concepts he'd never heard of in his time as a Collections Agent filling documents as though they'd become commonplace: essences that were never processed, souls refusing to leave their bodies after death, the population of ghosts expanding at an alarming rate. Even the verified existence of a Blind Spot, which had once been thought to be a myth but had recently been discovered in three separate locations across North America alone.

Jack reeled, the aches in his body paling next to the horror of what he was reading. Death really was broken, and souls were paying the price. Jack looked down at the gentle slopes and sags of the body he'd called home since he died. Possession was supposed to be impossible, and yet here he was, sharing a fleshy shell with a stranger. This glitch had enabled his extended afterlife. Which meant fixing it might be enough to evict him from the last thing holding him to this plane of existence. Jack shut the file in his lap and moved on to the next, a plume of dust scattering into the air with the action. He couldn't worry about his own soul now. At the moment, his soul was safe, tucked away in Margaret's body alongside her own increasingly active spirit. The same couldn't be said for anyone else entering the afterlife these days, and that was what Jack would focus on for the time being.

A tentative knock on the door to Section 301 D.

"Any luck?" Greta poked her fair head around the corner.

"Kind of," said Jack. "Things are bad. Very bad. I have no idea how I'm going to make them better, but I'll figure it out."

"You seem very confident about that."

"I've figured out a lot of stuff before," said Jack.

"Like this?"

"No. Never like this, but there's a first time for everything."

"Hmm." Greta fiddled with a small scrap of paper in her hands. "Restoring the balance of life and death doesn't seem like a one-person job."

"You offering to help?"

Greta scoffed. "I have shelves to organize."

Jack had to laugh at that. "Fair enough."

"But I think I might know of someone who can."

Jack looked up from his stack of disconcerting literature.

"It could be nothing," Greta added quickly. "I did a bit of my own research since you've been in here. There's this woman, she's the head of Murder at another branch. According to employee records, she has some experience dealing with afterlife anomalies. More than most people at the company, anyway. I think people around here are used to everything going smoothly."

"But not her?"

"There's a case she worked a few years back. The soul had been filed into the wrong department due to some kind of in-office corruption. She was the one who figured it out, apparently."

Jack silently watched Greta continue to rumple the paper in her hands, as blindsided by her sudden willingness to help as by everything he'd read. Greta shifted awkwardly under his gaze.

"Anyway," she said, crossing to him. "Here." She placed the small piece of paper in his palm and marched out of the room, back to the comfort of her standing desk and the computer with so many of S.C.Y.T.H.E.'s secrets.

He hauled himself unsteadily to his feet, hand pressed to the wall for support. He'd need days to recover from daring to crisscross applesauce as a senior citizen. He peered out of Section 301 D, but Greta had fully disappeared, leaving only shelves surrounding him.

Jack rolled the little paper scrap between his fingertips. It didn't hold the warmth or power of the Master List, but with any luck it held something more crucial to him, and maybe to death itself. Greta was right, he couldn't do this alone. And for once in his life, he wouldn't ask the You Agains for help. Eli needed to heal, Carter needed to work, and Greer needed to be with her family. They had moved on, and so had he. While they would always be his friends—his family, really—this new job required a very different kind of team.

He unfurled the paper.

Scribbled across the page was a name and phone number. The name was one he recognized from his time researching S.C.Y.T.H.E. From a memo about a soul-selling scheme and the agent who'd uncovered it.

Jack knew who he would be contacting next.

Kathy Valence.

ACKNOWLEDGMENTS

I still feel like I'm pulling off the ultimate heist by somehow being allowed to write books that people actually read. This would absolutely not be possible without my own gang of wonderful and absurdly talented coconspirators.

Endless thanks to my lovely and very patient editor, Tracy Bernstein, for your trust and your guidance. To my agent, Melissa Edwards, for always having my back. To my publicity and marketing angels, Natasha Tsakiris, Yasmine Hassan, and Elisha Katz, and everyone else who gets my words in front of eyeballs. To copyeditor Jennifer Sale for her expertise and for putting up with my rogue semicolons. And to the incredible design team for making a series about death look so dang pretty.

I also need to acknowledge the You Agains in my life: the P Girls and J Boys back in Canada, and my new community in Edinburgh, who have been a constant support on this wild literary adventure. Thanks as well to my fantastic family, who have always encouraged me to keep going. And to the entire nation of Scotland for being such a welcoming new home. And finally but most importantly, thanks to you, the reader, for hanging out with me in my goofy imagination. Without you there would be no S.C.Y.T.H.E.

ACKNOWLEDGMENTS

[illegible]

[illegible]

[illegible]

Photo by Madison Rose Photography

Maxie Dara is from a tiny, Hallmark movie–style town in Ontario, Canada, where she works as a writer and actress, because rejection-heavy careers are her passion. She is also a two-time award-winning playwright. Maxie knew she wanted to be a writer at the age of seven, when she first fell in love with the written word. She also wanted to be a mermaid but has mostly focused on the writing side of things.